Stormy Haven

'You're scared, aren't you, Decker? Scared I'm going to tell Daddy that you broke his trust, that you fucked his little girl. You should know damn well what he does to traitors, but I bet he'd find a special kind of hell for you.'

Daisy nestled into the pillows. 'So what are you going to do about it?'

Decker looked white as a sheet. 'Dig my own grave and jump in it?' he suggested dryly.

'Relax. I'm not that much of a bitch,' said Daisy. 'But it does put me in a stronger position for telling you to keep out of my face.'

'I'm here to look after you. And by the way . . . I'm coming with you on that tour.'

'Wonderful,' Daisy said acidly. 'Well try and blend in, for God's sake. You'll stick out more than Tom Jones's trousers in that suit.'

Decker turned to go.

'Wait!'

He waited. Daisy climbed off the bed and let the sheet fall from her, revealing her nakedness. He did not move as she approached him. Twining her arms around his neck she licked along his lips and backed away. More than anything she wanted him to push her back on the bed and fuck so her it hurt, but she knew he wouldn't. Not the way she had just spoken to him.

Author's other Black Lace titles:

Wolf at the Door

Stormy Haven
Savannah Smythe

For G.

Black Lace books contain sexual fantasies.
In real life, always practise safe sex.

First published in 2003 by
Black Lace
Thames Wharf Studios
Rainville Road
London W6 9HA

This edition published 2006

ISBN 978 0 352 34057 3

1

Daisy Mae Lovell considered her options through her mascara brush, carefully applying Max Factor to her fluffy eyelashes in the appalling light of the office loos. It was crunch time, but she knew the blonde would win. In the current climate they always did. Especially if they were fucking the boss. As for herself, a slim, dainty-chested brunette and almost 33, she was now considered a liability and had to go, even though she was a better woman for the job.

It was the look that irritated her. That smug, cat that gets cream regularly and copiously, look that Lydia had been wearing for the last three months. Before that, the company Daisy worked for had been aggressively taken over and most of the original workforce unconditionally axed. Daisy Mae had been kept on to boost morale and close the lucrative deal she had been working on, but her future had always been uncertain. Despite that, she refused to get drawn into office politics and, because of that, she was about to lose her career.

Daisy was a romantic and a firm believer in fate but, if they wanted rid of her, they were going to have to make her redundant. She knew the new regime didn't want to do it, because it would cost them too much money. So for months, she had also been enduring increasingly desperate attempts to get her to resign. This included undermining her authority, 'losing' work that she had spent five hours' overtime on, and other childish, petty indignities. But she had held on with the tenacity of a Jack Russell without the bark, quietly looking for any opportunity that might come her way to have the last word.

Val stuck her head around the toilet door. 'Dickhead's waiting.' Dickhead was the universal name for Jason Cordell, the imperious new boss of her department, used by all former employees of Data Supplies Ltd.

'Thanks, Val. I think he can wait a few minutes more.' Daisy continued to paint crimson Dior Addict on her bow-shaped top lip, finishing with a splash of Allure. As she walked back into the office, some of the others were watching her with delicious dread, as if they knew more than she did.

Jason Cordell's office was placed for maximum vision of everyone in the sales department. From his open door he could see everything, even when the office junior sneaked off for a quick fag in the toilet. They had all grown wearily used to the barbed comments that were flung from his desk.

Daisy shut the door and faced Jason, who was leaning back in his chair as if he owned the company. His desk was tidy, and on the blotter in front of him was a slim white envelope. He offered her a cigarette from a packet of Dunhills.

'No thanks, I don't smoke.'

'Good. It's a filthy habit.' He put the packet back in his drawer and smiled sympathetically at her. 'It's been a pretty tough time for you, hasn't it?'

She wasn't fooled. He and Lydia had been the main perpetrators of the stress she had been under.

'You could say that,' she replied lightly. She motioned to the envelope. 'Is that my Get Out Of Jail Free card?'

Jason smirked. He was a total snake, and just intelligent enough to be able to use his deep brown eyes to devastating effect, reducing the more gullible women in the office to quivering wrecks. He drove a red TVR and wore Paul Smith suits with Gucci silk ties, and obviously thought that he was above the lowly sales people that kept him employed, even though he was shorter than most of them. Now he was giving Daisy that lounge lizard stare, from her slim ankles up to her Stuart tartan mini-kilt, on to her rounded bosom, which was rising and falling gently under a black cashmere sweater. She had noticed him giving her the eye more than once, even though it was common knowledge that he was servicing Lydia at the time.

'It could be,' he replied. 'But I've been pretty impressed by you over the last few months. Your work is consistently excellent. You're popular with the others and you never seem to fold under pressure. We could use more like you.'

You had them, she thought tersely, but threw them all away in favour of beautiful young people who knew more about corporate image than selling telecoms equipment.

'It's very kind of you to say so,' she said calmly. 'May I have a look?' She took the envelope and opened it. Her face showed no reaction to the cheque and apologetic letter. They had chosen to pay her the minimum that they could get away with. Thanks for nothing after three years' service. She could tell him where to shove it but, the truth was, she needed the cash. She tucked the letter and cheque back in the envelope and resealed it. 'So what's your point?' She asked, keeping the tightness out of her voice.

Jason levered off his chair and came around the desk to perch on it opposite her. She could smell his spicy aftershave more strongly now and detect, if her eyes had not deceived her, a shifting under his trousers. He lifted the corner of her kilt and fingered the material thoughtfully.

'That's a really pretty skirt, Daisy. Do you have Scottish blood in you?'

She smiled sweetly. 'I'm American, so I could have anything in me.'

'Is that right?'

He had taken the ambiguous comment to another level. All her senses were suddenly on red alert. She knew he had been humping Lydia in this office, but would he seriously try it on with her in the middle of the morning with twenty people working just outside?

'Is there something you want to discuss with me?' she asked coolly, though her heart was beginning to thump. He was a very handsome man, even if he was a complete dickhead. She shifted in her seat, and found that her sex was hot and moist. She was just about to lose her job, and she was turned on by the man about to deliver the blow. How sick was that?

'I think we could get on a lot better without certain . . . disrupting factors. If I agree to remove those factors, and up your pay by five per cent, would you agree to stay? There would be other perks as well.'

'Oh? What kind of perks?' she asked, tossing her glossy chestnut hair back so he could see the pert fullness of her breasts properly. A measly five per cent. Was he really serious? He licked his lips and swallowed hard, staring at her breasts, his fingers twitching, wanting to reach out and touch. She subtly arched her back in subliminal invitation, and his eyes became glazed with surprised lust, as if he had not realised until then how eager she would be to play along. His hand dropped to her breast, his fingers cupping one full globe. She rubbed against his hand. Encouraged, he took the other breast as well, stroking up to each nipple with the tips of his fingers, licking his lips as he found each one already prominent.

'Big perks,' he whispered, taking her hand and placing it palm side down against the thrusting ridge in his trousers. For a moment she paused, feeling the pulsing of his cock, before looking up at him with her wide, golden eyes.

'That big?' She was being generous. His cock was rather like its owner, a short, thick snake, but he was vain enough to be taken in by her luminous expression. She squirmed in her seat, her sex all slippery now with anticipation. So he wasn't hung like a horse but he was randy as hell. Her earlier instinct was right. He wanted to take her right then, and boy did she need it, after almost a year without sex. 'Can I see just how big?'

'You may.' He reached down and flipped her skirt up so it exposed her black lace stocking tops, then spread her legs and stood between them. He leaned back against the desk and pushed out his hips, holding his jacket back so it would not get in the way. Smiling up at him, she tugged gently at his zipper, exposing white Calvin Klein trunks. A label man through and through. Was his dick Agent Provocateur, she wondered irreverently? It was certainly small enough. His balls packed the trunks well though, a neat load bulging between his legs, his short, thick cock visibly straining against the white cotton. As she trailed the tip of her fingernail along its length it jerked hard.

'Of course, this has to be a mutual arrangement,' he rasped. 'Show me your tits.'

Acquiescently she edged up her cashmere sweater, teasing him with a swelling underview of her breasts, encased in a sheer gauze bra. She liked her breasts. They weren't too big, and the fat, rosy nipples contrasted well with the chocolaty areolae, a legacy from her Scottish–Italian mother. As he visually feasted on her she eased each breast out of its lace cup and rubbed them together so the nipples almost touched, all the while watching his face flush with triumphant lust.

'That's very good,' he said thickly. 'Now let me see your pretty quim.'

'Of course.' She pushed her chair away and spread her legs wide across each chair arm, exposing matching black bikini panties. Through the sheer material her neatly trimmed bush could clearly be seen, as soft as sable fur. As she slipped her hand inside the panties to stroke herself, he rubbed his cock gently, pleasuring himself through the cotton. Daisy gently agitated her clitoris, letting her other hand drift up to her nipple and start tugging at it, teasing it out to an unbearable length. She was soaking wet, fired up by this gorgeous-looking creep and his stink of desperation.

'Take your panties off,' he commanded roughly. She obeyed, catapulting them cheekily at him. He caught them and pressed them to his face, inhaling her woman scent deeply. Her smile was feline. So he liked pussy. No wonder Lydia looked so satisfied all the time.

'I taste even better than that,' she said softly, offering him her glistening juices from her fingers. He sucked greedily on them with closed eyes, and the warm pulling of his mouth unleashed a fresh oozing of moisture, like the juice from a cut peach.

'Oh, yeah,' he muttered, licking lavishly at her fingers. 'I never realised you were so hot, Daisy. All this time ...' He sank to his knees and pressed his mouth against her sex lips. She could feel his tongue push into her, his hands under her buttocks to expose her further. She moaned as he probed and sucked, swirled and drank at her sticky nectar. She bit her lip as he found her clitoris, lapping at it so gently that, in the end, she ground herself on to him, her hands in his hair. Hair mousse. Never mind. She wiped it surreptitiously on his expensive jacket and rode his tongue, giving herself a lovely little orgasm.

'Oh, my, you are a bad boy,' she gasped.

'That's only the beginning, honey. This looks like the start of a beautiful friendship.' He sat back on the desk again, still rampantly hard. 'You still need to pass one test though.' He ran his hand lovingly up his cock. She licked her lips and fluttered her feathery lashes at him. The bad seed of an idea had started to form. Good idea, bad, bad seed.

'Sit down,' she said, vacating her chair. He sat down and widened his legs as far as his trousers would let him, letting his generous scrotum fall through them. She turned around and saucily pulled her skirt up, bending over so he could see how puffy and sticky her sex lips were. 'You've done that to me,' she murmured, running her finger between them and dipping it into herself with a soft squelch. Once, twice, staring boldly at him over her shoulder.

'Shit, Lydia isn't like you,' he gasped.

'There's no one like me,' she replied, straddling him and running her naked pussy up and down his enrobed cock. It rose desperately to meet her but was held cruelly back.

'Yeah?' His eyes drooped with wanton greed. 'I guessed it. That's why I want you to have this job.' His pelvis rocked, trying to reach her. She lifted the sweater above her breasts but did not take it off, instead exposing her nipples and pushing one into his mouth. His cock jerked and he mumbled, but the amount of breast in his mouth made his words indecipherable. He suckled greedily, sending electric tingles throughout her body. Then the other breast, until her nipples were fully distended and bright pink. She teased herself with them, trailing them along his lips, letting him suck, but only briefly, brushing his cock against her snatch and feeling it jump for more. Instead of letting him have it she peeled his trunks away, exposing him.

'It's beautiful,' she purred, sitting back down, and wrapping his cock in her wet pussy lips. She slipped the knot from his tie and removed it, putting it in a handy place for later. 'I want to be very naughty,' she whispered, undulating slowly on him. She had retrieved her panties and was rubbing them gently across her cleft, transferring more of her delicious musky scent before wiping his face with them.

'What do you call this, then?' He asked, before catching the panties between his teeth.

'Even naughtier,' she whispered, hot and tickly in his ear. 'Do you want me to suck you?'

'Oh, yeah,' he moaned.

'Run my tongue right up your cock, flickering it around the head and back, over and over, until you're desperate to get inside me?'

'Yeah, baby. Don't talk about it. Do it!'

'I want to, Jason. I want to fill my mouth with your cock. I want to choke on it and see how my poor pussy is going to manage it. I haven't had a man for almost a year and I'm so tight, I don't know if I'll cope with something so huge.' Don't overdo it, she warned herself. As she talked she tied his hands behind his back with the tie she removed earlier, looping it round the back of his chair so he was held fast. He did not notice until it was too late.

'Hey! What . . .?'

'Hush,' she soothed, kneeling in front of him and enveloping his cock in her breasts. His alarm was immediately replaced by greedy anticipation. He thrust between her breasts, grunting with pleasure as the very tip of her tongue lashed the great dewy hole at the top of his cock. She stopped just as the first beginnings of tension told her he was near to coming.

'Lick me,' he gasped. 'Suck me, you horny little tart!'

She straddled him again, this time holding his tie. 'Close your eyes,' she said, gyrating her hips only centimetres away from his cock. She could see he was reluctant, so she lowered her body and let the tip of him push into her weltering pussy. It felt rather nice. 'You want more?'

'Yes,' he moaned, and obediently closed his eyes. She sank down on him, blindfolding him at the same time. He moaned, incapable of doing anything but bucking against her. She did not hold back her own murmurs of delight. It was so good to feel something alive and warm and pulsing, as opposed to cool and rubbery and artificial, even if it didn't fill her as much as she liked. She undulated her hips against his.

'Oh, Jason, you're massive!' she cooed, feeling him throb in response to the compliment. She rocked on him, distracting him from the fact that she was undoing his shirt buttons. When she licked his nipples he gritted his teeth and bucked so violently she was sure he had come, but as she rode him he was still hard, still with that swollen look of need in his face. When she climbed off him again he looked around, pushing his cock forward hopefully. She drew it into her mouth, sucking her juices from him. His erection bobbed and swayed, kept at exploding point with anticipation by her warm, wet tongue. Still sucking him, she guided the chair closer to the door, then went back and grabbed the envelope from the table. Another long, slow suck, driving him on towards ecstasy.

'Oh, Daisy,' he moaned blindly, 'you are one hot babe...'

He heard the door open. At the same time, the blindfold was whisked from his eyes. Daisy stood, fully dressed, envelope in hand. Behind her were at least fifteen of his staff, open-mouthed, all staring at his lap. With them was Lydia, her pale millennium bob shimmering with outrage. Daisy grinned with impish glee.

'Thanks for the job offer, Jason, but you can shove it where the sun doesn't shine. I'm sure Lydia will know where to find it.'

And, after exchanging a high five with Val, she walked out.

* * *

'I'm going to chase tornadoes.' Daisy lifted her glass to the two friends she had spent three wild and irresponsible years with. Friends she had shared a messy flat with, got drunk on vodka at the weekends with, cried and laughed over men with. They had been great years but, with the loss of her job, they had reached their natural conclusion. She would be 33 this year, and her romantic side was telling her to find someone to settle down with, to make house, to make a life.

But before she did that, her adventurous side was telling her to have a bit of fun. Like countless other kids, she had always thought the best bit of the *Wizard of Oz* was the tornado, so she had signed up on a storm-chasing tour in the American Mid-West. She had been lucky, getting a cancellation with a group led by the brother of one of the country's leading maverick storm chasers. Daisy had seen Mike Bradley on the extreme weather programmes she like to watch on Channel 5. He was arrogant and unprofessional but, as he was prepared to take risks, the resulting footage had made him famous. Daisy was looking forward to see if the reality matched up to the hype.

Afterwards, she intended to cruise around the desert for a week or two, depending on her finances. Her late mother had always believed that everyone had a special place where they would find contentment and, despite her father dismissing the idea as romantic nonsense, Daisy still believed her, so she intended to continue her search. She had had no success in England but, now she had the opportunity to look again, she felt an unaccountable pull to see the Mid-West. Finding her old Minolta camera whilst she was packing up had also reminded her that she used to have hobbies, before work and partying took over. So, she would spend a month chasing wind and dreams before deciding which direction her life was to take next. One thing was definite. Unless she was down to her last dollar, she would never work in an office again.

But she didn't tell her friends that. They seemed to think that talking about photography and storm chasing was a tad too highbrow for their superficial sensibilities.

'OK, tornadoes, what else?' Suzie asked, clearly unimpressed. They were sitting in a bar in Windsor, overlooking the Thames, and it was a Friday night, two weeks after she had walked out on Jason Cordell.

'Then I'm going to go to Colorado to see lots of red rock, take lots of pictures and get laid, lots and lots of times,' Daisy said lightly. 'Who knows? Maybe someone will see my photographs and give me a job.' Realistically she knew that would never happen, but it was a nice thought.

'I'll drink to that,' Val said, with a grin, clinking her Metz bottle with Daisy's. They did the post-mortem on Jason's humiliation two weeks before. Someone had plonked a telephone directory in his lap to cover his modesty, and Lydia had dropped her ice-blonde coolness and had started shrieking, calling him every name under the sun. Then, Val said, laughing so hard that she could hardly speak, no one could untie the knot that held Jason to the chair, so they had to wheel him back into his office before cutting him free.

'Hey, you know Jason isn't called Dickhead any more,' Val giggled. 'He's called Free Willy!'

They dissolved into snorting giggles. When Daisy looked up she saw a man watching her. She noticed him because he was as sharp as an eagle's eye in a dark grey suit and black crew neck, unlike the normal male clientele of slightly sagging thirtysomething executives.

'Do you think you'll ever come back?' Val's voice pulled her attention back.

'I doubt it,' Daisy said honestly, sucking at an ice cube. She had missed the States, with shops that stayed open until late and real sale bargains, not to mention the privilege of getting a decent meal any time, night or day. 'Anyway, maybe it's time to put myself on the market for a man and a mansion.'

'Good luck, girlie. I've been on the market for years,' another friend, Suzie, said gloomily.

'You're too fussy, that's why,' Val said.

'There's nothing wrong with that. You don't want to end up with a man with scars, a load of emotional baggage and a messy divorce behind him.' As Daisy said it, she saw the man at the bar turn away and order another drink. She instinctively knew he had been listening to their conversation. She volunteered to get more drinks and went up to the counter, and stood beside him.

'Hi,' she said, after putting in the drinks order.

'Hi, yourself.' He was American, almost certainly from the North East, from his dress and slightly aloof attitude.

'You're a long way from home,' she ventured flirtatiously. He had very dark, straight hair brushed back in a style vaguely reminiscent of Elvis, and lazy green eyes. A nice mouth, slightly cruel, with a delicately bow-shaped top lip, suggested that he might be excellent at kissing.

'So are you,' he said. He was drinking bourbon, watching her guardedly over the top of his glass. She detected a very slight but unmistakable Northern Irish grit in his accent, but his attitude and sharp sense of style were pure Manhattan.

'Let me guess. New York, right?'

'Very good. Is it that obvious?'

'No. I've just seen too many gangster movies, that's all,' she said, grinning.

He visibly stiffened. 'What do you mean?'

'Relax! Welcome to England. Has anyone said that yet?'

'No, but nobody's accused me of being a criminal, either.'

'I wasn't ... oh forget it. What are you doing over here?'

'Looking for you.'

She giggled, checked it, and turned it into a womanly laugh instead. 'That's a great line, but you need to embellish it a bit. We girlies like a bit of flannel, even though we know its bullshit. Then the deal is, after you've screwed us, you can go all silent and moody.' What was she saying? It was all bollocks, and even her unspoken thoughts were sounding slurred. She backed away from him, feeling idiotic. 'That's just a handy tip for you, in case you get lucky.' She fled back to the table, her face bright red.

'Where are our drinks?' Val said accusingly.

She had forgotten them. She crept back up to the bar. He was watching with a vaguely amused expression. She decided to brazen out her embarrassment.

'So what do you do back in New York?'

'I'm a hit man. But it's okay, I'm on vacation.'

She closed her mouth with an effort. He was joking, of course, but it would have been funnier if he hadn't actually looked the part. Then she went cold inside. Surely her father hadn't broken his promise? And if he had, why would he send one of his lackeys to watch her?

No, it was her imagination. When she had spoken to him she had made the point of telling him she trusted him not to do anything stupid, as if she were a mother and he were her son. Anyway, he hadn't become a millionaire by sending hit men on expensive jollies to look after family business. She thrust the ludicrous idea from her mind. Time to get back to having fun.

'That's cool,' she said. 'What's your speciality?'

'In what way?'

'Gun, knife, bare hands? Let me guess.' She picked up his right hand, which was resting on the bar, and ran her fingers along his. They were slender and cool, blue veins showing prominently on the back of his hand. His nails looked buffed and well cared for. 'Hmmm, I bet you don't let these get dirty too often. I'd guess you use a gun, and you're probably a crack shot, looking at this trigger finger.' She waggled his forefinger gently, aware that the conversation could be getting dangerous. Being Irish didn't make him a criminal, but he had that same look she first saw after her comment about gangsters, earlier. He had to be joking, right?

But then he laughed. And although his smile was shark-like, his eyes seemed genuinely warm. 'I'm actually left-handed. You have a very vivid imagination.'

'So do you,' she countered. 'Blame mine on vodka.'

Val appeared at her shoulder. 'Drinks tonight would be good,' she said acidly, taking the tray back to the table. Daisy could see her friends peering at her, trying to see who she was talking to.

'I'd better go,' she said, although she did not want to. 'It's my party.'

'Enjoy it.'

She could feel him watching her as she went back to her friends.

'Is that your shag for tonight?' Suzie asked.

Daisy glanced back at him, but he had disappeared. 'Obviously not,' she sighed, surprised at the amount of regret that fact left her with.

'Well, this should cheer you up,' Val said, producing a brown paper bag and plonking it on Daisy's lap. 'We clubbed together to get you something to see you through all those lonely nights.'

Too touched to speak, Daisy tore open the paper and delved into the shoebox inside, drawing out a fat, veiny vibrator, with a huge, chunky glans. The latex was soft and silky, very expensive. There was a box beside it with three buttons that could be pushed to adjust the speed.

'That's the remote control,' Val said, taking it from her. 'Look. Vibrating action.' The vibe began to shiver in Daisy's hand. 'Squirming action.' It churned around in her palm, making her laugh. 'And this is the absolute best. Pumping action!' The vibe nearly jumped out of Daisy's grip. 'Sorry, that was full speed!' Val said, with a laugh. Daisy turned the vibrator around in her hands.

'This is the neatest thing!' She laughed, kissing them all in turn. 'Thanks, guys.'

'It's great. We've both had a turn,' Suzie said mischievously. 'Val didn't wipe, as usual.' They all pulled faces at the grossness of the idea. Daisy tucked the vibrator away, aware of the interested stares of a group of middle-aged, unattractive men.

'I'm going to miss you so much,' she said, wiping moisture from her eyes.

'Don't get all soppy on us,' Rachel warned. 'You'll start us all off.'

'Relax, I'm going for a pee. I'll cry in the toilet.'

'You want to take this with you?' Val cackled, holding up the vibrator.

'I might not need it,' Daisy chirped back at her, and not for one moment did she think it might be true.

The toilets were on the other side of the car park near the river. They were cold and damp but, as she sat there, she was thinking of the stranger at the bar. What a shame he had left. Another vodka and she might have had the courage to offer him something he couldn't refuse.

On the way out she bumped straight into him.

It was extraordinary, really. She did not even know his name. Yet when they crashed into each other, in the dark outside the toilets, it seemed only natural for their lips to meet in a hungry whisky and nicotine-tasting kiss. Instantly she forgot that men who smoked were usually repellent to her as he pushed her against the cold wall, hot and urgent as though he had been waiting for her all evening. She was so tall that she did not have to crane her neck to kiss him, and he was strong enough to hold her uncompromisingly against the white painted pebble-dash wall, grinding ruthlessly against her. Her body responded with an engulfing wave of desire that made her return his assault so readily it made him whimper with surprised lust.

In the cool darkness, with the twinkling lights reflected in the Thames and the smell of musty river water and beer kegs, the kiss continued, blindly, as hot as the sun. His hand was on her breast, kneading it greedily through silk and lace. She fumbled for the buttons so he could get to her flesh, feeling his moan as he hit second base, dealing swiftly with the catch on her Wonderbra. Her hand found his cock, very hard, very ready. As she squeezed his prodigious length through his suit trousers he groaned and broke the kiss.

'What's your name?'

'Daisy. What's yours?' She continued to massage him, feeling him throb strongly against her.

'I shouldn't be doing this,' he whispered, but he did not try to break away.

'Why not? Are you married?'

'No, but . . .' He gave in and kissed her again, pressing himself against her hand. 'I mustn't.'

'For God's sake, why not?' She ran her palm up and down the entire ridge of his cock, feeling him shiver. She wanted him, as suddenly and urgently as she had lusted for Jason. Her body was crying out with the desire to be screwed recklessly and anonymously, and from the heft of flesh filling her hand, she would not be left wanting. He did not stop her as she unzipped him and thrust her hand into his undershorts. Boxers, fine cotton, very nice. Her fingers tangled in thick soft hair and cupped under his balls, which were big and heavy and tight. She stroked their underside with the very tips of her fingers. In the dark recess no one could see them, though she could see people walking along the path by the river, and hear voices laughing nearby.

'If you don't fuck me I'll fuck you,' she whispered boldly.

'Daisy, please . . .' He grabbed her hand as it slipped up inside his thin, silky sweater and placed it on his cock instead. She wished she could see it properly and give it the attention it deserved, but he was kissing her again, rapaciously, his tongue so deep in her throat she could offer no resistance, even if she had wanted to. Then he was thrusting her hands behind her back, forcing her blouse open and baring her breasts so that he could suck greedily at each pronounced nipple until she wanted to come just with that sensation alone. She squirmed uselessly, her legs trying to scrabble up his in rapturous response. Totally entrapped, she could not help but plead with him in breaths of wonder to release her, to fuck her. Ignoring her pleas, his tongue continued to enslave her in a cage of pleasure, her breasts so overloaded with sensation that she felt drunk with it. She wanted to cry, to scream, to grind her body on to his but, more than anything, she wanted him to continue, to up the torture until eddies of sweet sensation, like fireworks on a distant hill, hit her one by one. As they faded away, she realised he had given her something totally new.

'No one's ever done that before,' she whispered breathlessly against his lips as he fumbled with her panties, wrenching them downwards. She worked one leg free, giving a loud, hoarse cry at the joyous piercing of his cock deep inside her. Her body reacted instinctively, undulating to experience every inch, sending pulsing echoes throughout her whole body. Two girls appeared around the corner, obviously coming to see what the noise was about. Their jaws dropped at the sight of Daisy being fucked relentlessly against the white pebble-dash wall. She waved them away and wrapped her legs tighter around his waist.

'More, you big brute,' she whispered, tugging on his earlobe with her teeth. 'Come on, give it to me!'

'If you want it you can damned well have it,' he growled, dropping her and spinning her around. He pushed her against a large beer barrel, his hands thrusting up her skirt, feeling her wet readiness. She bit her lip to stop from screaming as he pushed fully inside her hot, tight pussy again, his fingers digging cruelly into her hips. He fucked her hard, silently, intensifying the recklessness of the moment as she spread herself wide and let him take her. She felt his hand on her clitoris and she shrieked like a cat on heat, no longer caring who heard or saw her, her orgasm prolonged by the stranger plundering her depths like a man possessed. He came with a series of violent pulses. 'You've fucked me over, seduced me, destroyed me.' Murmured words to himself, not meant for her to answer. Totally spent, he rested on her for a moment before backing away, leaving her to scrabble to her feet, pulling her panties up from her ankles.

'Shit!' He said, looking at her with mounting horror.

'What it really that bad?'

'No, Daisy, that's the problem. Stupid motherfucker!' He backed off, his eyes feverish, said 'shit!' again several times over, and practically ran from the back of the pub.

'Wait!' She stumbled after him, confused and still so aroused she could hardly walk, but the last she saw of him was a dark car and tail-lights disappearing into the night.

She walked unsteadily back into the bar and carefully sat down with her friends.

'You guys won't believe what's just happened.'

2

Daisy arrived in New York the following Sunday morning, and her good friend, Chico Mendoza, was there to meet her, dandyish in Dolce and Gabbana. She ran to him with a whoop and leaped into his arms, her legs around his waist.

'Well, I see you've learned the art of discretion in England,' Chico said as she released him. She stuck her tongue out at him.

'Just preserving your reputation,' she replied gaily. With their arms around each other they went to his waiting limousine.

She and Chico had remained close even though her father tried to put the kybosh on their relationship. He obviously thought they were practically engaged by the way he had ranted at her. It wasn't the first time. He had played the heavy father with practically every boyfriend she ever had, and his behaviour had worsened with the death of her mother. But Chico was the last straw, because he was the son of Felix's worst enemy.

Felix Lovell's hatred of the Mendoza family began thirty years earlier when, as a thrusting exporter, he had been relying on Enrico Mendoza's investment to pull off a highly lucrative deal. But Mendoza had suddenly pulled out, leaving Felix high and dry and another five years away from multi-millionaire status. Since then, Lovell had a dislike of foreigners that boarded on the obsessive, and Puerto Ricans in particular. Drug runners, the lot of them, he said, dismissing his own dubious code of intimidation as being ethical business practice. And, as he was highly successful at it, no one was inclined to put him right.

So, when Daisy became friendly with Enrico Mendoza's son, all Lovell's old resentments were opened up, and visions of the two families unifying in marriage were intolerable. Not realising that there never would be any romance between them, he bluntly told Daisy that she was not to see him again. Daisy thought it best not to mention that she was actually sleeping with Enrico Mendoza at the time but having inherited her mother's determined spirit, she had confronted her father with all the other instances where he had been overprotective and unreasonable. So, when the opportunity came to work in England came up, she jumped at it. The irony was that no decent man had showed his face since.

'Let's look at you,' Chico said, critically assessing her glossy brown hair, chic black linen trousers and Office door-stop heeled pumps. She had changed on the plane just before landing, so that she didn't feel like a bag lady on the fashion-conscious streets of Manhattan. Now she was thankful she had.

'You'll do,' Chico decided finally.

'For what, you cheeky bastard?'

'Brunch at the Russian Tea Rooms. I thought we'd celebrate your homecoming in style.'

'Oh, you honey!' She flung her arms around him.

He gently extricated himself. 'Sweet Daisy. Always the affectionate puppy.'

It was a mild rebuke, and she found herself looking closer at him. The slim goatee beard and moustache were new, and gave his somewhat blandly handsome features a dangerous edge. He was also a good deal thinner than she remembered, showing his catwalk clothes to perfection. But it wasn't the old Chico, all muscles and hip-slung jeans and preppy sweatshirts. Something had changed, and not necessarily for the better.

'I've spoken to Phil and Paul,' he was saying. 'They say it's fine for you move in at any time.'

'That's great, Chico. I really appreciate it.'

'You're doing them a favour. Paul was beginning to be a bore about the house being empty for so long. They won't be back until the Fall.'

'I'll be long gone by then. I hope they know how grateful I am,' Daisy said with feeling. She would have to face her father soon, but she absolutely drew the line at moving back in with him. Since their last argument they had reached an impasse, but only after she had called him to make him promise not to keep sending his body-guards to keep an eye on her, as it was getting embarrassing. Now she had to find the mental strength to see him again face to face. It wasn't something she was looking forward to.

In the opulent surroundings of the Russian Tea Rooms they rubbed shoulders with the rich and bored, and feasted on tiny blinchikis with sour cream and cherry preserve. Daisy recounted her story of Jason and the chair, and Chico listened with great relish.

'The man who really decides he's in love with you had better watch out,' he said, pushing a lock of wavy hair away from her face. 'You've the eyes of an angel and the morals of a heavyweight wrestler.'

'You're too kind,' Daisy said, smiling angelically.

'I kept your letters,' Chico said. 'They were so amusing.'

'I'd like to say I kept yours, but you didn't send any.'

He waved her sarcasm away and lowered his voice to a conspiratorial whisper. 'You sure you weren't followed?'

'I changed planes twice, just to be sure,' Daisy replied, grinning. 'Daft fart. As if I care what Dad would say. I'm a big girl now. And don't change the subject. I also want to know why you never came to London?'

'Darling, you know I don't do long haul flights. Anyway, London's so ... grimy.' He squirmed with elegant distaste.

'I've really missed you,' she said, squeezing his hand.

'If you hadn't been so stubborn and insisted on being poor for years, you could have come back to visit.'

'I know,' she sighed, 'but I had to get away and keep away. Dad ... well, let's just say that everything comes with a price. I think I've paid it with every man I've ever met. Especially you.'

Chico rolled his eyes. 'Oh please, make me feel guilty, why don't you?'

'How's ... Enrico?'

'I was wondering when you'd ask. He's fine, spends most of his time with very expensive call girls, hoping that one of them might turn out to be like you. I hope he doesn't find her. I'd rather not have a 23-year-old whore for a stepmother.'

Daisy sucked cappuccino froth from her spoon. 'I was up front with him. I said I could never love him in the way he wanted, and I wasn't prepared to use him.'

Chico waved her words away. 'You don't have to explain to me. Personally I would have taken the money and run, but you have a perverse sense of righteousness that really has held you back somewhat in the financial stakes.'

'And there's you saying I have bad morals two minutes ago,' she retorted.

'Talking of which, I must go and powder my nose.' He excused himself and headed off to the restrooms. She anxiously watched him go. He had changed more than she first thought, with his new veneer of cultured distain. And there was she thinking she sounded English, whilst he was poncing around like an extra from *Brideshead Revisited*. Not the smartest of moves for a man whose inheritance rested on the illusion that he was straight.

When he came back he started to chatter like a clockwork monkey. The reason why suddenly hit her, and she felt stupid for not seeing the signs before.

'I think I've been in the provinces too long,' she said, reaching over and wiping a tiny trace of white powder from his nose. 'What the hell is happening, Chico? I thought you said you'd never touch coke?'

His brittle façade collapsed. 'It's the only way I can deal with it,' he muttered. 'Living a lie like this is driving me crazy.'

Daisy felt for him. She had once tried to broach the subject with Enrico. It was the only time he had been angry with her and, for a split second, she had feared for her own safety.

'Can't he see this is tearing you apart?'

Chico looked bitter. 'Well, either no, or he doesn't give a shit. Take your pick.' He patted his moist forehead with a pristine linen napkin. 'And just when I decide I can rise above the whole damned thing, I go and fall in love.' He swallowed a gulp of espresso as if it were life-giving water. She noticed how his slim brown hands trembled slightly.

'And ... that's a bad thing?' she suggested tentatively.

'It is when the object of my affection is in my face every day at the office, and someone else is moving in on them, and for the sake of my family's goddamned reputation I can't do a damned thing about it. I can't leave my job. I can't get him or the competition fired so they're out of my face. I can't do anything!' His voice had risen to a pitch that drew the attention of the people on the next table. Daisy covered his hand with her own.

'Keep your hetero hat on!' she whispered fiercely. 'What's his name, anyway?'

Chico's liquid dark eyes went briefly misty. 'Piers Molyneaux.' He rolled the name around his tongue like a fine wine. 'It's been like this for months. I don't know how much longer I can stand it.'

'OK, listen. Tonight we hit Chinatown for supper and we chew the fat. You're a mess, Chico. Someone has to tell Enrico that this has to stop, and I'm more than willing to do it.'

'Darling Daisy, always the would-be Fairy Godmother. You should know by now that I'm a lost cause. You can't just walk in and make everything better all the time. Life isn't like that.'

'I know!' She felt hurt by his mockery, but quickly reminded herself that he was the one that hurt more. 'OK, so I'm naïve and stupid, but I love you. I want to help and I've missed the Beijing Duck House, so humour me. Please?'

She could feel his reluctance but, to her monumental relief, he smiled again and gave her a return squeeze.

'You win.' He sparkled falsely at her. 'But first let's indulge in some retail therapy before your jetlag sets in.'

For a while they cruised around Bloomingdales. Living in England and being in professional business suits for most of the time hadn't prepared her well for life out on the Plains, so she went on a bit of a spree, despite her dodgy finances. After buying hip-slung Diesel jeans, some skimpy vest tops and two pairs of short shorts, she was also very tempted by some slim-fitting walking boots that laced up well past her ankles, making her legs look even longer and giving extra shape to her calves.

'Very Lara Croft, and they'll protect you from rattlesnakes,' Chico had pointed out practically, flipping out his Platinum Amex after she made some passing comment about being careful about her credit card bill. 'You should spend it, darling. Get some satisfaction out of having a rich daddy, for god's sake,' he had said impatiently.

'But I'm not like that,' she protested. 'I pay my way and rely on me. However much he irritates me, I'm not going to use my father as a commodity to be exploited.'

'Christ, you're so noble,' Chico said with disgust. 'You'll just have to use me instead.'

After much argument he also bought her a white Chloe dress, laced up at the front, with a cheesecloth cotton skirt that would be happy squashed in the bottom of her bag for hours at a time. A bronze Baja bikini completed her ensemble. She doubted she would need anything else. It would be hot on the Plains and in the bus, even though it was air-conditioned.

When they arrived back at his apartment they opened another bottle of wine and watched *Gladiator*. Despite the allure of Russell Crowe in sweaty leather, Daisy eventually fell asleep. It was only intended to be a five-minute snooze, but when she woke up she was lying on Chico's bed and it was dark. The clock by her bed said it was past eleven o'clock at night. She showered and put on a light silk chemise and robe. Voices floated from the large living room, so she crept past the door to make a cup of tea. There were fresh bagels on the side so she ate one with some smoked salmon she found in the fridge. She perched on a bar stool looking out over towards Macys and the Empire State Building.

Eventually she decided there was nothing better to do than go back to bed. As she passed the living room she glanced in, and braked fast.

Kneeling up on the silky sheepskin rug was the most beautiful man she had seen for a long time. His liquorice-coloured skin was complimented dramatically by white Calvin Klein trunks, half pulled down to free a hefty, thickly ridged penis. The other parts of his body weren't bad either. A long neck supporting an arrogantly defined African head with sharp cheekbones and tightly braided hair in tiny knots. His body was buffed up and glistening, with bulging pectorals aggressively defined. Chico was subserviently on his knees, worshipping his partner's cock whilst the man stroked Chico's backside with tenderness, slipping his hand into his boxers to fondle his balls. Chico gave a muffled moan of pleasure, arching his back, and Daisy moved away, not wanting to disturb such an intimate moment.

At that moment, the dark man looked over and saw her. She cringed with embarrassment as he smiled beatifically and climbed to his feet.

'Come on in, honey.'

His voice was as deep and smooth as bitter chocolate. Chico looked up. His eyes were hazy with lust and designer drugs. His friend was leading her into the room. On the zen-like glass table was a black slate block dusted with cocaine, together with two champagne flutes and a bottle of Bollinger.

'Get another glass, Chi. I think the little lady wants some education.'

She wasn't sure she did, or even what he meant. 'I don't want to interrupt,' she said hesitantly to Chico. It wasn't that she was scared of the two men, but she didn't know how Chico expected her to react. Chico stumbled over to a cabinet to retrieve another glass. She went with him.

'Where the hell did he come from?' she whispered.

'He's a dancer at a club I went to tonight.' He turned to the man. 'Hey, what's your name?'

'Jack,' the answer came back.

'So he's a stranger? And you've let him into your apartment? Are you totally nuts?'

A flash of annoyance passed over Chico's face. 'Relax, Daisy, he's a nice person. Anyway, sometimes I have to let off steam. It's the only way I survive.'

He wouldn't survive much longer doing reckless things like that, she thought, but knew better than to say so. She kept her mouth shut and sipped at the champagne Chico offered her. Jack came up behind him and encircled a thickly muscled arm around Chico's waist. He held a tiny cone of powder on the ball of one finger for Chico to inhale. He did, and sighed contentedly, leaning back against his lover's deep chest. Daisy should have been revolted by Chico's self-destructive behaviour, but the sight of the two of them, hands roaming around each others bodies, was actually turning her on. Jack's eyes were very wide, the whites showing all the way around his deep brown irises. She knew it was the coke but, eerily, it seemed as if he could reach right into her mind. He took her hand, and numbly she let him lead her over to the rug. His cock jutted out unashamedly in front of him, together with a pair of big, leathery balls that she tried desperately hard not to stare at. She glanced at Chico to check that her presence was acceptable to him. He shrugged peaceably.

'If you want to watch, feel free,' he said serenely. He motioned to a large, comfortable armchair at right angles to the couch. Obediently she sat in it, hugging her champagne flute and feeling slightly awkward.

'Why don't you tell us what to do? Our wish is your command,' Jack said.

She laughed at last. 'Don't you mean your wish is my command?'

Jack thought it over. 'No. My wish ... no ... your wish...'

'Is our command,' Chico finished for him, slipping off his boxers and tossing them over the couch. Daisy relaxed back into the chair. The unreality of the situation was playing havoc with her travel-weary brain. How many men were doing this right now, sitting in a big chair, hard-on in hand, waiting for two women to get into some hot lesbian action just for their benefit? The sensual role reversal sent a wicked pulse down to her most feminine of places.

'OK boys, go to the rug and start getting it on.'

The men started to kiss, their buff, beautiful bodies pressed close together, their limbs entwined like silken ropes. Watching Chico's fingers slip down the back of Jack's shorts and squeeze his hard buttocks, she began to get very moist. On the table beside the chair was a black mahogany humidor. She opened it and took out a short, slender cigar. She had never smoked one before in her life, but had seen her father clip and light up enough times in the past to do it right. The men watched her, still fondling each other, as she went through the process and took the first tentative lungful. It was sweet and fragrant, and didn't make her cough at all. She drew on the cigar again, aware that the men were waiting for her next order.

'You're the boss,' Chico said, a slight shake in his voice.

'The big cheese. We're your minions. We do as you say,' Jack added.

She caught on instantly, and struck an arrogant pose in the chair, legs splayed. Slowly she let the thick, creamy smoke trickle from her lips. 'Okay, Jack, get on your knees and suck his dick. Chico, turn this way. I want to see it.' She made her voice hard and authorative.

Obediently Chico knelt on the rug. They were both very handsome men, she thought wistfully. What a shame they weren't interested in her. The sight of Jack's taut buttocks moving slowly back and forth and the jutting spear of Chico's cock were making her very damp.

'Jack, use the tip of your tongue around the head. That's it. Tickle the underside. They all like that.' Chico moaned in agreement. 'And lick his balls, long and slow.'

As Jack did as he was bid, Chico collapsed suddenly on to the rug, his erection rampant. Jack kneeled beside him with his back to Daisy, lapping at his balls.

'OK, Jack, open those legs a little. I want to see your dick.' Even as she spoke she couldn't believe what she was saying. She fought the ever-increasing urge to stroke herself as she told Chico to finger Jack's asshole. Jack's heavy scrotum hung down between his thighs, swaying gently as he moved against Chico's finger. Chico looked over at her, a blurred expression on his face.

'Does this please the boss? Does she want to make herself come?' As if he knew she needed tacit permission, without breaking the illusion that she was in charge. She drew on the cigar again and threw him a steely look.

'Shut the fuck up and get down on him.' She slipped off her robe and sat back, just in her chemise. They would be able to see her soaking, swollen pussy but she didn't care. Her fingers found her nipples through the thin silk. They tensed at her touch and her vision clouded for a moment. She licked her fingers and sent one hand down to her cunt. Her sex lips were gaping and slippery, and her inner lips sucked at her finger as she pushed it inside herself. She visually feasted on Jack's thick cock, wanting so much for him to come over and give it to her, but there was some sick pleasure in knowing that Chico was going to get it instead. The men were on the rug, writhing together, their cocks rubbing together, their buttocks bunching, muscles shifting under their skin like ripples on a smooth lake. The fingers on her nipple sought out bare flesh and on contact she gasped, tugging harder at the prominent tip. She hardly noticed Chico coming towards her, holding a present: a thick, black dildo made of finest quality latex. The balls were big and squashy, unnervingly real. He stood in front of her, as did Jack, and watched her fondling it.

'Don't just stand there! Wank each other!' She tried to sound imperious, but the sheer size of the thing she was attempting to shove inside herself made her voice wobble. She slid further down in the chair to improve the angle. Her pussy couldn't be any wetter, watching two beautiful men pleasuring each other, but she still had difficulty easing the monster in. Her inner muscles strained, contracted against it, making her pant with pleasure. When it was in she could not move, so stuffed with cock that her clit was exposed to the air. Her nipples were huge and longer than she had ever seen them before, teased by her fingertips, each tiny sensation plummeting down to her clit, making it throb so wildly it reverberated through her whole sex.

'Give it to him,' she said to Jack through gritted teeth.

'Whatever you say, ma'am.' Jack led Chico back to the rug and pushed him over it, spreading his cheeks and licking lavishly along the deep crack. Chico moaned, his erection pressed into the silky wool, but Jack pulled up his hips and lubricated his back passage with saliva. As Daisy watched he eased his cock between Chico's buttocks. Her eyes widened as his whole cock disappeared, her own cunt throbbing wildly in response. As Jack began to move, she grasped the balls of the vibrator and moved it in and out in time. She had dried up with the sheer size of the thing, but feeling it move around inside her again unleashed a fresh flood of moisture. Chico's face was suffused with helpless lust, taking the other man fully, Jack reaching round and feeling for Chico's cock. Chico's tongue came out and his eyes half closed. His abandonment was total as Jack climaxed with thrusting grunts, hard, intense, totally male. Daisy rammed the dildo inside herself, building up for that final sweet surrender as Chico disengaged and moved behind Jack, now the one in control. Jack's cock was still rock hard and dripping semen as Chico mounted him. Daisy's fingers flew feverishly over her clit, her gaze fixed rigidly on Jack's massive, sagging cock. Her other hand was at her nipples, tugging each one, the chemise now down to her waist, all modesty forgotten. She started to come, bucking in the chair, the huge dildo stringing out her pleasure as she imagined someone just as huge as Jack, giving it good, giving it hard, as the mystery man had given it to her only a few days before. She peaked with a cry as Chico added his joyous yelps to the chorus of pleasure echoing around the room.

They drank shots of espresso on the balcony overlooking 33rd Street. The men wore trunks but nothing else. They all draped together on a couch. Chico had found his binoculars and was peering at the apartment block opposite, looking for any signs of licentious behaviour in the brightly lit windows.

'Nothing. Oh well, I guess we'll have to DIY,' Chico sighed.

'Surely you mean DIO?' Daisy pointed out.

'She's an awkward little cat, isn't she?' Jack commented.

'That's why I love her.' Chico hugged Daisy closer and buried his face in her hair. It seemed that their friendship was back on an even keel again.

When she woke up the next morning Jack had gone and Chico was curled around her. He woke when she turned around to face him.

'That was the best evening I've had in ages,' he said, stretching luxuriously. 'He was very good. My ass feels like the Lincoln Tunnel.'

'Good, but bringing him back here wasn't clever, was it? You might have been robbed or beaten up, or worse.'

He sat up, suddenly irritated. 'Oh, Daisy, that's so English of you. It's just as much of a risk for him. Anyway, I wasn't the one who walked in and took over.' He pulled on his robe and went out of the room. 'I'll make us some coffee.'

'Chico!' She padded after him. 'That's hardly fair. You were both really wired. The whole thing was . . . weird.'

'You know what's really weird? Someone I haven't seen for five years walking in, telling me how to run my life before she's recovered from jetlag!'

She felt like crying. This wasn't how their reunion was supposed to go at all. 'I'm sorry you feel like that. Do you want me to leave?'

Suddenly his face cleared and he threw his arms around her. 'Dear Daisy, of course not! You obviously need to relearn a few basic rules after being in that revolting country for so long.' He pressed a forgiving kiss on her forehead and held her for a long time, soothing away her confusion.

For the next three days he was extravagantly affectionate, as if he were trying in some way to make up for his strange behaviour. One part of her wished she wasn't going away, as it was obvious he needed someone sane around him.

They moved her belongings into Paul and Phil's house, a large, multi-faceted Colonial painted in Easter chick yellow with sparkling white fretwork and a covered porch that ran from one end of the house to the other. Four flags lined the balcony above the porch, as was *de rigueur* in most small American towns. They were The Stars and Stripes, a summer flag bearing a large red geranium and two bearing the symbols of Gay Pride, a pink triangle and a rainbow stripe. When her father found out she was staying in the house of a gay couple he would have apoplexy, Daisy thought gleefully as she opened the door.

Inside, the décor could best be described as eclectic. Upstairs there were frou-frou frills and a four-poster bed, together with a chair that looked as if it belonged in a torture chamber. When Chico sat in it and demonstrated what it was for, she began to wonder who the hell these people were. Downstairs were more, obviously expensive, pieces of English antique oak, a mahogany dining table and countless arrangements of dried flowers that made her nose wrinkle in anticipation of lurking dust. Fortunately Phil was anal about cleanliness, and had a woman come in weekly to do the necessary.

'Cows!' Chico exclaimed, looking aghast as he came out of the kitchen. 'This isn't good, Daisy. I'm going to have to seriously review my friendship with Phil and Paul on the grounds of good taste.'

Daisy looked in at the kitchen, and saw what he meant. There were cow oven gloves, cow storage jars, cow tea towels. A cow with a pink nose gurned at them from the wall, with cup hooks holding cow mugs. She shut the door quickly. At least she had a couple of weeks to think of ways to make it liveable with for the next few months.

The next day Chico took her back to JFK for her flight to Denver. As they said goodbye she could not resist telling him to be careful. Underneath the bright mask, his jaded expression made her heart ache. She promised to call as soon as she could.

3

Max Decker hovered outside a rundown apartment door in downtown Manhattan and yawned widely. He was still wiped out with jetlag, courtesy of British Airways two days before. His flight from London had been over-booked and then delayed by bad weather, forcing him to spend two extra nights in a hotel with no concept of air-conditioning, and windows that only just kept aircraft noise to acceptable levels. An exasperated Felix Lovell had finally sent him back home on Concorde. It was supposed to be a perk, sitting for three hours on an undersized pocket rocket with overfed and overfunded businessmen, but he wasn't convinced. However, the food had been excellent, and the cabin crew easy on the eye. He had sat mid-section, kept his Hugo Boss shades on and had tried to look inconspicuous. Not that it had worked. It seemed the more drably he dressed the more people were likely to mistake him for some celebrity striving for anonymity. 'Was that Christopher Walken?' someone had whispered behind him. He was used to it, though no one ever approached him. He had perfected a glacial stare to prevent unwanted attention.

In the gloom cast by a single bare bulb his dark auburn hair looked black, brushed back from an unlined forehead and narrow, almond-shaped green eyes. Those eyes held the look that liquefied the bowels of any scum-bag criminal unfortunate enough to cross his path, sec-onds before they felt the whispered finality of a silenced bullet. But tonight his weapon of choice was the blade concealed in his left shirtsleeve. The unsuspecting punk on the other side of the door was about to have a very bad evening.

When Felix Lovell had learned that Decker was stranded in England, he had panicked and asked a small-time private investigator to follow Daisy once she landed at JFK to see where she went. Now he was going to get more than he bargained for. Tommy O'Brien was a sleaze-bag of the lowest order, not long out of jail for defrauding old ladies out of their life savings, and well known to Decker from the past. He had recently set himself up as a private eye, but the temptation to cream off more cash from his clients had already proved too much. The photos he had developed that afternoon had shown Daisy getting very friendly with two half-dressed men, so he had called Lovell that afternoon, asking for another five thousand.

Decker listened for a minute. No television, no movement to suggest that someone was behind the paper thin wall. As he raised his hand to knock gently, he noticed that the green paint on the door was peeling. He pulled a bit off, then another. It came away in long, satisfying strips. He dropped them to the floor and crushed them with an elegantly pointed steel-capped shoe. As he reached for another green curl, footsteps approached from the bottom of the stairs. Quickly he concealed himself in the dark space underneath the stairwell, trying not to inhale the smell of piss and old takeaways.

Footsteps. Tommy lurched drunkenly up the stairs, eventually making it to the top. He couldn't find his keys. Decker waited impatiently as he dealt with the lock, but he smiled as he saw the door stop on the latch. With quick, efficient movements he attached the silencer. He waited a couple of minutes, then gently pushed the door open.

Tommy was sitting in a chair with his back to the door. In one hand he held a porno mag. In the other was his pathetic little dick. He was pulling on it absent-mindedly, concentrating on a pneumatic redhead falling out of her redskin costume. She had two somewhat larger dicks in either hand, her glossy red lips stretched around one of them.

Decker coughed discreetly. The startled man's eyes flew open, seeing the gun first and then Decker's tall, dark presence, holding the weapon as if it were a natural extension of his rock-steady right arm.

'I was going to wait a while but you were taking too fucking long.'

'Please don't kill me,' Tommy whispered. His cock had shrivelled back to nothing. Decker was shaking his head.

'No, what you should be saying is, "please don't hurt me."' He stood at ease, relaxing his gun hand. 'Do you remember me, Tommy?'

The man's eyes widened in recognition.

'That's right. I'm the cop that put you away. Pity you only got five years. You gave all those nice ladies a life sentence. Now I hear you're a private investigator. How's business?'

'What do you want?' Tommy stuttered. 'You here to arrest me? What for?'

'I left the NYPD a long time ago, Tommy. I work for Felix Lovell now. You've been trying to shaft him like a bitch, and this is his way of saying he doesn't appreciate it.' He drew out a wad of notes from his jacket and threw them on the bed. 'Five thousand, as agreed. What have you got for me?'

'The photos are over there,' Tommy said sourly, nodding to a large brown envelope on a messy table. Keeping him in sight, Decker picked it up and looked inside. He recognised Chico Mendoza, which wasn't going to please the boss, and Daisy, and a big, Afro-Caribbean man. They were all barely dressed. In one picture, Daisy was draped languidly over the stranger whilst Chico played with her hair. She looked blissed-out, her short chemise falling down around one shoulder. There was no doubt how they had been entertaining themselves that evening. The grainy, monochrome images filled Decker with an all-consuming jealous rage, which he hid behind a neutral façade.

'And you think these are worth another five thousand?' His voice was dangerously quiet.

'Why not? He can afford it.'

'That isn't the point, Tommy. Business is business. You don't welch on a deal, especially with someone like Felix Lovell. Did you take stupid pills this morning?'

'The flaky little slut should have stayed in Sluff,' Tommy said bitterly.

Decker didn't bother to reply. He lazily squeezed the trigger. Tommy jerked once and was still, a small hole in the centre of his forehead. 'It's Slough, you moron.'

He pocketed the money, together with the photographs. As he left the apartment he tripped over something soft. Looking down, he saw a Siamese cat curling around his ankles. It meowed softly, regarding him proprietorially with narrow blue eyes. Something about the creature appealed to him and, as it was now a stray, thanks to him, he couldn't help but feel sorry for it. Voices from the stairs above helped him make up his mind. He scooped the cat up and tucked it into his jacket, then left the apartment building as swiftly and silently as a shadow.

Out in the deserted, rain-washed street he pulled his collar up around his neck to keep out the sharp wind. The cat rumbled warmly against his skin, reminding him of his new responsibilities. He went to an all-night store and bought a tin of kitty chow before taking a cab back to his apartment in Greenwich Village.

The place was spartan, like his life. A comfortable bed, a minimally equipped kitchen, a few items of furniture scattered here and there were only a few clues to what kind of man he was. The one shelf in the main living area held a sloping mix of Dean Koontz, James Ellroy and James Herbert, and a couple of hardcore glossies, barely touched. For the past few years he had been living simply whilst he decided what to do next. Now his bank account held upwards of eight hundred thousand dollars, boosted by the compensation payment he had received for injuries in service to the NYPD. It wasn't a fortune, but enough to enable him to walk away from Felix Lovell for good. He had started working exclusively for him soon after Daisy had left for England. The money had made him do it. Lovell was prepared to pay over the odds to keep ahead of the game, and he wasn't fussy about asking questions about Decker's methods. However, after a couple of years, Decker realised he was prostituting his talents to line another man's pockets. It wasn't that he minded breaking a few limbs, but the smell of death had started to sicken him. At 42 he was already getting too old for that shit. It was putrefying his soul.

After feeding the cat he resisted the temptation to reach for the bourbon. Instead he lit a few candles, giving the room a soft, unobtrusive glow and the woody scent of hemp, and stripped off his clothes. Exhausted as he was, he needed to exorcise the last hour.

After the brief telephone call that always preceded his t'ai chi routine, he put the Verve's *Urban Hymns* on his CD player. As the streaming violins of 'Bittersweet Symphony' began to play, he began to move slowly and insinuatingly, critically watching his reflection in the window. Daisy Mae didn't want a man with scars, emotional baggage, a divorce. Her words had branded themselves into his brain, because that was him, down to the last detail.

His skin began to glisten with sweat in the half light; hard muscles rippling under flesh as smooth and hairless as satin as the discipline intensified. In his reflection he could see the slim scar running from his throat to his navel. That didn't bother him as much as the star-shaped patch of twisted flesh in the centre of his chest, just below his collar-bones, where his attackers had also used a serrated knife to gut him like a fish. They had failed only because a police raid in the apartment next door had made them jumpy, leaving him for dead on the floor.

Even after three years the sound of his flesh being torn still made him shudder, in the night when there was nothing else to think about. The crack-dealing punks who did it fared worse though, when Decker was fit enough to hunt them down. He had sliced and diced them like provolone, and because he was still a cop at the time, no questions had been asked.

But his career played hell with his marriage, which had failed after only two years. His refusal to take a desk job and more money was the trigger for the downslide. He was happier out on the street but, after he was attacked, he was no longer fit enough to be considered for promotion. So goodbye wife, goodbye career.

Since then he had shed the pain of his failed marriage and the Catholic guilt indoctrinated in him by his Irish father and Sicilian mother, and emerged a new man. He was fitter than he ever had been in his thirties, and wealthy enough to leave the security business behind for good, as and when the right time arose. Soon, he knew. The time was coming soon.

Almost an hour later he stood poised on one foot, the other leg at a perfect right angle. Calmly balanced, he could feel the stress flood down his body and mass at his groin. He lowered his leg, stretched his arms out in a slow crucifix and felt the nervous energy flow to his fingertips and fall from them like invisible drops of rain. A slow lunge, his right foot out in front of him, he lowered his body with his back perfectly straight. There was a soft knock at the door but he ignored it, repeating the movement with the other leg, cooling his strenuously worked muscles, letting his heart slow down. Only when he had completed his routine did he pad to the door, still naked. The woman on the other side averted her eyes from the scar running down his body and smiled when she saw his heavy, semi-erect cock. She reached out to touch it but he caught her wrist, so hard she cried out in pain. He pulled her into the room and shut the door.

No words were said. She knew from past experience that he disliked small talk. He handed her a slim embossed envelope, which she tucked inside her short leather jacket. He sat in a large, comfortable chair and motioned to her. She sank to her knees and cradled his balls in her hand. They were heavy with seed, and he drew in his breath when she rolled her tongue around them. His cock thickened instantly, though the cool, dispassionate expression on his face did not change.

As she sucked and licked professionally at his cock he watched the cat watching him. It seemed curious, wondering what the hell was going on. Then his physical need took over and all he could imagine was Daisy Mae again, and the illicit feel of her he had snatched so hazardously. He had found her fascinating before that, hearing the story of what she had done to Jason Cordell. Now he could picture her, having tied him to a chair, sucking him, ravishing his mouth with her tongue, slapping him around and telling him he was an evil cocksucking bastard. But all the while she was straddling him, her soft, furry mound millimetres away from his cock, rubbing her rose and jasmine scented breasts all over his face, before easing him fully into her tight, pulpy depths and squeezing . . .

'Oh, Christ,' he gagged suddenly, letting go with a huge pulse that shot come deep into the hooker's throat. She wouldn't like that, but he was past caring. He slumped in the chair, his heart pumping wildly as the hooker lapped gently at his balls, calming him down. She didn't seem to mind the impromptu snack he had given her. She looked up, grinning.

'That was a load off your mind.'

'Get me a drink.' His eyes were closed, but he motioned in the general direction of the bourbon and waiting tumbler. She poured and placed the bourbon on the table next to him. 'Now leave,' he said, in a voice that left her in no doubt that she had to go.

He drank in the dark and watched the candles burn to nothing. Despite the physical exercise and the drink and the hooker, he was getting hard again. It was as if his body had woken from a deep coma and wanted to grasp every opportunity for pleasure before it sank back into oblivion for good. Gloomy thoughts did not help. He stared down at that reddened, betraying organ, beating gently against his belly, hating it for exposing his weakness. Sleep would not come until he came again. He had to be honest. Since he had first set eyes on her he had done nothing but eat, sleep and breathe the memory of Daisy Mae Lovell, with her melting caramel eyes, rich, sensual laughter and hot, supremely tight cunt that fitted him like a glove. It was as if his life before their brief meeting had been erased totally, and telling himself to get a grip just wasn't working. Idly, he picked up the candlestick nearest his chair and looked at the clear wax sliding slowly down the stubby remains of the candle. Pain might help him exorcise her from his head. He tipped the candle to let a slender trail of hot wax drizzle on to his shaft but, at the last moment, realised what a bad idea that was. A drop of wax fell on to his cock and he leaped to his feet, swearing and wiping it away. The cat watched him incredulously, sitting with her paws tucked under her chest. He glared at her.

'What's your fucking problem?' Then he laughed deprecatingly to himself. Seducing the boss's daughter, rescuing and talking to a cat, resorting to torture to stop his dick ruling his head. Was this what normal men did when they were horny and alone? He slumped on his bed, still hard, and closed his eyes. He sighed deeply and resignedly curled his hand around his shaft.

'OK, puss, avert your eyes. Max is going into orbit.'

It was unthinkable, but it had to be faced. Max Decker was in love.

Night passed. It always did, eventually. Decker woke to the sound of trashcans being noisily emptied and a meaty purring in his left ear. Diesel fumes from an unnecessarily revving dump truck drifted in through the half-open window. The night before he had forgotten to close it before falling into a bourbon-soaked slumber. Now his mouth tasted like the bottom of a canary cage and his head was pounding with every crash of metal on concrete.

After showering he surveyed his monochrome wardrobe. His suits hung in laundry bags from Jays Cleaners in Delancey Street, where he sent them after only one wearing. He chose a charcoal grey Armani and a fine cotton black shirt from a neatly stacked pile on the shelf above. He buttoned it up to the neck to hide the scar. Even after all this time it still made him feel like a freak. After checking his reflection in the full-length mirror by the door, he left the apartment to find some breakfast.

The late spring heat hit him as he stepped out on to the street, together with the stink of rotting trash from the bags split open in the night by hungry cats. The usual oddball crowd were out: a tall youth with bright red hair, leading a small puppy on a studded leather leash, two thickset women with their arms around each other and matching T-shirts proclaiming 'She's My Man'; and the old woman who always sat on her step opposite his apartment, chewing tobacco and spitting it at anyone she didn't approve of. She had never done it to him.

Half an hour later, fortified with espresso and a cinnamon doughnut – the only habit that had stayed with him since his NYPD days – he rescued his racing green 8 Series BMW from its rundown lockup and drove to Long Island.

The old white house was situated just outside the Hamptons, on the edge of Long Island Sound. Felix Lovell sat dwarfed in the massive bed, which was an achievement because he was not a small man. Huge brocade drapes flanked wide French windows that opened out on a long expanse of immaculate lawn, running down to the Sound. Fresh air blew in, ruffling the pages of the *New York Times* slung carelessly at the end of the bed. Lovell's back was propped by mountainous pillows. On the table beside him was a tray bearing fragrant vanilla coffee, pastries and freshly squeezed orange juice. He smoked a hand-rolled Cuban cigar.

'Did you deal with the problem?' he demanded as soon as Decker entered the room. Decker's look told Lovell two things. The question was redundant and he wouldn't like the answer anyway.

'I guess that's a yes,' Lovell grunted.

'The Perez faction will take the rap. He owes ... owed them around fifty thousand dollars. Gambling debts.'

'Huh. Did he get anything for me?'

Felix Lovell's loud, grating Texan accent reminded Decker of the dumpsters working outside his apartment early that morning. He knew that Lovell would go up like a rocket when he saw the photographs.

'Right now Daisy is en route for Denver, Colorado,' he said, evading the question.

'I know where Denver is! Why the hell didn't she come home first? That's what I want to know!'

Decker sighed, wearily used to Lovell's irascibility. Lovell had married late in life, and it was a cruel irony that his beautiful young wife had died before him. Now Daisy was all he had left, and he was getting increasingly obsessive about her protection. In fact, he was getting obsessive about everything, from the trumped-up war with Enrico Mendoza to how his laundry should be dealt with.

Decker opened his mouth to speak, but Lovell's mercurial mood had shifted again.

'Tell me again what she did to her boss when he fired her.'

Decker told him in detail, and the old man's face split into a wide grin.

'She's such a cunt, just like her mother. Sophia could be the biggest one of them all.' His eyes went briefly misty, remembering his dead wife. 'But she was a real lady. Daisy takes after her, doesn't she?'

Decker pictured the last time he had seen Daisy, with her skirt up to her waist and her panties around her ankles. 'The resemblance is uncanny,' he said politely, looking up at the huge oil painting of Sophia Lovell. She was perched formally on a chair in a white flowing dress that seemed too prissy for her flashing hazel eyes and the wicked smile playing around her lips, making one wonder about her relationship with the artist behind the canvas. Yes, the resemblance was uncanny.

'You didn't make yourself known to her, did you?'

'You told me not to, boss.' If it was possible to sweat inwardly, Decker was doing it. *Hi, I'm a hitman. Can I suck on your tongue?* Jesus, he was in trouble, especially if Daisy had a good eye for remembering faces.

Lovell demanded to see the photographs, and turned pale as he saw his daughter draped all over two practically naked studs, with just a scrap of silk to cover her modesty. Then he propelled himself out of the bed with the force of a bull elephant in full charge.

'It's that goddamned Mendoza brat! What the fuck is he playing at?' Lovell began to stalk the room, venting his spleen against the Mendoza family, whilst Decker gazed absently out of the window and waited for the tirade to pass. He had heard it all before.

'She isn't with him now,' he said calmly, when he got bored with Lovell's dark ranting. 'He didn't go with her.'

'He could have met her there! Enrico Mendoza must think I'm a blind fool! Get him on the phone. No, get my car ready. I'm going to have this out with the bastard.' He went into his walk-in closet and slammed the door.

Decker knew better than to try and dissuade him. Half an hour later they were driving to Enrico Mendoza's luxurious office in the heart of Manhattan.

'Jesus, look at it,' Lovell said with disgust as they walked through the corridors filled with thick pile carpet and original Gabriel Orozco prints. 'I bet these are all originals, and the poor bastards paying for them are out on our streets, littering them like rubbish.'

He was astoundingly rude to the receptionist and to Mendoza's personal secretary. Unruffled by Lovell's bull-in-a-china-shop demeanour, Enrico Mendoza offered fresh Colombian coffee from his own plantation, and did not demure as it was rudely rejected.

'I want to know what you're playing, Mendoza. Setting up meetings between my daughter and your son.'

Mendoza paused behind his dainty coffee cup, one dark eyebrow raised. 'This is news to me. When did they meet?'

'Don't mess me around, they were together last night! He had her involved in some orgy! And she had only just got off the plane from England for Chrissakes!'

'Did he give her a ride from JFK? How thoughtful of him. If I had known she was coming back I would have done it myself.'

'Where is he? I'll ask him myself.'

'I'd be happy for you to talk to my son, but he isn't here.'

'Where the hell is he?'

'That isn't your business. I can tell you one thing, though. He isn't in Colorado. Storm chasing isn't quite his thing. And with due respect, Felix, I think they are old enough to decide for themselves what they want to do, whether it be share a cab, have a meal or screw each other senseless.'

Lovell's close-set eyes narrowed into evil slits. 'Do you think I'm prepared to let my daughter by soiled by a spic brat with a drug-dealing bastard for a father?'

Mendoza merely looked amused. He plucked a long, juicy cigar out of a leather-bound humidor on his desk and lit it with impeccably manicured fingers.

'The one thing I've always admired about you, Felix, is your well-balanced view on your fellow man.'

'Well? Say it ain't so!'

'I don't give a damn what you think of us,' Mendoza drawled lazily. 'And I don't intend to justify myself to a man so eaten up by jealousy. Daisy is a very attractive and intelligent young woman. She always knew to aim a lot higher than Chico.' He allowed himself the glimmer of a smile. 'She obviously didn't inherit that from her mother.' He hit the security button under his desk just as Lovell grasped his meaning. Immediately the door burst open and two hefty bodyguards waded in as Lovell swung a punch at Mendoza's calm face. One of them took the full body blow as Lovell hit him like an express train from the momentum of the swing. He bounced off the barrel-chested man and stumbled to the floor. When he looked up, Mendoza still had that supercilious look that deserved to be wiped from his face.

'You're finished, Mendoza,' Lovell whispered hoarsely as he staggered to his feet. 'Anyway I can do it, I'll have you put away for a long time.'

Mendoza's expression turned icy. 'It's a bad move to threaten me, Felix. You know how we drug-dealing bastards like to deal with our enemies.'

Decker steered Lovell back towards the door, murmuring, 'Let's go, boss. Ignore him. He's doing it deliberately.' As they left Lovell heard Mendoza speak again, and the words made him feel sick inside.

'Daisy's a beautiful woman, isn't she? Let's hope she stays that way.'

Decker poured two stiff bourbons in the car, one for Lovell, one for himself, to see him through the inevitable tirade. Instead, Lovell stared morosely into his tumbler.

'She wouldn't do that, would she? He was lying. He had to be.'

'About what?'

'Wake up, Max! About Daisy sleeping with him! He's old enough to be her...' Lovell couldn't go on. The scenario was too horrible to contemplate. What made it worse was that Enrico Mendoza did not look his 59 years, but at least a decade younger. He buried his head in his hands and groaned.

'You heard him, didn't you? He's going to hurt my little girl. There's only one thing for it. You'll have to go after her and make sure she doesn't get hurt. But you mustn't tell her. I broke my promise to her once by sending you to England. If she finds out about this she'll never talk to me again. But if you even *think* she's in danger, bring her in. We can't risk it, not until we get that cocksucking bastard's number and nail him to the floor with it.'

Decker cursed inwardly. He wanted more than anything to see Daisy again, but not in circumstances like this. One slip and his career and balls would be toast.

But there was no getting out of it. For the second time in his life he had let his dick rule his head, and again he was paying for it. After taking Lovell back to the house, he went home to pack and find someone he trusted to look after the cat.

4

Daisy called her father when she was already in Denver. He sounded annoyed that she had not gone straight to see him on reaching New York. She had side-stepped his delicately probing questions as to whom she had stayed with and instead broke the news that she would be living in New Jersey for a while. As predicted, he didn't take it well, but was slightly appeased when she agreed to spend a few days with him after her vacation was over.

The next call was to Chico.

'Hey, what's up?' he drawled. He sounded stoned. There were mens' voices in the background. Actually, not voices but grunts, almost drowned out by thumping Snoop Doggy Dog.

'Sounds like one hell of a party,' she said.

'Yeah, we're playing who can pop the most times. Jack's winning so far.' He dropped the phone with a clunk. 'Oop, sorry,' he giggled. 'It's hard to fuck and talk at the same time. Guy, say hello!' There was a breathless 'hello', from a distance. 'Honey, I'd love to talk but we're busy getting coked up and fucked up. Oh, yeah, that angle feels good, baby . . .'

'I'll leave you to it, then,' Daisy said dryly, and hung up on him. She knew he was trying to wind her up for the way she had nagged him. The old Chico wouldn't have done that. It was hard to admit that she no longer liked the person he had become, but she wasn't prepared to give up on him. She resolved to wait a few days before ringing him again, and tackle the issue head on when she returned to New York.

It was day four on the Storm Troopers tour bus, and she, along with her eight companions, was casting hopeful eyes at the heavy line of cloud ahead. From the start they had been warned about the grotty motels, the suspect food, the long hours in the bus and the eternal gazing at the skies waiting for something to happen.

They had not seen any tornados, but had learned a lot about Doppler radar, flanking lines and Mike Bradley, the famous maverick storm chaser. He seemed to be regarded as some kind of god, even by his professional older brother, Keith, who was running the tour. Though when Daisy spoke to other chasers in the bars they ended up in each night, it appeared that not everyone shared the same opinion. At least two amateurs had been killed thinking that they could be the next Mike Bradley. The words 'unprofessional', 'irresponsible' and 'asshole' were among the kinder things said about him when Keith was out of earshot. And Keith's girlfriend, Karen, who navigated and kept an eye on the radar, froze whenever Bradley's name was mentioned.

The only other single woman on the trip was a pretty, collagen-enhanced blonde called Clare. At 23, she seemed to think that every woman over the age of 30 should be shot on sight and, very early on, she had deemed Daisy to be some kind of threat. By her own admission, her agenda was to bed Mike Bradley. She had already started on Keith, draping her D-cup implants all over him in front of Karen, a slim, earnest brunette whose small, heart-shaped face only lit up when she smiled. Unfortunately, she didn't seem to have much of a sense of humour. Not that Daisy thought there was much to laugh about when studying radar reports and low pressures, and having a blonde nymphomaniac trying to steal your man. As for Daisy, she had no hang-ups about Clare or anyone else. She knew she looked good, with her chestnut long hair tamed in two fat bunches that hung low behind her ears, and her long legs looking shapely in the Lara Croft boots, teamed with short khaki shorts and subtle pink lip gloss. It would be her dress code for the next ten days.

That night the bar was quiet. A dry electric storm was rumbling around outside. Some of the chasers, including Clare, had gone out with Keith to a cliff top to learn about photographing lightning. Daisy stayed with Karen because that wasn't her thing. As they talked, Karen wasn't giving much away, but Daisy reviewed her opinion of her. She wasn't sour, just hurt, and she guessed that Mike Bradley was the main culprit. Eventually two more people joined them, ones that Karen knew and obviously felt more comfortable with. Daisy left them, wondering what to do next. There didn't seem much option but to go back to her room. She would call Chico and see what he was up to, she thought, going first to the rest-rooms for a pee.

When she came out, she heard faint sounds coming from down the passageway separating the bar from another building at the back. Curiosity aroused, she went down to see what was going on. As she drew nearer, she recognised the sounds of heavy sexual activity. Never one to pass up on the opportunity for a sneaky look, she slunk into the dark passageway, stood on a handy beer crate and peered through the window.

What she saw nearly made her fall off the beer crate. On a pool table, Clare was splayed, surrounded by at least ten men, including most of those in the chase group. Daisy could see her long legs spread wide, and a man standing between them, pumping rhythmically away, his hands kneading her fat tits like bread dough. At the other end she was preoccupied with another man's cock, thrusting it so deep down her throat she looked like one of those pythons that swallowed its prey whole. The other men were watching, some drinking, openly masturbating, others just looking sick with lust. The man between her legs began to grunt louder, then uttered one long drawn-out howl as his back arched. Daisy could see his buttocks bunching under his jeans, the final deep-felt thrust before he pulled away, leaving Clare in full view. Her pussy was pink and open, glistening with his semen. The man she was fellating staggered round and took the other man's place, and she beckoned the next in line with a greedy smile, unzipping his trousers and taking his cock into her mouth. Daisy's mouth was also open. This was industrial-strength fucking at its most brutal. She had never seen anything like it before.

'Come on, Rob, shoot and let me at her,' one growled. It was mild-mannered Keith, jacking off to keep hard, his usually bland countenance twisted with anticipation. Daisy slipped off her beer crate with the shock. For a moment she stayed down, afraid that they might have heard her, but when she hazarded a look back through the small window, the action was getting hotter. Come was on the floor beneath Clare's feet and all down her thighs. Her pretty face was overblown with greed. Some of the men who had already fucked her were waiting for another turn, stroking their cocks to make them hard. Through the small window, Daisy could almost smell the sleazy, smoky atmosphere as they reamed Claire's mouth and cunt. Her face was wet with spunk, her hair ratty and tangled, but Daisy at once felt incredibly jealous that she would have the balls to open herself up to so many men and be so lasciviously wanton. As she watched, the next man quickly shot his load and was pushed out of the way by the next, who immediately plunged into her and began humping her like a dog. He too did not last. Man number five was spraying come all over her pneumatic tits, whilst man six was fucking her mouth. She had one hand on her clit, agitating it with sparkly tipped fingers, squirming and squealing like a baby piglet as she came. There seemed to be no correlation between her pleasure and theirs. Despite the most intimate of acts being performed, they were separate beings, clawing at satisfaction, devoid of any emotion other than the common need to get off. She turned around and presented herself to man seven. The insides of her thighs were slick with sperm, her hole a dark, wide tunnel, but he was pushing against her backside, taking her right up the ass. Daisy's own bottom tightened at the thought. She had only been ass-fucked once and, afterwards, she couldn't shit properly for a week. But another man was manouevring under Clare's crouched body, guiding his cock into her pussy until she was stuffed in both holes. Daisy looked at the next man, wanking hard with a club-like cock that made her own pussy go very damp. Go on, take her in the mouth, she urged silently and, as if he had heard her, he did, grabbing her matted hair and forcing her lips over his cock. They moved in one seething mass, like some monstrous animal, Clare almost lost between the men. Between her legs Daisy was as wet as if she had been in there herself, her clit throbbing out of control. She could feel her nipples, nut-hard and tingling against her shirt. She had no desire to be part of it, but the need to relieve some of that pulsing tension in her sensual places was overpowering. Holding that last horny picture in her head, she went back to her room.

Not wanting the erotic tremors in her body to go wasted, she quickly stripped down to her panties. They were damp and, inside, her sex was puffy and open. After rummaging in her bag for the vibrator Val and Suzie had given her, she slipped between the cool cotton sheets and put it inside herself. There was no protest as the thick, ridged tool nestled deep inside her. She was so wet that she could hardly feel it until she tried to move. Then she was reminded of just how long and heavy it was, held in place by her panties so it did not slip out. It nudged against her cervix as she wriggled to get comfortable. The room was cool and quiet, the fan over the bed sending little waves of cool air over her nipples. The sophisticated remote control for the vibe was ready by her fingers, but she was content just to let her internal muscles squeeze the hefty tool for now. Her nipples were so aroused by the touch of her fingers that she almost came right then. The sensation sent an electrical impulse down her body to her clit and she whimpered. Soaking her fingers, she stroked the swollen organ, keeping her other hand on her nipple, moving her lower body slowly to keep herself aware of the thick vibe stretching her inner muscles. For a while she kept herself on the edge, enjoying the sensuous pleasure of fingers and latex cock, before lightly tapping the remote control. Inside her, the vibe began to move, quite slowly, churning around inside her. She moved with it, conjuring up confusing images of Clare and all those men, morphing into her and the stranger in England, and how big and right and desperate he had felt, fucking her blind over that beer barrel. In her mind they found a patch of warm grass and continued the fuck, mindless of people walking past, until another couple decided to join them, then another, until the riverbank was covered with people making it, swapping, sucking and fucking, another stranger kneeling above her and pushing his cock into her mouth as her man (what was his name?) started to eat her out with those lovely cruel lips and long, thrusting tongue. Spreading her legs wide, she pressed another button and the vibe began to pump up and down until her eyes rolled and her moans became gritted cries. As her fingers agitated her clit, faster and faster, the images became a blur, with only her and the strange man in focus. She was teasing him, not allowing him anywhere near her as she brought herself off, her gaze fixed firmly on his cock as it jumped and yearned for her, his face stricken with need. She came in a series of deep felt shudders, wringing every pulse out of her clit as the vibe pumped at her, giving her another shuddering orgasm, deep inside her body this time. Exhausted, she turned the thing off and removed it.

'Damn, I'm good at this,' she said out loud as she lay sated, breathing heavily.

'Yes, you are,' a laconic voice replied from the end of the bed.

Too shocked to scream, she scrambled to a sitting position, holding the sheet tightly to her body. In the next moment she thought she was hallucinating. Her clit was a genie's lamp, and touching it had made him appear, the stranger from the bar in England, five thousand miles away. But how come, and why, and all those questions she was too terrified to ask.

'You have five seconds before I start screaming,' she said tremulously.

'It's OK, I'm not going to hurt you. I...' He seemed supremely reluctant to finish the sentence, before presumably deciding he had no choice. 'My name is Max Decker. I work for your father.'

'My father,' she repeated dumbly.

'Yes. Do you mind if I...?' He motioned to the end of the bed. She shook her head rapidly and he sat down. 'He sent me to find you.'

'You found me in England. Why didn't you say anything then?' She quelled her shivering with an effort. Not for the first time in her life, she wished she had a nicotine habit.

'I couldn't, not after ... I guess I didn't deal with the situation too well.'

That slight Irish accent made his words sound almost like an apology, and she found herself forgiving him. 'It's OK. Right then I wasn't looking for dinner and dancing.

It's the first time a man has ran out on me within five minutes of having sex, though.'

'I usually like to do things properly.'

'But that isn't why you're here, I guess?'

He seemed to remember what he had come for. 'I'm here to look after you.'

'Oh, please!' Daisy's eyes rolled and she flopped back on the bed. 'I'll be 33 in a few weeks, I think I can look after myself!'

Decker didn't reply. Following his stare, she saw that the sheet had fallen away from one creamy breast, and that the nipple was still perky and pink. She covered herself up.

'Did you say look after me or look at me?' she said pointedly.

'I'm more professional than that.' He coughed to disguise the desire in his voice but she had already detected it.

'And in England? Oh, that's right. You were on vacation.'

He ran his fingers through his hair, clearly agitated, and began to prowl the room. 'He told me not to tell you.'

'I bet he did! So how come it was the first thing you told me?'

'I didn't have any choice! You were going to start screaming, remember?'

'Well, excuse me, Mr Professional, but what were you doing at the end of my bed? Anyone with an ounce of initiative would have joined the tour anonymously and observed me from a safe distance. Is this your creative side coming out or what?'

He glared at her. 'You were supposed to be in the bar! How was I to know you would come back early? It was either do it that way or let you discover me in the bathroom! Then, believe me, you would have started screaming!'

She cocked her head at him. 'Rather like you are doing now. You're scared, aren't you? Scared I'm going to tell Daddy that you broke his trust, and . . .' her eyes widened in mock horror, 'you fucked his little girl! You should know damned well what he does to traitors, Max Decker, but I bet he'd find a special kind of hell for you.' She nestled deeper into the pillows. 'So what are you going to do about it?'

Decker looked whiter than he had before, if it was possible. 'Dig my grave and jump in it?' he suggested dryly.

'Relax, I'm not that much of a bitch,' she said mildly. 'But it does put me in a stronger position for telling you to keep out of my face. And I want to know what drove my father to break his promise to me and send my own personal guardian angel. He knows what is at stake. So tell me.'

'I'm here to look after you.'

'Not good enough. Try again.'

'That's all there is, Miss Lovell.'

'It's more than I got in England, I suppose,' she sighed, 'and I think after what we did we should be on first name terms at least.'

'That's fine by me.' Decker stood up and headed for the door. 'By the way, I'm coming with you on the tour.'

'Wonderful,' Daisy said acidly. 'How much did Dad pay to wangle that?'

'More than enough, believe me.'

'That's fine, but take some advice. If you're coming with us, try and blend in. You'll stick out more than Tom Jones's trousers in that suit.'

Decker involuntarily glanced downwards and closed his jacket.

'Don't flatter yourself! I meant the New York wiseguy look doesn't look so great on the Plains. I guess Dad didn't pick you for your ability to go undercover. How long have you worked for him, anyway?'

'Long enough to know what he's like. I'll see you in the morning.' He turned to go. He looked so repressed and grim that she had a strong desire to throw him off balance.

'Wait!'

He waited. She climbed off the bed and let the sheet fall around her feet, revealing her nakedness. He did not move as she approached him. Twining her arms around his neck, she licked along his lips and backed away again. His breathing was shallow but he was trying very hard to conceal it. More than anything she wanted him to push her back on the bed and fuck her so hard it hurt, but she knew he wouldn't. He seemed to be possessed of superhuman self-control, obviously only compromised when off American soil.

'I'll give you a day, Max Decker. If you irritate me any time between now and this time tomorrow I'll just have to phone home.' She waggled her fingers at him. 'Bye!'

He seemed to want to reply, maybe even to spit something obscene at her. Instead he strode out and slammed the door with a resounding crash. Daisy rolled over on to her back again, closed her eyes, and let her nasal senses pick up the lingering scent of Hugo Boss aftershave. After four days of endless wheat and corn-fields, of dustbowl landscapes and grungy men in baggy denims, his scent was like a breath of fresh air, a distant echo of the slick city he inhabited, and she felt a brief pang for civilization again.

But hang on, what about the small issue of her father sending him in the first place? She rolled again and lunged for the phone, then hesitated. Demanding to know what he was playing at would land Decker in shit so deep he would never resurface, and she wasn't sure whether she wanted that to happen. Sighing, she cradled the receiver. Wait and be happy, she told herself. Storms were building, and not only in the West. It could be an exciting ride.

5

Just after seven the following morning Keith called at her room to say they were leaving. The supercell they had been discussing the previous night was forming faster than anticipated, and they had a two-hour drive to catch up with it, as it was moving west.

The men were gathered around the van, looking hungrily at Clare, who looked as fresh as a virgin, apart from the smug look on her face. She stared curiously at Max Decker as he added his own smart leather holdall to the motley collection of old rucksacks.

'Okay, everyone, Steve had to leave us last night because of family issues and Max here as taken his place. He's from New York,' Keith added, as if that explained everything. As he made introductions, Daisy noticed how bright-eyed and bushy-tailed he was. It could have been something to do with Clare, or the large amount of cash her father had paid for him to accept Max Decker's presence and keep his mouth shut.

'Karen's just been talking to the National Weather Service,' Keith was saying cheerfully. 'The supercell is on the Texas–Colorado border and it's looking good. You folks ready to see some action?'

There was a good-natured cheer. Decker grimaced and Daisy laughed at him. It would serve him right if the next week was purgatory.

In the event, the hottest action she saw that day was in the back of the van, where Clare was offering sneaky blowjobs to the men nearest her whilst everyone else, except Daisy, seemed oblivious. Decker was content to stare out of the window, earphones stuck to his head, listening to what sounded like Moby. Occasionally he lost himself in the music, much to Daisy's amusement. His sleepy green eyes would close and his slim, rather elegant hands would move slowly, sinuously, as though conducting under water. Then he would realise what he was doing and stop abruptly, glaring at her when he saw her smiling at him.

All that day he kept out of her way. He had taken her advice and wore chinos and chunky Timberland sandals. And, hallelujah! No socks. To complete his wardrobe, he wore an olive green cotton shirt that complemented his green eyes and dark hair, which was definitely dark red, not brown as she had first thought. The shirt was buttoned up to the throat. It looked good but she didn't understand why he thought it necessary to be so formal. And who the hell was it that he reminded her of? Clare homed in on him, and Daisy heard him telling her he was a cop. He talked so knowledgeably that even she was convinced. Clare asked if he carried a gun and his succinct answer was not on vacation. But he wasn't on vacation, Daisy thought. She shuddered inside, not knowing whether to be reassured or alarmed at being shadowed by an armed man.

That night most of the men were too preoccupied with Clare's charms to be disillusioned by the continuing elusiveness of their prized tornado. Max Decker did not talk much, content to merge into the background with his bourbon. Daisy could see him acutely observing the crowd, and more than once she saw him watching her exclusively. It stirred conflicting emotions inside her, and she found herself watching him as well, until he suddenly looked up and caught her. She reddened and looked away, cursing silently the fine silver threads of electricity flowing between them. It was hardly surprising, remembering what had happened in England. He obviously regretted it, which made the mixed signals he was giving her even more confusing.

'Am I still on trial?' he asked later.

'Are you going to tell me why you're really here?'

'I'm protecting you.'

'And I think you're lying, so you're still on trial. Oh, and if you even think about getting sucked off in the back of the bus tomorrow, I'll be straight on that damned phone,' she added vehemently.

'I'll give that careful consideration, Miss Lovell.' He stalked off, out of the bar.

Watching him go, the thought of Clare getting her chubby little hands on him made her feel physically sick. She hardly heard Keith talking about the following day when, weather permitting, Mike Bradley would finally grace them with his presence.

'Daisy? I said it's good chase weather tomorrow. You OK?' Keith looked concerned. It was hard to imagine him sticking his dick into Clare with such force the night before, like Paul McCartney screwing Pamela Anderson. Daisy blinked and focused on him. She could see Decker outside, talking on his mobile.

'Yeah, sure! A great chase day. Good!'

Keith seemed reassured by her bright smile. She could tell he wanted to ask about her relationship with Decker but didn't quite know how. And as he seemed a man thrown by complications, apart from those in his love life, she decided not to enlighten him.

Later that night she waited impatiently as the bath filled with scented water. She was grubby and nervy and needed to slough off the grime of the day. When the bubbles were satisfactorily high she stepped in, and with a huge sigh relaxed back in the water. With her eyes closed against the brightness of the tiles she put her headphones on and began to sing. 'I–I want to thank you, for giving me the best day-ay of my life.' OK, she wasn't Dido but with no one else to hear her it didn't matter. Anyway, her voice wasn't that bad. She sank down lower until the bubbles were up to her neck. Despite Decker's brooding presence on the tour she would sleep well tonight.

Max Decker also sat in the bath, but he was fully dressed, and the bath was empty. He knew he was crazy and accepted it as he sat concentinaed in the small tub, his long legs aching in protest. Right now he could be easing the continual ache in his groin with that fluffy little blonde girl at the orgy someone had given him the nod was happening that night, but he was happier right where he was. It was nothing to do with Daisy's threat. In fact, hearing it had made him happier than he had felt for years. He pressed his face to the cool tiles, savouring Daisy's warm, husky voice and the little splashing noises as water flowed round her body, inches away on the other side of the thin partition. In his heated imagination he could watch her soaping between her toes, lifting each long brown leg out of the water, letting the suds slide down her skin. Caressing with loving hands her belly and breasts, fingers brushing over each stiff little peak, touching between her legs, the soft hair floating like sea kelp in a secret cove.

'Daisy,' he murmured softly, 'oh god, Daisy.'

Eventually he heard her climb out and all was quiet. Decker unfolded his protesting body from the small space with some difficulty and undressed. He too was travel weary and nerved up. It was going to be a long night.

The heat was intense but dry. He lay there on his back, his fingers laced behind his head. In the darkness of the room his eyes remained open, staring sightlessly at the ceiling.

With the smallest of sounds, the internal door opened.

He should have reached for his gun but he was unable to move, transfixed by the sight before him.

Daisy stood just inside the door. She wore a translucent white shirt that ended just past her thighs. From the lights outside the window he could see she wore nothing else.

She walked over to the end of the bed and stood there, drinking him in with her eyes. With sensuous grace she slipped the flimsy garment over her head. He could see the outline of her full breasts, with delicately upturned erect nipples, curve of waist and a dark triangle of soft hair between her legs. His breathing quickened and grew ragged. He could not see her face.

She crawled like a cat on to the bed, straddling his legs, and arrived with her breath fanning his face. Nothing was said. He could feel the heat of her whole body, intensely concentrated at her very centre, poised directly above his groin. He strained to touch her, but she remained teasingly out of reach, moving instead to pin his hands above his head.

He chose not to fight the strong hands that held him, concentrating on the hard nipples grazing his chest, the heat of her pussy torturing his cock. Her body moved fluidly, her breasts warm like satin against his skin. His jaw clenched as he made futile attempts to reach her.

'Bitch,' he muttered helplessly as she snaked above him. She remained silent, communicating only with her eyes. His frustration grew as she denied him. She played him like an instrument, drawing out his anticipation with every move. He ached for her with need that bordered on pain. When she found the sensitive tip and sucked him in, he cried out at her scalding heat. She rode him with skill, using her superbly toned inner muscles to squeeze and massage his whole length, making him harder than he thought possible, his hands itching to keep her locked on to him, wanting to bury himself in her so deep she would cry out.

He could not bear it much longer. The dizzying sensations were too much. The warmth of her soft breasts and the wet tightness of her cunt were too great. He came with a harsh cry, shouting her name.

Gone. She was gone. He sat up suddenly, drenched in sweat. An uncomfortable trickling sensation made him look downwards.

'Shit,' he muttered with some feeling.

The last time he had a wet dream he was fifteen.

It was early the next day. Everyone except Daisy, Max Decker and Karen looked a tad out of sorts. Daisy clocked a couple of the men giving her admiring glances as she joined them on the bus, her crisp white linen shirt and the Lara Croft boots showing off her subtly tanned skin. It wasn't exactly surprising. Clare looked as if she needed her beauty sleep. Her eyes were puffy and her pouty mouth was bad-tempered, especially when she heard Daisy's light laughter ringing down towards the back seat.

Keith had advised them that when they found good food, it was wise to stoke up as much as they could just in case the next place was lousy, which it invariably was. So they had stowed away bacon and waffles and eggs for breakfast before gassing up and setting off towards New Mexico. A hundred miles passed, and most of the group were in buoyant mood. By now they all knew 'Bad Moon Rising' by heart and gave it some, loud and proud.

The storm was girding its loins, fuelled by the heat of the New Mexican desert floor, but it hadn't been very showy about it. Things started getting interesting as they backtracked towards the Texan border. They stopped at the end of a long line of chasers, in an otherwise lonely spot where the endless verdant plain seemed to merge into the threateningly green sky. Thunder rumbled almost continuously around them and, in places, threads of black cloud seemed to brush the top of the young corn. As ever, Daisy had the Minolta by her side. She took a couple of shots of the menacing wedge-shaped gust front, before deciding that it was better just to watch it. One cloud would look very much like another when she was back in New York. She watched Decker light up a cigarette and head in her direction.

'I'm going nuts,' he said tightly. 'I've had supercells, stovepipes and the wonders of the Real Time Weather Radar Display System, not to mention Credence Clearwater Revival every five fucking minutes, right up to here.' He turned to go, then paused and asked wearily, 'And what, in the name of fuck, is a mothership?'

She laughed out loud. 'You should pay more attention, Deck. The mothership is the reason we're here!'

Decker rolled his eyes. 'Christ, I'm in the Twilight Zone.'

'Look.' She pointed to the swollen, boiling sky. The supercell had been causing considerable excitement as they charted its development. Now they were close enough to see the underbelly, and smell the electricity crackling in the air. The outer edge was smooth and striated, like the underside of an enormous galleon, or an otherworldly space station. 'The mothership. See?'

'Yeah, I get it.' He didn't sound that bothered. She suddenly felt like shaking him.

'Look at it! Don't tell me you don't feel anything!'

His voice was as flat as the Plains. 'I don't feel any rain, if that's what you mean.' But when she looked at him again his gaze was fixed on the developing storm. Way above, a Daz-white atom-bomb-style cloud was topping out at around forty thousand feet, while the base was the colour of brushed steel, darkening by the minute. Arrows of lightning dropped to the ground some miles away, generating considerable excitement in the thirty or so chasers gathered to watch it.

'Keep away from the fence!' Keith yelled as Decker inadvertently brushed against the wire. He had told them previously about the danger of being electrocuted by lightning hitting the fence five miles down the line, but Decker hadn't been there for that part of the briefing. He backed off and leaned against the bus instead, lighting his next cigarette with the butt of the old one, getting in as much nicotine as he could before being denied the pleasure for the next three hours.

A solid block of thunder took them all by surprise. Low-slung rolling clouds swirled across the highway. A big black Ford pick-up tore past them, into the storm. The licence plate said 'Warrior', announcing that it was Mike Bradley's truck. They could hear whoops and thumping hip-hop receding into the distance. Before their eyes the landscape blurred and disappeared behind streaks of white.

'Hail's coming!' Karen shouted.

'OK, back in the bus! Move, move, move!' Keith yelled, just as Daisy felt a rush of cold air on her face. As they picked up speed away from the rolling gust front, the first heavy lumps of ice banged on the roof like bullets. When Daisy looked back, the road was no longer visible, hidden behind a grey wall of rain. Hailstones the size of walnuts assaulted the bus with deafening force as the wind buffeted the bus from behind, shooing it away like a small fly. Daisy was fearfully excited. The chase was on, but this time it was nature chasing them.

They passed through a small town, busy with people running for cover and battening down hatches. Keith opened his window a crack so they could hear the haunting wail of the tornado warning system. Over it Karen was shouting at him to find shelter, and why the hell had he taken them so damned close? He parked behind a large municipal building that looked strong enough to withstand assault, close to the wall. Decker immediately moved to Daisy's side. She found it rather touching, until she remembered he was being paid to do it. They heard a constant rush of sound like an express train travelling over a metal bridge.

'We're going to have to sit this one out, guys! This is a classic PDS!' Keith yelled.

'What's a PDS?' someone called out.

'Particularly Dangerous Situation,' Karen called back, with another angry look at Keith.

'Something you know everything about then,' Daisy murmured to Decker.

He stared penetratingly at her. 'And you,' he said quietly.

Debris scattered across the road. Some hit the van with deafening clunks. Instinctively Decker put his arm around Daisy, ready to bear her to the floor if the windows caved in. The lid off a trashcan spun like a childishly thrown frisbee and bounced off the roof, but everyone else seemed to be enjoying themselves. Keith looked rapt, his attention glued to the back of the van.

'It's moving away,' he said eventually. Decker hesitated slightly longer than necessary before releasing Daisy.

'Well, folks, that's what it feels like to be sideswiped by an F2.' Keith sounded supremely cheerful. They all climbed out after another cautious glance at the skies. Keith inspected the outside of the bus. Apart from a few more dents, there was no major damage. The rain was light and warm in the aftermath, punctuated by receding thunder and half-hearted flashes of lightning. Daisy closed her eyes and lifted her face to the rain, letting each drop cool on her skin.

'Next time you want a vacation, go to the Caribbean and spend two weeks on the beach,' Decker's terse voice said beside her. She opened her eyes and caught him looking at her breasts where the rain had turned her white cotton top slightly translucent. When he saw she had found him out he glared at her as if it were her fault.

'This isn't you losing your nerve, is it, Deck?' She grinned at him.

'It takes a lot more than that to make me lose my nerve.'

'Like what? Fucking the boss's daughter?'

The white heat in his eyes told her she had hit home. Watching him walk away, she wondered what it would take to make him lose his cool. With that dark red hair and Irish blood, he was bound to let go eventually. Keith cut through her musing by offering to buy them all lunch at the Blimpie up the road. As they trooped off behind him Daisy heard Decker muttering, 'Great, now he wants to poison us.'

She also noticed Clare sneaking off with three of the men. They came back fifteen minutes later, the men looking smug, Clare licking her lips. She gave Daisy a bitchy smile as if to say, how much have you been getting lately? Daisy smiled benignly back. Yes, in her fantasies she wouldn't mind getting brutally banged by more than one man at once, but she had standards and was going to stick to them.

After what nearly passed as food, they followed the storm back west. When they reached the leading edge they stopped. Along the roadside there were at least ten vehicles, the leading one being Mike Bradley's. Keith parked at the other end and they all piled out.

Daisy wandered through the crowd, taking photographs. She had decided that people interested her more than landscapes, and there were enough little dramas going on in each group to keep her amused for hours if the storms didn't do their bit. She ended up near a tall, fit-looking man in flashy designer sports gear. Mike Bradley, storm-chasing uberbrat: it couldn't be anyone else, though he looked coarser in the flesh. His white blond hair was closely cropped under a Chicago Bulls baseball cap and his face held the flush of winters spent on ski slopes and summers on the surf. He scowled at the weather through Police mirrored sunshades as if it were inconveniencing him personally. She took a photograph of him while he wasn't looking, then approached him.

'How far away is it?' she said, nodding to the storm. It was densifying, getting closer. The under cloud was a thick, menacing green.

He looked amused, and not in a pleasant way. 'Why? Scared you'll get your hair wet?'

'Asshole,' she muttered.

'Is everything okay?' Keith had come up behind her, looking anxious. Mike slapped him painfully on the back.

'Hey, bro, you caught yourself some action at last back there.'

'It nearly caught us, you mean,' Daisy said. Mike Bradley looked at her with fresh interest.

'This is Daisy Mae. She's in my group,' Keith said. 'Daisy, this is . . .'

'I know. I've seen you on *The World's Worst, Wildest Weather*, or something like that,' she said carelessly.

'Daisy Mae,' Mike Bradley said, instantly turning on the charm and holding out his hand. She could practically hear his pheromones tuning in. Keith's attention was back on the storm but Mike still held her hand. 'Daisy may or Daisy will?'

'Make that Daisy won't,' she said, pulling her hand away. At least, unless I choose too, she added to herself.

'Oh man, look at that,' someone gasped, and at once cameras and camcorders swung into action. The twister started as an elegant white rope, and moved sinuously across the sky almost at a 45 degree angle from the ground. Daisy heard a sharp intake of breath beside her and saw Max Decker, his eyes fixed on the twister. Impulsively she grabbed his arm and squeezed it. He immediately curled it around her shoulder, probably because it was his duty, but it still felt nice. Her heart was pumping with excitement. As the twister touched down there was a loud cheer. Daisy whooped with triumph as the tornado picked up desert dust and darkened, spinning and dancing harmlessly across the plain like a gay, benign dervish. Caught up in the exhilaration of the moment, she flung her arms around Decker and kissed him full on the lips. Their tongues met, entwined and for a moment it seemed as if the world had stopped spinning, leaving them floating in their own private universe.

He let go first. The look in his eyes was so close to revulsion that she felt like screaming at him, what the hell is wrong with you?

'Sorry,' she muttered, forcing her attention back to the tornado. This is why she had paid two thousand dollars, after all. It lasted for another seven minutes before fading away. The noise of whoops and high fives was deafening.

That night they celebrated their success with massive slabs of Texan steer and beer. Daisy watched Keith watching Clare making heavy play for Decker, who was ignoring her completely. Karen was watching Keith. Daisy knew it was all going to get very messy, very quickly, if Keith couldn't keep it in his pants. As for Decker, he drank bourbon and effortlessly put away an eighteen ounce steak, eating with neat, nervous energy. He did not look her way once.

After the meal they sought out the bar. It was noisy, packed with chasers and gum-snapping women, wearing the seemingly obligatory South Western uniform of tight blue jeans and shirts tied at the waist. Fluffy big hair, lots of lip gloss, and a hirsute male in tow. Daisy clocked a few of them giving her admiring glances when their girls weren't looking. As she moved her slim shoulders to the music she hoped that Decker was taking note of the male interest she was generating, then wondered why the hell she was getting so obsessed about what he thought. She ordered a whisky on the rocks and went to the jukebox in the corner, selecting Eric Clapton's version of 'Black Magic Woman'.

'Good choice,' Decker said behind her. She felt inordinately pleased until she saw that Clare was with him, all sparkly and perky, tits on show. He seemed annoyed at her presence, as if she were a piece of fluff that kept appearing on his jacket, but it was obvious that Clare's skin was as hard as leather, and she wasn't going to go away. Daisy looked over to the bar where Mike Bradley held court, surrounded by chase groupies, male and female. He caught her glance and smiled, but she assumed he was smiling at Clare, giving him a cute little wave beside her.

'Mike was saying that the Navajo call him "Wind Warrior". Isn't that the coolest thing?' Clare twittered breathlessly.

'I can think of better names,' Decker said witheringly, and left them to it. Clare laughed at his retreating back.

'I really like that guy. He doesn't give a shit about anybody.'

And that was just the reason she had begun to hate him, Daisy thought irritably. To avoid watching him, she looked over instead towards Mike Bradley's group. Again her eyes met his, and this time she was sure he was purposely seeking her out. The possibilities sent an excited little shiver to the bottom of her stomach. He wasn't her type, but he was attractive in a thuggish way and she was feeling the need for a bit of rough to flush out those ambivalent feelings she was cultivating for Max Decker. The next time Bradley looked at her she offered a cool smile. Clare chatted on about superficial things, laughing prettily and casting long, meaningful glances in Mike's direction. If she thought her chances would improve by sucking up to her, she was wrong, Daisy thought cynically. It was interesting watching her try though.

'I wonder what Karen's problem is with Mike?' she mused when she tired of hearing about when Mike was on the set of *Twister*.

'They were an item once, apparently. He slept with someone else when they were supposed to be engaged.' Clare's voice was low and gossipy.

'Did Keith tell you that when he was screwing you?' Daisy murmured. Clare looked both guilty and defiant at the same time.

'A couple of fucks isn't true love, is it?'

Daisy nearly choked on her whisky. 'A couple!'

Clare tossed her long blonde hair. 'Serves Karen right for being such a sour bitch. Anyway, Mike's hornier, richer and better looking. I'll have him bagged by the end of the night.'

'Maybe I'll beat you to it,' Daisy murmured. 'Just for the hell of it.' Or just to get back at Decker, an annoying little voice said inside her head.

'I thought Max Decker was more your type by the way you were snogging him this afternoon,' Clare said accusingly.

'Trust me, Decker is more of a dickhead than Mike Bradley.'

'Oh? How come?' Her eyes were bright and greedy for information. Daisy realised that having mentioned it, she really didn't want to talk about it. 'Past history,' she said shortly. She looked over to where Mike Bradley was standing. He raised his beer bottle and smiled. Easy meat then, Daisy thought, deciding to go for it. But she wasn't going to make him think that it would be easy.

She left Clare and went up to the bar. She stood some distance away from the group, thinking that if he were really interested, he would have to come to her. She watched Decker shooting pool with two of the other chasers. He looked quite good leaning over a pool table. Pretty damned good, actually. He looked up and met her eyes, then shot the ball decisively into the hole. Slick bugger, she thought, capturing that look in her mind and holding it. It was the eyes that did it. Green eyes like those of an angel or a psychopath. At last she knew who he reminded her of.

'The King of New York,' she said softly to herself. 'Christopher Walken.'

'No, Mike Bradley,' a voice said next to her, reminding her of what she was actually up at the bar to do. 'Can I buy you another drink?'

A quick close-up appraisal revealed a strong, tanned face, sparkling white teeth and a lean physique under a Hilfiger sports shirt and pristine white Ralph Lauren baggy jeans. Another label man, another Jason, another asshole, but tempting all the same and a bargain too. She smiled sweetly at him.

'A Miller Lite, but only if you promise to be patronising and rude. I really get off on being treated like shit.'

He snapped his fingers at the bartender, who produced two more beers at lightning speed. 'I get kind of tense when I'm on a chase. I've been on the road almost seven hundred miles today and all I've got is a sore ass and a twister the size of Mickey Mouse's dick.'

As apologies went, she had heard better. 'Do you chase full time?' she asked.

'As much as I can, between May and August. The rest of the year is taken up doing docu's. I guess you've seen me a lot on TV.'

'I've been in England,' she said dismissively. 'I haven't spent my time there watching it much.'

Cue him asking about her, but surprise, surprise, he didn't. 'I don't spend all my time working. I have other ways of getting my kicks.'

She laughed at him. 'Because you're so desperate for me to ask how, I won't.'

'Suit yourself. I skydive and bungee jump . . .'

'Snowboard in the winter and surf in the summer?'

'Yes.' He looked genuinely surprised. 'How did you . . .?'

'Wild guess. Ever jumped into a tornado?' The question was facetious, but for one alarming moment he looked serious. All balls and no brains, she thought.

'Wouldn't that be a rush?' He was grinning.

'Sure, for a total idiot. Anything else, Mr Action Man?' She motioned to his wide, large knuckled hands. 'You've even got the handjob grip.'

'You're mocking me.'

Daisy shrugged. 'You deserve it. I'm too sensible to throw myself off a bridge with an elastic band around my ankles. Or do anything else that might end in the word "ouch".'

'That's a shame. The anticipation of pain is half the pleasure.' He gave her a frankly sexual once-over, all the way down her body and back up again, smiling warmly into her eyes. 'Although sometimes pleasure can be a pain. It's difficult to surf with a huge hard-on.'

She bit back a derisory laugh and returned his suggestive smile, licking the rim of her whisky tumbler. There was a rather attractive cluster of creases at the corner of his eye, only there when he smiled. She could almost smell the raw energy radiating from his athletically tuned body.

'So you've never done a parachute fuck, then?'

Bradley spurted into his beer.

'Or a bungee fuck? No? You're an adventurous guy, so why not?'

She had obviously disconcerted him, but he hid it well. 'I can't say it's ever appealed. Until now, that is. Are you offering? Two experiences for the price of one?'

'I might just have to slap your face for that, Mr Bradley.' She put on her best Southern Belle accent and smiled coyly. The smile was wiped off moments later when she saw Clare talking to Decker. Bradley turned and saw them.

'Is that your man?'

'No. Right now I don't have one.' She tore her eyes away and smiled flirtatiously at Bradley.

'I can't say I'm unhappy about that.'

'And I can't say I think it would stop you,' she said pertly as Decker left Clare and joined them. 'This is Max. He's on the tour with me.'

'Yeah?' Bradley looked at Decker's casual dark suit, unimpressed. 'I don't think I've ever seen a chaser dressed in Armani before.'

Decker gave him a cool stare. 'It's Helmut Lang, but I forgive your ignorance. You're from Arkansas, yes?'

Bradley bristled visibly. 'And you have to be from the Bronx,' as if it were the worse insult he could think of.

'Actually my father was from Belfast and my mother was Sicilian, so maybe you'd like to watch your mouth.' He smiled to soften his words, but the warning was implicit. Daisy watched with interest. The antagonism between the two men was palpable, but the smirk on Bradley's face held the assuredness of the young confident pup knowing he could conquer the older dominant male. She inhaled deeply, closing her eyes and letting out a deep, satisfied sigh.

'My, I just love the smell of testosterone in the evening,' she purred.

Bradley ignored her. 'So are you here for the storms or is there another reason?' he asked Decker.

'The storms. What other reason could there possibly be?'

Bradley glanced down at Daisy, or rather, at her breasts. She hoped he wouldn't say it, but he did.

'I can think of a couple.'

'Fair enough. I'm sure you'll share them with me one day. Excuse me.' His final look at Daisy said it all. If you want this asshole, you deserve him. She watched him go, wondering at the ambiguity of his reply. He was such an intriguing man, far more articulate than she had expected. He certainly had the edge on Bradley when it came to duelling with words. He was a wall cloud, a dark, ominous presence concealing a turbulent core. She laughed deprecatingly at herself. This storm chasing was going to her head.

'Well, that's got rid of him. You want to cut to the chase and go back to my room?'

She had been thinking of a snog and a fumble outside the bar, maybe developing into something more later on. This offer of full-on fucking threw her completely. She scrambled for her composure and shrugged, thinking fast.

'I have to make a call first,' she said quickly, buying some time.

Bradley looked slightly annoyed. 'Can't it wait?'

At last she found her feet. 'Can't you?' She challenged.

His jaw tightened, and she knew she had gotten to him. 'Room 21,' she said quietly so no one else would hear. 'Give me fifteen minutes. If you can't wait that long, I'm sure Clare will oblige.'

Back in her room she checked her text messages. There was one from Chico. She decided to call him and was relieved when he sounded like his old self.

'So tell me about the men. Have you been balled senseless yet?'

'Not yet, but give me ten minutes.' She told him about Mike Bradley, going into loving details about his coarse good looks, his spiky cropped hair and ghetto-fabulous wardrobe.

'What about his schlong? Any idea how big it is?'

'Not yet. I hope it's not a wiener. If he turns up I'll let you know.'

'Hmm, good luck. Anyone else?'

She paused a little too long before replying.

'That means there is,' Chico said. 'Come on, spill the beans.'

'He's kind of weird, very moody.'

'OK, weird, moody, what else?'

'Check this out. He's my own personal bodyguard, sent very kindly by my father to look after me.'

'What!' Chico was stunned. 'What the hell for?'

'He won't say. He wasn't even supposed to tell me.' She told him about their first two meetings. Chico thought for a while before replying.

'So you've got famous surf bum with big ego and white teeth, dick an unknown quantity, versus weird, moody, Irish and repressed, but you know he's hung. On balance, I know which one I'd go for. Live dangerously for once. All it'll take is one spark to light the blue touchpaper and Wham! Your feet won't touch the ground.'

'That sounds nice, Chico, but he's afraid of my father.'

'Honey, read between the lines will you? I have enough male chromosomes to know how these things work, believe me, and I doubt this guy's afraid of anything.' He sighed down the phone. 'I have to go. Alfonso will be here any time and I'm not dressed yet.'

'Alfonso? Who's he?'

'Now don't give me the lecture, but I met him two nights ago at the Red Room. Cock like a watermelon, muscles like a bag of basketballs.' Distantly she heard his intercom buzz. 'He's eager, poor lamb. Call me soon. I want to know how sporty Mr Bradley has violated your luscious bod. Take special note of his peachy ass, just for me. And I want you to cocktease your bodyguard outrageously and tell me how he reacts.'

'Will do, Chico. Have a good time. I love you.'

'Yeah, yeah, you too, honey. Ciao.'

As he rang off she felt happy that he was sounding more like the old Chico. If only he would drop that ghastly faux English foppishness. It really didn't suit him.

6

Decker was outside having a smoke when he saw Mike Bradley going towards Daisy's room. He wished he had his blade so he could liberate the redneck from his dick or, at the least, wipe that smug grin from his white trash face. His only comfort was knowing that Daisy was playing him like a fool, using him as a tool to satisfy her own ego. Had she been doing that with him as well in England? He didn't think so. Then it had been mutual, instinctive and raw, almost spiritual in its divine intensity, for all its brevity. That was why he had run from her. And why he had spent every living second since regretting it.

He approached Bradley just as he was about to knock on the door.

'Hey, Mad Max,' Bradley said cheerfully. 'Don't bother trying to get some nice Texan pussy tonight. She's already taken.'

'Don't count on it.'

'Sorry, my friend, but I do. Take my advice and get into television. Then picking up these cute little bints is easier than falling off a log.' He chuckled smugly, but checked it when he saw Decker staring at him.

'You just don't get it, do you? She isn't interested in you because you've been on the Discovery Channel! You're a notch on her chalkboard, someone to satisfy her curiosity, that's all.'

'Well, consider her curiosity well and truly satisfied. She won't forget this vacation in a hurry.'

'I don't doubt it, but not for the reason you're thinking

of.' Decker lit another cigarette and blew smoke into the night.

Bradley smirked at him. 'Oh I get it. She hasn't put you on her chalkboard yet, is that what the problem is? Or has she, but you didn't manage to satisfy her curiosity. Is that right?'

Decker moved into the light so that Bradley could see his face full on. 'You're scratching an itch, that's all. I can guarantee that by this time next week, she won't even remember your name.' He threw the cigarette butt at Bradley's feet like a dart and crushed it, the symbolism tacit but unmistakable, before walking away.

He found a quiet spot to make his nightly call to Felix Lovell. He was wracked with pain and confusion, and it all stemmed from that captured snippet of conversation he had heard between Daisy and Chico Mendoza. But if she loved him as much as she proclaimed, why was she still sleeping so willingly with Mike Bradley? A very small part of him actually felt sorry for Chico, but a larger part, like the hidden underwater massive of a floating iceberg, felt a vicious satisfaction.

He called Lovell and told him what had happened that day. As predicted, Lovell wasn't too happy about his only child being sideswiped by a recalcitrant tornado, and the thought of a redneck, especially one involved in the media, sniffing around her ankles didn't please him much either.

'How the hell did you let it happen?' he demanded belligerently.

'I'll blow my cover if I get any closer,' Decker pointed out.

'So blow it. Protect my little girl from any more assholes. What about Mendoza?' he asked tightly.

Decker thought of the phone call Daisy had made to Mendoza, and the potential consequences of telling Felix that the romance was back on. As much as he wanted the little fucker out of the way, he also wanted to deal with him personally.

'No sign of him, boss. Everything's fine and dandy.'

'That's easy for you to say.'

After the phone crashed down Decker allowed himself a small smile. He was taking a certain sick enjoyment in watching Daisy, even though it hurt like a persistently picked scab.

The heat was stifling, the darkness cloaking his skin like wet silk. Satisfied that he was alone, he undid his shirt and let the pitiful breeze attempt to cool his scarred skin. It felt tight, as it always did when his body got overheated. He had cream to ease the stretching of the new tissue, but he didn't want to go back to his room just yet. He knew what he would hear on the other side of the wall – Daisy and that fuckhead, making it like cats. He lit another Marlboro and sat with his back against the wall, trying not to let his mind run wild.

'Why are you out here all alone?' A playful voice said next to him.

He wasn't fooled by Clare's casual tone. She had been loitering around him since the day he joined. Now she had better watch her step. He had consumed enough bourbon to dispense with niceties.

'I like being on my own,' he said tersely, hoping she would go away.

'I thought you liked Daisy Lovell.' He could hear the sulk in her voice. He stood up before she had the chance to get cosy next to him and clouded her with smoke.

'Why should I? She's in her room, fucking Mike Bradley.'

Clare's eyes narrowed at his bitter tone. 'And you're not jealous?'

He laughed mirthlessly and did not answer.

She stepped closer. 'I bet I could easily take your mind off her.' She reached out to slip her hand into the waistband of his trousers. He grasped her wrist before she got even close. 'Hey, what's your problem?' Then her eyes zeroed in on his body. In the half-light the skin on his chest looked even more disfigured. He let her look, for the first time ever, savagely pleased at the repulsion in her eyes. She fought free and backed away from him.

'What's the matter? I thought you fucked anything with a cock,' he sneered.

She did not speak, but ran from him back to the bar. He went back to his room to finish the bourbon and think about how to persuade a fresh, beautiful woman like Daisy Mae to love an embittered, flawed man like himself.

In the darkness Daisy lay on top of the bed, letting the fan blow cool air over her body. She had decided on saucy red and cream gingham panties, with *broderie anglaise* daisies holding them together at each hip. The matching balcony bra had daisy straps that matched the panties, and it held her bosom in a very inviting way, as if enticing a man to bury his face between her breasts. She had sprayed herself with Allure and brushed her long wavy hair into a nut brown gloss, thinking she would feel a real fool if Bradley decided not to turn up. But he would. She had him pegged as a greedy opportunist. He might even be banging Clare in the parking lot on the way to her door. That was fine, but if she detected Clare's Tendre Poison on him she would just send him right back out into the parking lot.

She tried to calm her heartbeat with slow, sensual images of how he would undress, and his big, capable hands running tantalisingly over her body. Mike, not Max. Mike, not Max. Remember that when you come, a small but irritating voice said at the back of her mind.

There was a soft knock on the door, almost undetectable under the buzz of the air-conditioning. She switched it off and opened the door, then sauntered back to the bed, draping herself across it in a feline pose that accentuated every curve.

'So, Mr Extreme, do you think you can handle me?'

'I've handled forty-foot tubes in Hawaii. I think I can handle you, pussycat.'

She heard the door close and the bed dip behind her, then his hand, warm and confident on her stomach. She fell back against him and he enfolded her in his arms, their mouths meeting in a deep, tongue-aching kiss. Outside she could hear people laughing as they went past, and saw their shadows through the thin drapes. Occasionally cigarette smoke would drift in, along with drunken singing and the shuffling of feet. She wondered if Max Decker was out there, listening in. Stop. Behave and focus, she told herself severely, watching him peel off his T-shirt. His muscular chest was matted with soft dark hair, his small pink nipples like puppies' noses. She ran her fingers through the soft fuzz and licked each nipple with a pointed tongue, feeling them stiffen. He shrugged out of his baggy jeans. Under dark boxers, a thick, not overly large but very eager cock strained for release, and when she ran her fingernail along its length a tiny dark stain appeared at the top.

'Wicked woman,' he rasped as she straddled him, pinning his arms above his head.

'Let's have a look at you, then,' she said. Her mouth left a sleek trail of wet hair between his nipples and down towards his navel. She shuffled down between his knees and tongued out the deep well, being careful not to touch him anywhere else. She blew on the dark wetness and felt him shiver. He lifted his hips as she eased his shorts down and tossed them away, somewhere across the other side of the room. When she hovered over him again his face was flushed and narrow-eyed with lust. His cock was pumped to bursting along his hard belly. Her own sex moistened in response.

'Not bad,' she said lightly. He did not move, lazily enjoying the warmth of her body over his. 'Don't just fucking lie there, Bradley. Do me!'

Rising to the challenge in every sense, he rolled her back on to the mattress. His eyes were greedy as he grasped her breasts in his large, shovel-like hands.

'Let's take this off,' he said, unhooking her bra. He had hardly bothered to look at it. Throwing it across the room, he squeezed her breasts together and slurped at her nipples. Despite the slightly repellant sounds he was making his eagerness did the trick, her back arching as electricity fired from each tip to her clitoris. She was really wet, her pubes were sticky with female honey, and she could smell her own excitement, oozing from every overheated pore. He seemed insolently pleased with her body's rapturous response, as if it was no more than he had expected, and for a moment his complacency angered her. His cock felt very nice pushing up against her pussy lips, but a tool was only as good as the man who could master it.

'Now show me how you use it,' she said boldly. She held on to the bed head as his reaction to her challenge to his pride showed angrily on his face.

'I'll show you, lady.' He stripped her panties off and turned her over, then pulled her hips up to meet his, slamming deep into her with a force that crushed her against the pillows. And again and again, until her cries ceased and she was stunned into panting silence by the intensity of his thrusts. The bed banged against the wall, but she was too turned on to wonder about the occupant on the other side, listening to them inches beyond the plasterboard.

'Is that the best you can do?' She threw back at Bradley.

'Give it harder, you useless fuck!' He banged relentlessly at her, his heavy balls slapping against her thighs. Then he was throwing her over on to her back again and fucking her missionary style before pulling her on to his lap. She leaned back, steadying herself on the bed with one hand and watched their bodies move in the same, sensual dance. He carried her, still joined to him, and screwed her hard and slow against the wall, his mouth locked on to her breast, almost engulfing it. He lifted her legs and pinned her to the wall with his cock, grinding ruthlessly against her until she was out of her mind with fucking overload. Then they were back on the bed, she sitting on the side as he fucked up into her flagging body. She felt like a rag doll, tossed around by a petulant child. It was all she could do just to hold on and take the hammering he was giving her. His muscles bulged and sweat began to bead his brow, but still he screwed her until she pleaded with him to stop.

'You've had enough?' He challenged, pressing hot, wet kisses all down her throat and neck. 'You want big bad Mike to soothe that poor beaten pussy?'

'Oh, God, yes!' She melted against him, almost weeping with relief. 'Give me your tongue. Show me how good you are.'

He smiled against her mouth. 'I'm very, very good,' he whispered hoarsely. 'I know what my ladies like.'

She broke her lips away from his. 'Ladies?' She asked in mock disapproval.

He winced at his error. 'Well, you know . . .'

'I do. A man with experience means more fun for me.' She licked him lavishly along his jawbone, swirling little kisses that made his cock throb deep inside her. As he sprawled her out on the bed and drew out of her, her pussy seemed empty and bereft, until the undulating length of his tongue filled her so unexpectedly she screamed softly.

She tried to keep still. She tried not to churn and moan and wriggle, but he seemed to possess the longest tongue on the continent. She abandoned her sense of shame at being so desperate and just opened herself wide to let him feast on her. He wasn't as accomplished as he thought he was, but by this time her body needed release so badly that even the most inexpert of lovers could have brought her off. She felt the first waves of orgasm, fought them to draw out the exquisite pleasure, then found it was no use and let them crash over her, vibrating through her body, making her moan with abandonment. She spread her legs so wide they ached, quivering as he lavishly licked her, pushing all her buttons over and over, until she needed him to stay right there and finish her off. She peaked three times, dousing him in her juices. Her overflow dribbled down into the crack of her ass and he lapped it up. He blew on her distended, overwrought pussy lips and cooled them down as she lay replete amongst the thin cotton sheets, dampened with the sweat of their loving.

'Oh, my,' she breathed as he kneeled next to her. Opening her eyes with an effort, all she could see was cock, the circumcised end red and gaping. He guided it to her lips and rubbed it along them. She smiled.

'You don't believe in giving a girl a break?'

'If you have the energy to talk, you have the energy to suck. Blow me.' He nudged his cock against her lips again, and obligingly she gave him a swirling lick over the very tip. He tasted musky and sweet and of her as well, the whole length of his cock sticky and glistening and harder than ever. His hand was in her hair, guiding her mouth down on to his cock. She didn't like the way he was controlling her, fucking her mouth and not giving her a chance to make it good, but his lewd encouragement was turning her on again in a very tawdry way. She cradled his balls in her palm, gently scratching the underside of his scrotum while continuing a smooth sucking, licking motion, up and down, over and over. His knees gave out and he collapsed back on the bed, letting her continue. She recognised his groans as those of a man who could have his cock sucked all day and not get off until he chose to. It probably happened every week with willing young things wanting to bathe in reflected fame for a while. But she wasn't one of them, and he was taking her expertise for granted. What she needed was a way of distinguishing herself from the crowd.

'Oh, baby, that's good,' he moaned. He was splayed out on the bed, eyes closed, lazily enjoying her attention. He did not move when she went into the bathroom. She sloshed Listermint around her mouth for a few seconds, then went back and sucked as much of his cock back into her mouth as she could.

The extreme cold of the menthol, followed by the heat of her mouth made him cry out. She felt his cock sagging with shock and then recover as she sucked him fiercely, feeling for her vibrator under the pillow. He moaned harshly again as her cool, saliva-soaked fingers found his backside and probed his puckered hole.

'Oh, God, yeah,' he muttered thickly. 'Finger fuck me, baby, go on!' Then as she pushed the blunt end of the vibrator against his hole and turned it on his body jerked, sending his cock deep inside her hot, wet mouth. 'Oh, Christ,' he gurgled as she pulled on him. She muffled the stream of profanity by sitting on his face. It was her turn to gasp as he probed her pussy with his tongue, opening her bottom cheeks wide and dousing her entire crack with a salivating tongue. She turned the vibrator on, letting it send buzzing sensation up from his ass to his balls, then stroked the vibe all over his balls and cock, all the while lavishing wild attention on him with her tongue. He grunted like a pig beneath her, out of his mind with pleasure, as she brought him close to coming again and again. Finally he slapped her buttocks hard and pushed her away. His cock was still rock hard, but he looked haggard, as if she had wrung him dry. She stretched like a cat and played with her hair, letting it fall over one shoulder to tickle her nipple.

'You want to finish the job?' she asked in a sultry voice.

'I want to finish you, you frisky bitch,' he muttered, and grabbed her legs, throwing them wide apart. She splayed her pink pussy lips to invite him to enter, and he sank into her as gratefully as entering a hot bath.

'Not my neck!' he said hurriedly as she nipped his throat. 'It looks bad on camera.'

She really wished he had not said that, but his cock felt strong and deep inside her, and she could forgive him a lot. As he began to pump long, hard strokes she felt her own excitement building again as her legs wrapped around his waist.

'More,' she whispered greedily, goading him further. 'Give me more, mighty Mike. Drive that cock into me. Go on!' She hardly knew what she was saying, but each word was like a spur to drive him further and deeper. 'Remember that bungee fuck? Imagine your woman all wet and sticky, bound up in safety harnesses, unable to move as you fuck her. You're at the edge of the bridge. The people round you can't help staring at your huge cock, the woman with her pert little tits painfully pushed up by the harness, and her sopping, open pussy. The drop is at least two hundred feet. You are bound together, your cock deep inside her, pulsing, throbbing, the anticipation of free-fall fucking almost too much to bear. You can feel her warm flesh, the way she trembles with fear against you, unable to escape your cock, driving deep into her very centre.'

'You're a crazy woman.' Bradley rolled his eyes and pumped harder.

'Then you jump. You're falling, your stomach swooping, for a split second gravity is zero and all you can feel is your cock and her pussy, clenched tightly around it. Then the rebound, pulling you back up, forcing you so deep into her that you start to come. Each bounce brings another surge, her cunt contracting all around your cock, squeezing every last drop...' Daisy ran out of words as she felt him tense and screw her harder. His face was a blank mask, trying to hide a raw and terrible lust that he was trying to hold back, but the wave had been restrained for too long.

'Uh, uh...' Bradley grunted as he started to come. Daisy felt her own orgasm overtake her, excited by the impossible scenario she had painted, the helpless free-falling, the hard driving cock from which there was no escape. She came suddenly with a guttural shriek, just as Bradley emptied himself into her with slow, intense pulses, punctuating each one with a heartfelt grunt. He paused for a moment, his back arched, his lips drawn back from his teeth in an ecstatic grimace before he collapsed on her like a pack of cards.

'You're something else,' he sighed happily, but she wasn't sure whether he was saying it to her or to himself. She smiled inwardly. Jason had said the same thing. Was that the measure of a true asshole, that phrase, 'you're something else'? He rolled away and lay on his back, breathing heavily. She curled away from him and snuggled into the pillows, sated and happy and ready for a good night's sleep.

'I'll see you at breakfast,' she murmured, dismissing him.

'You want me to go?' He sounded slightly stunned. She turned to face him.

'I'm making it easy for you, Bradley. Did you really want to stay all night?'

He moved closer to her. 'Yeah, I do.' He kissed her neck

and inhaled the fragrance of her hair. 'I like you, Daisy Mae. Would you tell me another bedtime story?'

This was a development she hadn't anticipated. His body felt good, spooned around hers, warm and hard, and having someone else in her bed was strangely comforting but, being a woman, she was already fighting guilty feelings about using him. Remember what he did to Karen and get a life, she told herself. Enjoy your vacation.

'If you insist,' she sighed happily, and allowed him to roll her over and take her in his arms again.

Decker had hit the bar again and was staring moodily into his shot glass. All around him was music and laughter that he had no interest in, but he couldn't bear to listen to the heavy sounds coming from just beyond the wall any longer.

'Can I join you?'

He glanced up and saw a slim brunette in a very short white denim skirt, one of the prostitutes that frequented chasers' motels. Their collective name was 'lot lizards', but this girl seemed too pretty to warrant such an unattractive title. Still, he wasn't in the mood for flirty chit-chat, or even company at all, right at that moment.

'No thanks,' he said shortly.

'Oh come on, don't look so blue.' She moved in beside him. 'You were watching that sexy long-haired girl earlier. I guess she blew you out, huh?'

He opened his mouth to tell her to go to hell, but she had moved closer and was running her soft, warm hand up his arm to feel the hardness of his bicep. 'If she did, she's crazy. I bet you're a real tiger in bed.'

'Spare me the sales pitch, honey, I'm not in the mood.'

'Fifty dollars and I could get you in the mood.' She moved closer, so he could smell her heavy fruity perfume and see down her small blouse to her plump, swelling breasts. 'What do you think? If we make enough noise, she might regret being mean to you.'

Now there was an idea, Decker thought grimly. The brunette's face was in shadow, but her hair was wavy and long, like Daisy's. And her legs were long as well, reminding him of Daisy in those sexy lace-up boots she always wore. She was shorter than Daisy, and her perfume was too heavy for his taste, but her offer suddenly made his libido explode into life. Everything that was bad about Daisy seemed personified and magnified in this woman. She was a slut, her dress was too short, her smile too knowing, but he needed to release some of that angry lust that had been brewing faster than the desert storms. He slammed the glass down on the counter and nodded curtly for her to follow him.

Outside, she whimpered in surprise when he pulled her into his arms, pushing her up against the wall, his mouth hot on her throat. His hand pushed up the tiny skirt and cupped her buttocks, suddenly hungry for the feel of flesh and blood moving against his.

'Easy, lover. It's cash up front,' she murmured. He fumbled for his wallet, drew out a fifty and stuffed it into her blouse, despising himself for his lack of self-control. But now the need to feel a woman in his arms was purely physical. They stumbled together to his room. He could feel her hands all over his crotch, his butt, up his shirt and in his pants. He didn't care. All he could think of was Daisy, in the room just beyond his, just inches away on the other side of the wall.

'Strip,' he said harshly as soon as the door was closed.

'I don't usually undress for my clients,' she said, as he pushed her breasts together and licked along the deep, tight crevice.

'I'll make it a hundred if you do.' He showed her another fifty. She hurriedly stowed it in her denim baguette bag.

'Be as loud as you like,' he said, peeling the skin-tight blouse away, letting her breasts tumble from a too-small black satin bra. She wriggled out of the short skirt and displayed her tight, round butt, the string of her thong tight up the crack. He slapped her buttock cheek, leaving a red blush.

'Bad girl,' he muttered, smacking her again. 'Show me your cunt.'

Obligingly she pulled the thong to one side and let him see her puffy, shaven cleft. He almost buried his face into it and thrust his tongue into her hole before remembering. This was not really Daisy, and that hole was probably slick with someone else's semen already tonight. He collapsed back on the bed instead.

'Blow me,' he commanded, in a voice loud enough to penetrate through the thin wall. He grabbed the metal bedhead and braced himself as the hooker stripped away his trousers and shorts and began paying slavish attention to his cock. There was no denying she was good at her work, he thought as he closed his eyes and imagined Daisy down there instead, her laughing mouth wrapped around the root of his shaft. At least twice he thought he was going to lose it, and each time his hoarsely uttered obscenities floated through to the next room. He knew Daisy would be able to hear him, as clearly as he could hear her breathy little cries that wrenched his soul apart.

He told the hooker to sit on him. She guided his cock inside her open, willing pussy and sat up, undulating her hips.

'Come on, lover,' she whispered huskily, 'fuck me.'

'Louder,' he commanded, his hips moving with hers.

'Fuck me!'

'Louder!'

'Fuck me!' she screamed, and he tipped her on to her back, still imbedded deeply inside her. He gave her his pile, driving energy full throttle, hammering the bed against the wall, aware that he was competing against the sounds coming from next door. Hardened by triumph, he felt as if he could go for hours, showing the bitch next door that she could not beat him. The hooker was whimpering, exhausted by his pounding, her hair all over her face. He lunged into her again and heard an answering thud on the wall. Then again and again, until he knew they were as aware of him as he was of them. It was the trigger he needed. He steadied himself on the wall behind the bed and began to fuck the poor little hooker's ripe body with such deep intensity that she was wiped out and Daisy was in her place, a challenging smile around her lips, her body lifting to meet his, her expression changing as he wrung out her pleasure, becoming desperate, wild, her hands all over her breasts, teasing the nipples . . .

'Play with your tits,' he rasped and obediently the hooker did so, jiggling them in her hands, tugging on each dark nipple. He wondered whether Daisy was responding to his order, tormenting Mike Bradley with her wondrous breasts, teasing out those long, dusky nipples. The thought tilted the balance, urging his body into overdrive. He began to come, pulsing into the hookers tight little cunt as Daisy's answering screams seared across his brain. An explosion of white heat erupted from his cock as he banged on the wall. 'Fucking bitch! Can you hear me?' he shouted.

'Yes, yes, yes!' Daisy shrieked in reply. He could picture her, sitting astride Bradley and slamming down on to his cock with every ounce of strength. He could hear her hands slapping the wall, mere inches away from his, the sound connecting them as intimately as if they had been face to face. The crazy eroticism of being so near and yet so far from her tempered his joy, but not the raw need that emptied his balls as well as his soul. His last sobbed curses punched through the wall before he fell back on the bed, breathing heavily. After a moment he looked at the hooker, lying exhausted beside him

'You can go now,' he said calmly.

7

The next morning the sky was gunmetal grey and rain was falling steadily. Daisy was glad that Bradley had stayed and they had given Decker and Clare a run for their money. It had been ugly and exciting and incredibly confusing, and she wondered what exactly he was trying to tell her. Bradley, the dope, had no idea that she was using him as a living, breathing dildo. As they walked together to the diner to join the others he was strutting, wrapping his arm possessively around her neck as they went through the door. She pushed him away, sensitive to the fact that Karen would be upset by seeing them together, but Bradley had no such hang-ups.

'Did you have a good night's sleep, mad Max?' he bellowed to Decker as they passed his table. Decker glared at them but did not answer. Everyone else turned to look at them. Irritated, Daisy separated from him and went to the Ladies. When she came out, Clare approached her, all approachable and smiley, but her eyes were unfriendly.

'Max wasn't the only one who heard you. I was with him for most of the night.'

'Did we disturb you? Oh, I'm sorry.' Daisy flashed a tight grin at her, resisting the temptation to punch her smug face in. Behind Clare, she saw Decker's brooding face in profile. He didn't exactly look as if he had spent the night in the arms of a nubile blonde sex maniac. 'Well, I wouldn't advertise it if I were you. If anyone I fucked looked that miserable in the morning, I'd know I was doing something seriously wrong.'

Clare's lips compressed and she bounced back into her

seat. Daisy saw Bradley with his buddies, back-slapping and talking in low voices. She turned away, not really wanting to know what was being said, and ran straight into Karen.

'It's OK,' Karen said, seeing her embarrassment. 'I'd rather it was you than her.' She nodded disdainfully at Clare and went on her way. Decker caught Daisy as she went up to the counter to order breakfast.

'I guess you didn't sleep that well.'

She fought the desire to throw coffee in his face. 'Actually I did. Better than you, anyway. Just don't look for sympathy once you start scratching your dick,' she retorted.

'I'll buy some cream, just in case,' Decker replied casually. 'Then when you start scratching, you can have some.'

Daisy wasn't given to flouncing off, but she came dangerously close right then. What made it worse was the way they were being secretly observed by the other members of the tour group as if they were an excruciating, but addictive, soap opera. As she turned to go Decker held her back.

'Felix is happy for me to blow my cover in the interests of protecting you from assholes like Mike Bradley, so whatever you say now won't make any difference,' he said quietly.

'I don't suppose he said anything about protecting me from assholes like you. By the way, I'm quite capable of handling Mike without your help, thanks very much.'

'So I heard. Quite the little ballbreaker, aren't you?'

'It's better than being an emotional cripple.' She went back to her table, knowing that he was still watching her.

'When are you two going to stop fighting and get it on?' Karen asked.

'Excuse me?'

'You and Max. I know you're just using Mike and that's

OK. It's about time he had someone turn the tables on him, but everyone's wishing you would screw Max senseless so we can move on and be happy. Can't you see how he feels about you?' She sounded slightly exasperated.

Daisy toyed with her orange juice. 'I didn't realise we were attracting that much attention,' she muttered, knowing damned well they had been. She looked over to where Decker was reading his *USA Today*. If he looks up she's probably right, she thought. But he didn't. So much for that theory.

'Let's put it this way. The last time I was this close to so much chemistry I was in the science lab at Junior High. Clare practically laid herself on a plate for him but all he could see was you. The hooker was just a cipher, trust me.'

Daisy laughed then. 'A hooker?'

Karen nodded. 'He blew Clare out last night and chose to pay for his kicks instead. She wasn't very happy. Spent the rest of the night dissing the hell out of him. God knows what he said to her.'

Just then Keith appeared and the Troopers gathered around while he went through the itinerary for the day. The previous night's storm was the only one they had and, as the air was still unstable, it was worth checking out.

They drove for a hundred miles before stopping at a gas station to fill up and grab coffees. The rain had stopped, but the atmosphere was humid and expectant. People were theorizing about the collapsing storm, trying to second-guess its next move. The air was still, with a silence that made their voices echo around the parking lot. Daisy could feel the steam rising up from the tarmac, drifting around her bare legs. She saw Decker standing by the road, looking up at the sky. Something in his stance told her that he was reading the cloud. His eyes were searching, his face lifted to the breeze.

'Deck? What is it?' He was making her feel uneasy. It was as if he knew exactly what was to come. Thunder rolled, but the leaden cloud above didn't look as if it would produce anything more sinister than a light drizzle.

'It's reorganizing,' he said. 'We can't see what's happening on top because we're right underneath it. A tornado could drop right on us and we wouldn't even know until it was too late.'

He sounded convincing, but there was nothing in the sky to back him up. Mike strutted over, having heard their conversation.

'Hey, city boy, leave the predictions to the experts, will you?'

But Keith had also heard him, and was looking more worried. 'How do you know this, Max?'

Decker turned his green eyes on to Keith. 'Like the man said, I'm not an expert.' He strode back to the bus. Daisy was about to follow when Mike stopped her. He picked up one of her bunches and ran her hair through his fingers.

'I hate to say this but he's right. It's stoking up something good. Just like me, watching that nice tight ass of yours. You want to ride with me? We'll catch the others later on.'

She hesitated, but Decker was watching her from a distance, looking as dark as the growing storm. It made her angry, the way he was hanging around in her peripheral vision like a tortured soul. If he really wanted her, she wished he would damn well say so.

'It's OK,' Bradley was saying. 'Keith made me promise to keep you safe.'

She gulped a disbelieving laugh. 'So you've already cleared it with him?'

'You coming or not?'

Decker was still there, radiating hostility. She forced

down her disquiet at his absolute conviction about the storm and turned her back on him.

'Sure. Why not?' She flipped her coffee cup into a trash can with feigned nonchalance and walked to Bradley's truck. He leapt in beside her and pulled out of the lot with a spit of gravel. In the wing mirror, she could see the Troopers' bus fall in behind. The radio crackled and the disembodied voice of his navigator, who had been relegated to the next truck, told him to take the next turn left. The highway stretched out like a grey ribbon in the distance, with a dark swathe of woodland to their left. Bradley took Daisy's hand and placed it on his crotch. Her palm brushed against a large, stiff lump.

'I've had this all morning, thinking about what we did last night. You want to help me out?'

'What, now?' She was incredulous, with the weather developing fast in front of them. The road ahead was now blurred, as they approached a dark curtain of rain. He grinned sharply at her.

'Why not? I always get a boner when I'm chasing something hot, but it's the first time I've been able to do something about it.' He pulled his shorts down to reveal his erection, like a big pink strawberry popsicle, sticking up to the sky. 'Come on, baby. Get your hand round that.'

He was so vulgar, she thought sadly, but the opportunity for some salacious behaviour couldn't be passed up. Obediently she curled her fingers around the root of his shaft and began to stroke him, up and own, very slowly. He was very hard, excitement showing in a red stain on his cheeks and all down his neck, his expression now concentrated on the road ahead. Seeing him so turned on excited her deeply, despite the hazardous nature of their situation. She said nothing, just in case they could be heard over the CB, but she lifted her T-shirt so that he could see how hard and prominent her nipples were. With her free hand, she played with them. Bradley was looking increasingly desperate.

'God, I want to fuck you,' he said through gritted teeth as she made little sounds of pleasure from the feel of her own fingers sending tiny shivers down to her clit from her nipples. She kept her hand on his cock, her nipples kept hard by the constant stimulation by eddies of cool air rushing through the open windows of the truck.

'Yeah, keep that up, baby,' Bradley said shakily, and she could see the effort it took him to concentrate on his driving. The rain now lashed at the windshield, making a mockery of the fast wipe he had employed to clear it. Then she heard hail, small patters of ice at first, then getting louder.

The radio crackled again, causing her to jump back guiltily, as if they could see what she was doing. She tucked her breasts back into her T-shirt, suddenly aware of the severe deterioration of the weather. It seemed that Decker had been spot on. The radio fizzed at them.

'Er, Mike, if that wall cloud keeps coming at the current rate it'll bring you right into the core,' Keith said cautiously.

'Roger that.' Bradley disconnected him and carried on, but his concentration was now on what was happening outside the van.

'What did he mean, into the core?' She looked behind. They were now on their own. She could see the headlights of the other vans receding in the back window. 'You're not going to punch it, are you?'

He smiled at her easy use of chaser terminology. 'Why not? I've never had a blowjob from Mother Nature before.'

'Mike, you've got to pull back. You're too close!' Keith sounded frantic. Bradley switched him off and veered off down a small farm road. It was wooded on one side and not very well made, and Daisy's teeth rattled as they hit one pot-hole after another. The hail was deafening, hitting the windshield so hard Daisy was afraid it would cave in. An excited shriek pierced the interior of the truck.

'It's on the ground! A big rope on the ground, south 28. Can you see it?'

'No, not yet. Shit!' The trees suddenly cleared and they were staring at green open fields. The hail stopped abruptly, replaced by torrential rain. They were inside the wall cloud and, to the right of them, no more than half a mile away, was a thick, grey, roaring vortex, flinging debris petulantly around like a child in a tantrum. Bradley kept abreast of it, steering with one hand and adjusting his video camera with the other. 'God, this is beautiful. Look at it, Daisy. Mike Bradley has delivered your own, up close and personal twister!'

Daisy held on to her seat and tried not to scream. She stared at the tornado with horrified fascination as it munched through the fields next to them.

'OK, this is about as close as we're getting, right?' she shouted, above the fearsome shrieking. A chunk of wood hit the bonnet and she cried out. Bradley grinned at her.

'Not scared, are you?'

The radio hissed again. 'Mike, get out of there! It's an F2 and it's turning!'

'Give me some bearings, Rob.'

'You'll hit the main highway in thirty seconds. Get going before it overtakes you!'

Bradley cut the hysterical voice off and put his foot to the floor. 'Seatbelt on?' he demanded of Daisy, who nodded speechlessly. She was mesmerised by the swaying, hungry spike, sucking up huge lungfuls of dirt, beautiful and horrifying and deadly all at once. Bradley was whooping beside her, thoroughly enjoying the teasing game he was playing with the tornado. She looked back over his shoulder and wished she hadn't.

'It's getting closer!' She yelled suddenly, and his face changed.

'Fuck!' He floored the accelerator, not breaking when they hit the main highway again, swerving so hard they almost ended up in the field on the opposite side. He glanced at the mirror again. 'It's gaining on us.' His eyes had a mad sparkle. The speedometer showed seventy-five. The tornado was still a looming presence behind them. In the distance there was an underpass and he went for it. Daisy's fingernails dug into the seat. She wanted to scream at him for getting her into this situation but kept silent, not wanting to break his concentration. The concrete bridge beckoned like an oasis in the desert. When they reached it he slammed on the brakes and they scrambled out, the wind snatching at her hair and plucking at their clothes. They ran up the slope underneath the bridge and he pushed her on to her front and lay on top of her. The surface was gritty and hard, but the large warm lump pushing into the crevice of her backside was harder. His breath was hot in her ear.

'What about finishing what you started?'

'Now's hardly the time,' she shouted back as he pushed his hand up her skirt, into her panties. Frozen with terror, she felt rather than heard his approving groan as he sank his fingers into her moist pussy. She felt a hysterical laugh bubbling up from deep within as he tore her panties away and thrust her legs apart. He was going to fuck her right in the path of an approaching tornado. The hot probing of his cock confused her into pushing back at him, the tornado roaring so close it made her ears pop.

'Yeah, baby. Ride it like the wind!' Bradley hollered, plunging into her again and again until she was filled with a deep and terrible longing to come, coupled with fierce anger that he would do that to her when she was unable to escape him.

'Fuck you!' She screamed hysterically, over and over as

the tornado thundered against the bridge, spitting dust and fury.

'Yeah, that's right. Come on baby, give it your best!' Bradley was yelling as he continued his brutal assault on Daisy's body. The truck was moving, being sucked towards the tornado. Under the shelter of the bridge Daisy was screaming, unable to do anything but want Mike Bradley to screw her harder. The truck spun around to face the other way as Bradley purged himself inside her, howling, 'oh Jeez, what a fuck!' Oblivious of her own howls of terrified joy, she bucked back on to him: the feel of his cock and the awesome danger of their situation spiked an adrenaline rush she had never before experienced. For a long moment they were still, panting heavily.

'That was intense,' Bradley said at last. The tornado had died away, having given up on them. Bradley pulled away from Daisy, leaving her to spit horrid gravelly dust from her mouth. Her palms and knees felt skinned, and when she looked at them they were red and raw. Now the tornado had gone she felt sick with the shock of how close they had been to getting killed. She desperately needed a drink, preferably something alcoholic and 150 per cent proof. Bradley had already forgotten about her. He had climbed out from under the bridge and was staring at the sky. It rotated and heaved, but the tornado was moving steadily away from them. Daisy limped towards the truck to look for water, uncomfortably aware of the semen oozing down her legs. She found some Evian in the back of the truck and washed out her mouth. On the radio Karen was asking if they were still there. Daisy called to Bradley, as she had no idea how to answer it.

'Yeah, we're OK. It went right over us. It was awesome, man and most of it's on video. It's award-winning stuff!'

'Forget that. Is Daisy Lovell okay? Keith is shitting his pants,' Karen said tightly.

He glanced back at Daisy. 'She's fine.' He motioned to the glove compartment where she found a box of Kleenex. She cleaned herself up, starting with the stickiness to her inner thighs. Bradley gave the co-ordinates and they waited for the other trucks to join them. He pulled her into his arms.

'Baby, you are so hot.' His kiss was deep and wet, only ending when the convoy of trucks pulled to a halt beside them. A figure jumped from the last van and started running towards them. With a sense of unreality Daisy watched Max Decker catch Bradley by the throat and slam him against the truck. His fist was white-knuckled and drawn back, ready to reduce Bradley's face to a pulp, and his face was white with primeval fury.

'You fucking idiot, you could have killed her!'

For the first time, Bradley seemed to realise what Decker was capable of. The fear in his eyes was not a pretty sight. He looked feverishly at his entourage for help, but none was forthcoming. Everyone seemed frozen to the spot.

'Get this maniac off me!' he gasped through a painfully squeezed windpipe.

'It's OK, Decker. Let him go.' Daisy put her hand on his arm. For a moment it seemed as if he was unaware of her presence, then he gave Bradley one last vicious shove before backing off. As he stalked away, Bradley looked around and saw that his macho image was in jeopardy. With an outraged curse he charged at Decker's retreating figure.

Decker deflected the attack with precocious ease, rolling Bradley over his shoulder and sending him sprawling on his back in the dirt. Before he could get up Decker was standing over him. With a practised flick of his wrist he had produced a slim switchblade from underneath his shirtsleeve. He held the point to Bradley's dimpled chin for the briefest of moments before it disappeared up his sleeve again, leaving a tiny pinprick of blood. Then he walked away, leaving Bradley to scramble to his feet. Without saying a word, Decker had made his point.

'Someone should report that guy,' Bradley said shakily, wiping at his chin.

'Well it wasn't your cleverest move, was it?' Keith said. He sounded terse, more like the older brother he was, without a hint of his earlier admiration.

Bradley rubbed at his throat. 'Whatever. Just keep that psychopath away from me.' He cast an evil look at Daisy. 'Tell your guardian angel he should keep a hold of his temper.'

'You got off lightly,' she retorted. She went over to where Decker was standing with his back to all of them, staring across the plains. His back was ramrod straight and shimmered with tension.

'You OK?' she asked tentatively.

Decker glanced at her. 'I should be asking you that. I'd lay money down that he didn't.' He tossed his head contemptuously in the direction of Mike Bradley's truck, rapidly disappearing in a cloud of fumes.

'You're right, he didn't, but I always knew he was an asshole.'

'So why did you screw him?'

'Don't start on me, Deck. Near-death experiences don't exactly put me in the mood for it.'

'I guess they put you in the mood for fucking Mike Bradley, though.'

'Screw you, Decker!'

'No, screw you!'

The sudden whip crack of his voice was like a slap across the face, sharp enough for everyone to look round to see Decker aim a vicious kick at a fence post and disappear inside the van. Karen appeared with steaming coffee and moist antiseptic wipes.

'Here, let's look at that.' She examined Daisy's reddened hands and knee, then handed her the wipes. 'Are you sure you're okay?' She sounded genuinely concerned.

'I'll live. He's not the brightest of bunnies though, is he, our Mike,' Daisy said dryly, dabbing at her sore spots. She took the coffee from Karen and thanked her.

'I should have warned you about him earlier. He uses people. He doesn't give a toss about anyone else,' Karen said angrily.

Daisy shrugged. 'It's OK. Up 'til now I was just having fun.'

Karen's laughter was tinged with bitterness. 'I wish I could say the same thing. Keith's so struck by Miss Drop-Knickers over there he's forgotten what sex I am.'

'Then he's a bigger fool than his brother and he doesn't deserve you.'

'Thanks.' Karen looked a whole lot more friendly than she had before.

Despite Daisy's assurances that she was absolutely fine and she wasn't going to sue Storm Troopers for stress and negligence, Keith decided that they needed a break. The motel he found had a pool and a good steak bar, used by truckers on their way to and from the West Coast. No one seemed to mind as the sun had come out, luring them to the cool blue waters of the pool. They stayed there all afternoon, drinking beer and behaving like tourists.

Decker didn't join them, probably to avoid any awkward questions about his new-found skill at weather prediction, not to mention his masterclass in self-defence. He was far away on a piece of waste ground, practising his aim with the switchblade against a slender fence post. Daisy could see the darkness on his shirt between his shoulder blades as he backed away from the post, fifteen feet, twenty feet, she couldn't really tell, and let the knife fly with telling force, hitting his small target with killer accuracy time after time. She was tempted to go over to him, but the thought of getting another public brush-off didn't exactly appeal.

Bradley didn't show his face, either, which annoyed her. He could at least have said he was sorry but, according to Karen, that was something he just didn't do. As she stewed with indignation, a very bad, exciting idea began to form. It felt similar to the feeling she had had in Jason Cordell's office. After giving it some thought, she turned to Karen, who was rubbing suncream into her legs on the lounger next to hers.

'What would you say to teaching Mike a lesson?' she whispered so that no one could hear.

'What do you mean?' Karen whispered back.

Daisy told her. Karen's face showed disbelief, then feline glee.

'It might turn him on though,' she murmured.

'Well, that's good for us, but it doesn't have to be good for him, does it?'

Karen hesitated, but only for the briefest of moments. Then she smiled, lighting up her dainty features.

'It won't be,' she whispered.

Just then the man himself made an appearance. He approached Daisy, obviously primed by Keith to make a formal apology, but she could see in his face how much it cost him to do it. She let him suffer for a few moments before waving his painfully forced words carelessly away.

'Just remember that the next woman will sue your ass off if she has any sense.' She smiled to soften her words. 'Listen, just to show there's no hard feelings, why don't we have a little fun tonight? I've someone who'd really like to join us.' She nodded to Karen, sitting a short distance away. 'That is, if you're interested.'

Bradley looked over at Karen, very lovely now she was smiling at him, with dainty, tiny, high breasts and a neat ass in a tiny blue bikini. He relaxed and grinned stupidly.

'Are you kidding? Of course I'm interested.'

'OK, we'll come to your room tonight.' She dismissed him with a sultry smile. 'Run along, big Mike. We ladies need to conserve our energy for later.'

'I look forward to it,' he said huskily, and she could tell he meant it.

'Like shooting fish?' Karen asked as Daisy lay back on the sun-lounger next to her.

'Easier,' Daisy murmured, closing her eyes again and lifting her face to the sun.

By four o'clock the sun was even hotter, casting shimmering mirages in the middle distance in every direction. Daisy left Karen by the pool and went to find some shade on a grassy hillock overlooking the motel, so that she could read her copy of *American Psycho* in comfort. From her vantage point she could also see the monstrous eighteen-wheelers pulling into the parking lot. The truckers that emerged from them were mostly slim and as small as ants next to the big beasts they drove. How did truckers stay so fit, she mused, watching one in particular, climbing out of a black rig with 'Spunky's Wieners' emblazoned on the side in red and yellow. He was short and wiry in dark blue Wranglers and a black sleeveless vest. As if knowing he was being watched, he turned and looked straight at her, flashing a rascally grin.

'How ya doing, sweetheart?'

'Pretty good, thanks!' she called back. For a moment she hoped that he would come over, but he didn't. He gave her a friendly wave and went into the diner.

Minutes later he was out again, bearing two large Diet Cokes and a paper bag. He was walking over to her.

'Can I join you?'

She closed her book and sat up. 'Sure,' she said diffidently.

'Huh, I thought you might like this.' He proffered the Diet Coke. She thanked him and took it. 'Doughnut?'

She laughed and delved into the bag. 'Why not?'

'I'm Ricky. You are?'

'Daisy Mae,' she said through a mouthful of cinnamon sugar.

'I bet you've heard all the puns about that.'

'Yep.' Daisy licked sugar off her fingers.

'You won't hear them from me then.'

He was interested in the tour and what made her go on it. She was interested in what made a man live such a solitary life for weeks at a time. He was en route to Phoenix to deliver frozen hotdogs before visiting some friends in Flagstaff. As well as being good company he was also very pleasant to look at. He was shorter than her, wiry and tan, with dense black curly hair escaping over the top of his clean black vest. And his muscles were sinewy and hard, making her entertain thoughts of how sinewy and hard he would be everywhere else.

While they were talking Daisy thought of Phoenix, of sun hotter than this and the freedom to eat, pee and sing whenever she liked. She had had enough of the tour. Storm chasing wasn't as much fun as she thought it would be. There were too many hours in the bus, too much time waiting for something to happen. Most of all, there was too much of Max Decker, watching her every time she turned around. Or not, as was the case that day. Then there was what she and Karen had planned for Mike Bradley. He would not forgive her for a long time, so making herself disappear would be no bad thing. The thought grew and grew, and by the time she had finished her Coke she had made up her mind.

'Ricky,' she said at last, 'when are you leaving?'

'Tonight, after some shuteye and a good steak. You want to join me?'

It was as easy as that. They arranged to meet in the parking lot at midnight.

8

Daisy's last meal as a Storm Trooper was fittingly delicious and gargantuan, and appropriate for her farewell, though no one else knew of it. She knew she had made the right decision, and was looking forward to the next step of her adventure. Meanwhile, she watched Mike Bradley sizzle like a ribeye steak with anticipation all evening. She could almost smell it on him, and see it in the heated glances he was giving both her and Karen throughout the meal. Eventually he approached Daisy, his face hot and flushed with excitement.

'I've had a boner all evening watching you two. When are you coming to see me?'

'Give us a few minutes to powder our noses,' Daisy whispered, tweaking his cock through his baggies. It was as hard as a tree trunk.

She packed her belongings for her great escape, exchanged phone numbers with Karen, and then they made their way to Bradley's room. In Daisy's bag were three pairs of No Nonsense pantyhose, a can of shaving cream and a packet of disposable razors. Karen carried a tub of ice cubes. Underneath her short khaki skirt Daisy wore a black thong and a matching balcony bra. Karen wore a very small string-strapped vest top with nothing underneath it, and girlishly innocent white panties. She had shown them to Daisy, anxiously asking if they looked all right as she wasn't a thong type of girl. Daisy assured her that they looked great, and her confidence seemed boosted by that small compliment.

'I've never done anything like this before,' she confided

as they approached his door. 'What if I screw up and look a complete dork?'

'I'm not going to judge you.' Daisy squeezed her hand reassuringly. 'Go in there, screw him any way you want and have some fun. You deserve it.'

Karen sparkled at her. 'Yeah, I do. Fuck 'em! That's what I say!'

'Fuck 'em!' Daisy repeated with a grin, and knocked on the door.

Bradley opened it, practically rubbing his hands with glee.

'Hey Kaz. I always knew you'd be back for more.' She shocked him by putting her hand directly on to his crotch and squeezing. 'Jeez, have you been taking lessons from her?' He nodded at Daisy.

'You just never gave me the opportunity to reach my full potential,' Karen replied silkily, and Daisy felt absurdly proud of her. She greeted Bradley with a deep, sensuous kiss and another squeeze. He was already massively erect, staring at them as if all his birthdays had come at once. Karen pulled the cord on his baggy shorts and let them drop to the floor. He stood with his hands on his hips, like a young sun god, golden skin glowing except for the small white triangle above his buttocks and under his pubic hair. His cock stood out like a club, brutish and thickly veined. The two girls prowled around him, fondling his buttocks and feeling the weight of his balls. They were heavy and full.

'Enough for both of us,' Karen purred to Daisy.

'And more,' Bradley replied arrogantly.

'Stop bragging and get on the bed,' Daisy said softly, pushing him back on the mattress. She stood over him, dropping her shorts and kicking them away. She dropped to her knees and toyed with her thong, pulling it between her pussy lips so they puffed over the thin strip of material.

'Oh, baby, lovely pussy,' he gasped, running his hands up over her thighs. Karen took one hand and tied it to the bedpost, then the other, as far apart as they would go. He let her do it, too enraptured by Daisy's breasts falling out of the tiny bra. His cock bounced on his stomach as she wet her fingers and played with her nipples, making them glisten and pucker.

'We're going to give you such a treat tonight,' she said, letting her breasts drift over his face, distracting him from Karen securing his ankles to the bottom of the bed so he could not raise his knees. Too late, he noticed that he couldn't move very much.

'What is this?' he said, wriggling to get comfortable. They saw lust and slight concern battling on his face. His cock wasn't quite as hard as it had been before, now lying softly along his belly. The girls knelt before him and took a testicle each, sucking, licking, blowing, not touching his cock. As he relaxed and began to enjoy the attention, it thickened again, swelling like an inflating balloon. At Daisy's encouragement Karen straddled him and teased his lips with her tiny pointed breasts. He snuffled greedily at them, slurping at each long nipple like a big puppy. Daisy concentrated on his cock, running her fingers up and down its length as if she were playing the clarinet. As he looked up from Karen's breasts his eyes were hazy and his mouth soft and red.

'Come on, Kaz, get stuck on my cock,' he said with crude languor, pushing the distended member up towards her. Karen took his cock in her mouth and began to suck him with such expertise that Daisy was enraptured just watching her.

'You should give Clare some tips,' she said. Karen smiled around Bradley's cock. He bit his lip and churned his hips as far as he was able, which wasn't that far. Daisy licked at his balls with a pointed tongue, her eyes smiling at Karen's as she continued to fellate him. When she felt him tensing, Karen pressed the base of his cock hard to quell the desire to come, and he sagged, gasping. Daisy could see him getting angry.

'Let me free, you fucking whores,' he snarled, and Daisy shook her head disapprovingly.

'I don't think you're in any position to call us names, Mr Bradley.' As she picked up the shaving cream the first inklings of real dismay showed in his eyes. She took the shaving cream and shook it, then sprayed it all over his chest. At that point he started to yell. Karen pushed her panties into his mouth and the yells became enraged mumbles, his face going puce with fury. Karen masturbated him slowly, keeping him hard for Daisy, who positioned him inside her and fucked him slowly, enjoying the mixed emotions playing on his face. Then she sat comfortably, with his cock still buried deep inside her, squeezing it regularly with her inner muscles as Karen handed her a Bic razor. Bradley began to wriggle violently, but all it did was push his cock deeper into Daisy's hot, tight pussy.

'If you don't keep still you could get hurt,' Karen said sternly, wagging an admonishing finger.

'He won't mind that, Karen. He said himself that the anticipation of pain is half the pleasure!' Daisy said, laughing, skillfully disguising the need the feel of his cock had aroused in her. Karen was ready with a flannel and warm water and a towel. Daisy shaved Bradley's chest with long, careful strokes, taking particular care around his nipples. His eyes bulged with fury but he dared not move. Whenever she felt him relax slightly she squeezed his cock with her internal muscles and felt him pulsate. His eyes grew hooded. He seemed enraged by the strength of his cock, revealing him to be so enslaved by it even in the face of his humiliation. When Daisy had finished, his chest looked curiously naked and very smooth. Daisy moved off him and knelt down by his legs.

'What do you think, Karen? The razor or the wax?'

Bradley shook his head frantically. Daisy rescued her bag and pulled out some hair removing cream. 'This will only take a few minutes,' she said, smearing it on and around his balls. She looked at her watch. 'Time for a break, I think.'

They turned the television on and opened a packet of Doritos, washing them down with Bacardi Breezers. They talked about the tour, totally ignoring Bradley, helpless and ridiculous on the bed, his cock limp now and rather pathetic. Eventually Daisy looked at her watch again.

'OK, let's see what's going on.'

Karen brought out more hot water, and together they washed away the cream, together with all of Bradley's pubic hair. His cock was like a newborn puppy, flaccid and pink, his balls also a soft baby pink and smelling unpleasantly of the cream. Karen wrinkled her nose.

'I don't really fancy those right now, do you, Daisy?'

Daisy lifted Bradley's cock and peered at them. 'They look a bit raw. Maybe we should cook them first.'

Bradley looked as if he would be sick any minute. Karen patted him on the shoulder. 'Relax, Mike. We're not going to hurt you.'

Daisy continued to fondle his balls. They were pleasingly soft and velvety, though next to his legs, covered in tight curls of hair, they looked very strange. She picked up some baby oil and poured it on to her hands, then rubbed it into his chest. Her oily, glistening hands ran down to his balls, all around his cock, until it began to shift and swell. As Karen rubbed her breasts all over his face, he began to growl deep in his throat, his pelvis pushing back and forth. Karen slid down on to his cock and began to ride him, pleasuring herself at her own pace, ignoring his increasingly desperate thrusts. Her body became slick with baby oil, glistening on her thighs.

'Oh, this is good,' she gasped, frantically agitating her

clitoris at the same time. She fucked herself to a hectic orgasm, her short swingy hair whipping all over her face. Out of breath, she climbed off him. 'You try it,' she said to Daisy.

Daisy climbed on Bradley and guided his cock into her honeyed pussy. He jerked and throbbed inside her, moaning impotently.

'Don't worry, honey, I'm going to make you come,' she said soothingly, and gasped as he thickened instantly. His face was red, his eyes bulging as she rode him, her fingers on her clit. She let her imagination go wild, seeing Max Decker underneath her instead, boiling mad and ready to fly. Bradley jerked his hips as Daisy soared into ecstasy, screaming Decker's name, grinding herself on to Bradley's cock. As the orgasm ebbed away she grew still, while Bradley bucked underneath her with increasing desperation, his muffled cries sounding like, 'fuck me you bitch', but it was difficult to tell. When she drew away the great dewy hole at the top of his cock was open and ready, but he sagged with exhaustion as the waves of lust were snatched cruelly away from him. She pulled on her clothes.

'Fancy a beer?' she asked Karen.

'Yeah, why not?' Karen was already dressed. They paused by the door and looked back at him, still gagged and bound, his cock still sticking up but looking distinctly ravaged.

'This is for being a total shithead,' Daisy said, and threw the ice cubes into his lap. They closed the door on his muffled roars.

Back in Daisy's room, Karen hugged her fiercely. 'Thank you. I can safely say I have Mike Bradley out of my system now.'

'Good. What about Keith?'

Karen grinned. 'I was thinking of dumping him anyway, but I think I'll have some fun with him first.' She peered out of the grubby net curtain. 'OK, Ricky's waiting. Shit, Max is coming!'

Daisy hid her packed bag under the bed and Karen hid in the bathroom. Daisy unfastened one braid and was combing it through when he knocked on the door.

'What do you want?' she asked, more rudely than she intended. His voice was just as abrupt.

'Who was that you were talking to earlier?'

So he wasn't stupid, and he had his suspicions. She continued brushing her hair, using the calming motion to steady her nerves.

'Someone pleasant and undemanding, unlike you.' She hoped she didn't sound too desperate or guilty. 'Is that all you wanted to ask me?'

'I just came to see you were OK.'

'I'm fine! It isn't as though you really care anyway, so cut the concerned crap.'

'I am concerned. You could have been killed today. Is all this hostility just because of last night?'

'Go to hell, Decker.'

'I'll see you there,' he said loudly as she slammed the door in his face.

Daisy watched him leaving through the curtain. Ricky's rig looked miles away, and if Decker saw what she was doing there was no telling what he would do to stop her. She took a deep breath, feeling as nerved up as if she were doing an Olympic sprint. Karen looked out of the window. Decker was out there, loitering around.

'OK, I'll divert him while you run like hell. See you around, kid.' They hugged hard and Karen left.

Through the grubby net curtain Daisy could see her talking to Decker and motioning to the bar. Decker followed her with a final look back at Daisy's room. Daisy opened the door, her heart thumping, and ran as if all hell's angels were after her towards Ricky's rig.

Ricky was behind the wheel with the door open and the engine running. His grin was white and cheeky, as if he could not believe his luck, as she threw in her bag. He told her to keep down and they pulled out on to the highway. As the motel lights disappeared from view she felt her spirits lift. Ricky was good company, undemanding and totally laid back. It was going to be an easy ride to Phoenix.

After a while she flipped through his CD collection. He was a lover of the ladies, Belinda Carlisle, Shania Twain *et al.*

'Don't you have any garage music, Ricky?' she asked dryly.

He shrugged. 'Nah. I never did go for that punk rock stuff.'

He was absolutely serious. She laughed, shaking her head. At length she found some common ground. Texas, which seemed appropriate. She even had the CD somewhere at home. Home, wherever that would be in the future. Her father would be as mad as a bull, knowing Decker had lost her. Later, she wondered how Decker had reacted when he realised she had gone, and what he was going to do about it. But it was time to forget about him. Push him out of her mind. She had better things to think about now.

The cab was almost better equipped than her flat in England had been, with a small television with built-in video, a pull-down bed and a mini-fridge. All along the edge of the windows were amateur crotch shots of half-dressed women, all in panties, but far more erotic than they would have been naked. He saw her looking at them.

'I like pussy,' he said, somewhat bashfully.

'You know, Ricky, I find that quite comforting.'

They were driving down the empty highway, the white lines mesmerising as they disappeared under the wheels of the cab. Eventually she fell asleep, but didn't realise it until the hydraulic brakes hissed as the truck came to a stop outside a gas station and small motel. It was just before dawn, a red stain on the horizon behind them.

'A leak stop,' Ricky said. 'I need some gas as well.'

Daisy jumped out to stretch her legs. It was dark but she could still feel the heat radiating up from the tarmac road. Apart from the ramshackle motel, strip lighting over the petrol pumps and the red neon arrow advertising their existence for miles around, there were no other lights. No tiny pinpricks of civilization. She headed over to the bar. Rock music blared out, Guns 'n' Roses, to be exact, which was disorientating so early in the morning. In the parking lot were at least ten other big rigs, and she guessed that their drivers would be in there, propping up the counter.

She was right. As she walked in, ten pairs of eyes turned in her direction. Truckers from scrawny to verging on the obese, all varieties catered for. They raked her with their eyes until she felt naked before them. And she hadn't noticed until then how much her butt wiggled when she walked. She headed for the restrooms, trying to check the inviting sway of her hips, painfully aware that they were watching her every move.

She used the toilet and splashed water on her face. Some of it dropped on her thin jersey top, and the dark drops of water and the slight sheen of moisture on her skin made her look hotter than ever. Those truckers had looked at her as if they had never seen a woman before. She bet that some of them had gone for weeks without a decent fuck, lot lizards aside. Now she was in their midst, smelling of roses, despite the dusty lace-up boots and khaki skirt, exuding a fresh sensuality that few men would be able to resist. And she could bet what they were thinking. She fluffed up her hair and tweaked her nipples and went to run the gauntlet again. Enjoy, boys, she thought, this time walking in her usual loose-limbed way. They all watched her, not speaking, as she ordered two Pink Lemonade Snapples and went to find Ricky back at his truck.

Two other rigs were filling with gas and Ricky was standing a way off, talking to the drivers. By the huge cab of Ricky's truck the heat smelled of oil and dust. She wandered round to the petrol pump. The pipe leading to the pump was long and thick, drooping towards the ground. She accidentally brushed against it and found the buzzing sensation very pleasing against her thigh. After a moment she moved so the vibration agitated her pussy through her short skirt. It felt even better, and she realised that teasing those truckers in the bar had turned her on. What would Chico make of her frigging herself with a gas pipe, she thought to herself, closing her eyes and enjoying the sensation? Soon her whole sex felt heavy with need. Unable to deny it even more pleasure, she straddled the pipe and crouched down on it, feeling very licentious. No one could see her. She was obscured from view by the rig and Ricky was far away, having a smoke. She pressed her sex against the thick pipe, too greedy for pleasure to mind the grubby oil marks on her thighs and clothes, letting the vibrations judder through her pussy, right through her whole body. It was as if breaking free from the tour group had liberated her sexually. Today a gas pipe, tomorrow, who knew? She remembered her vow, back in England, to get laid lots and lots of times. Then it had been a joke; she wasn't really that kind of girl, but it was an incredibly erotic thought to know she could walk back into the bar and push her breasts into the face of the first man sitting there, knowing he would fall on her like a dog. From then on she would be systematically screwed, cocks big and small, fat and long, her legs open and her eyes closed,

feeling bearded mouths on her breasts, beer- and nicotine-tasting tongues in her mouth, semen spilling over
her lips. She could be like Clare, reduced to a human
blow-up doll, with men fighting over her, spurting over
her and inside her. The dirty fantasy aroused her so much
she could hardly stand up. She leaned on the pipe as it
acted like a huge vibrator, pleasuring all her sexual ori-
fices at once, hot and dirty and very sensual.

Ricky chose that moment to reappear. His mouth
dropped open.

'What the fuck! Oh, you crazy little slut!'

Helpless with the need to continue what she started,
she lifted the front of her skirt so he could see her
sparkling clean panties being made all dirty. Instantly he
was on the pipe with her, his fingers on her plump cleft.
She had her hand on his crotch, feeling for his cock, the
other pulling down her top so that he could suck on one
of her nipples. For a few mad moments they frotted each
other frantically until the petrol cut out, the tank filled to
bursting. Ricky looked up from her breast, breathing
heavily.

'You're all dirty now,' he said hoarsely. 'I'll get us a
room with a shower.'

He staggered away to pay for the gas. When he came
back he gave her a key and said sternly, 'I need to move
the rig. Stay exactly as you are. I want to wash you clean,
you dirty little tramp.'

The room was a pit-stop, nothing glamorous at all, but
cool, clean and possessed a big bed and a reasonable
shower room. She waited, feeling all quivery and highly
excited, her nipples as hard as pebbles. This was what
she thrived on, spur-of-the-moment, raw sex with one
man, not anonymous, mechanical fucking with several.
Her decision to go with Ricky to Phoenix had been partly
guided by her attraction to his husky good looks and lean,

wiry body. The bulge in his Wranglers looked promising, too. And he was a sweet man, which helped a lot.

Ricky came back quickly, shut the door and purposefully rubbed his hands. 'In that bathroom,' he said, marching her towards the bath. She kicked off her shoes and dropped her skirt, bending over so he could enjoy her tight white thong disappearing between her buttocks. Only it wasn't white, it was filthy with oil and dust.

'Leave your top on,' he said. Considerately making sure the water was warm, he made her stand under the shower, watching greedily as her T-shirt turned transparent and her nipples showed through. She arched her back and pushed them out to him. He peeled away the thin fabric and tightened it over them, again and again, enjoying how the soaking fabric clung to her skin. Eventually he peeled her panties down and threw them aside. He soaped his hands and ran them all over her thighs and bottom. His fingers slipped briefly into her sex, into the crack of her bottom as the water washed the oily grime of the pipe and grey bubbles away. She moved with his hands, liking their assured gentleness.

'OK, you can take your top off now.'

She eased it down over her breasts, taking her time, letting sparkling drops of water hang from her jutting nipples. The soap was in his hands, making them all bubbly. As he applied them to her breasts they, too, were slippery through his fingers.

'You're dirty too,' she said. 'Why don't you let me wash you?'

He wrenched his T-shirt over his head and shrugged off his jeans. His stomach was hard and flat, a slim line of hairs going down from his navel to below black bikini briefs restraining an enormous bulge. She went a little weak-kneed, looking at it. Seeing where her gaze was fixed he hefted his balls in both hands and grinned at her. He was obviously proud of the prodigious gifts the Almighty had bestowed upon him. Teasingly he peeled away the grossly misshapen briefs. Underneath them, his cock was hugely erect, priapic against his small frame, curving gently like a bow. She took the soap and foamed her hands, then washed his balls, which were hot and tight, but left his cock well alone. She could feel it, nudging against her belly, hot and hard and ready, but she knelt and washed his thighs, his calves, up again towards his chest. She made him turn around and washed his back, between his buttocks, pressing her warm breasts against his back and letting him feel her pebble-hard nipples. He turned around again and took her in his arms. Their bodies rubbed sinuously together like two glossy eels and, as he was shorter than her, he could suck on her nipples easily and slide his cock in and out of her thighs, rubbing along her outer sex lips. In the mirrored tiles, she could see the red tip protruding just under her buttocks and see his dark, tanned arms starkly contrasted against her creamy flesh not yet touched by the sun. His hand slid between her legs, finding her sex all receptive and open and slippery with her juices. He stuck two fingers inside her and slid them in and out, slowly, lasciviously, judging each thrust with a tug on her nipple, his palm rubbing indistinctly against her pussy until she was almost too aroused to stand up. She felt for the soap and applied it to his cock, then ran it through her hands, over and over, until the friction made him groan and churn his hips. He backed away from her, letting the shower rinse the remains of the soap from their bodies. Daisy turned around and presented her pouting pussy lips to him.

'Oh, God, you're a peach,' he groaned, pushing grate-fully into her. Her clit pulsed in appreciation of his size and she widened her legs to let him in further. The tip of his cock knocked against her cervix, bruising her slightly and forcing her to tell him to go easy. As he gently rocked against her she reached down to stroke herself whilst bracing herself against the wall with her other hand.

'I'm going to come if we carry on like this,' Ricky gasped, never ceasing his rhythm.

'Isn't that the idea?' she panted, pushing back at him.

'Yeah, but not like this. I want to taste that pussy first.' He pulled away and stepped from the bath. He gave her a towel and began to dry himself. Suddenly a thought occurred to her.

'Do you mind if I take a few photographs?'

Her camera still had the black and white film in it. She took a couple of shots of him drying himself. On her instruction he acted naturally, not looking at the camera. The contrast of his dark, angry cock against the white towel pleased her. Its weight made it hang at right angles to his body as they went into the bedroom.

'Sit on my face,' he ordered.

Acquiescently she crouched over him and took another couple of shots of his cock, from an angle that accentuated its length and immediately gave away her position. His tongue swarmed all over her pussy, up to her clit, driving deep into her until she was squirming and panting, unable to concentrate on taking any more pictures. She put the camera away, took him in hand and sucked contentedly on the great circumcised glans, her eyes closed with pleasure. He settled down to a gentle exploration of her cunt as she licked along his shaft. They sixty-nined each other for a while, too lazy to do anything more, until she decided to up the tempo by plunging his cock as far as it could go down her throat. She gagged as he jerked upwards, but did it again, rising to the challenge of taking as much as she could of him into her mouth. His body bucked and wriggled, muffled sounds coming from her cunt until she felt him tense for the final shot. She pulled back to let him concentrate on her.

His tongue zeroed in on her clit, his saliva cooling on her thighs. He wasn't the most accomplished of pussy eaters but he found the spot, strumming it until she was shimmering with orgasmic joy, flooding his face with her juices, taking his cock back into her mouth so he could feel as well as hear her moans of ecstasy. He began to tense again so she pulled back, her orgasm over for now, and climbed off his face.

'I'll get blue balls if you carry on like that,' he muttered. 'Get on my cock and stay there next time.'

'And what if I refuse?' she said playfully. He turned her over and sank into her as far as he could go.

'Then I'll fuck you raw,' he growled.

'Do it,' she said.

9

They left just after seven o'clock so he could reach his deadline in Phoenix. On the way they chatted and drank Sprite, and the morning passed very pleasantly as the vermilion rock and tall, spiky saguaros drifted past. She called Karen and was somewhat disappointed to learn that Decker hadn't gone on a frustrated killing spree, but had been left behind at the motel to make his own arrangements. She felt she owed Karen a full explanation, but didn't want to reel it off with Ricky tuning in beside her. They discussed meeting in New York later that month and, when the call ended, Daisy felt as if she already had a close friend.

Business done, she decided to have some fun, subtly flashing her panties at Ricky, knowing it would drive him wild.

'I wish you'd behave yourself,' he said sternly.

She snuggled up closer to him and ran her hand up and down his leg. 'I can't help it,' she murmured. 'Watching you drive this big beast makes me feel very horny.' She breathed hotly into his ear. 'All horny and wet.'

He gulped, his Adam's apple bobbing under his black open-necked shirt. She stretched out on the long seat with her head leaning against his thigh and pulled her skirt up so he could feast his eyes on her tightly encased snatch. The steering wheel wobbled. She slipped her finger down into her panties and stroked herself, and the truck swayed.

'Shit, you're going to be the death of us,' he gasped, regaining control. She pulled her panties down around her thighs and continued to stroke her clit, guiding his hand down to her breasts. As he plucked gently on her nipples, trying to keep his eyes on the road she agitated her clitoris, imagining how his huge prick must be feeling, uselessly trapped inside his jeans. Then she could imagine the truckers back at the bar, watching as she cockteased them before letting them ravage her swollen, sopping pussy, one after the other, until her legs were slick with sperm. Her climax left her breathless, straining against Ricky's thigh. Then she noticed he had stopped the truck. He jumped out and ran around to her side, climbed in again and set his cock free to plunge straight into her waiting, open cunt.

'You can't do that and not expect me to fuck you,' he growled, pumping hard against her. In less than ten strokes he was there, his face brutal with lust, staccato grunts coming from his lips as he purged inside her. The raw urgency of his fucking set off an echo of an orgasm inside her, making her screech like a banshee. It was fiery, quick and left them breathless, balancing precariously on the narrow seat. As Ricky grinned at her they lost their balance and ended up in a tangled heap in the footwell of the truck, still joined by his cock, giggling like children. It took several moments to disengage themselves, still laughing.

'I really need to make this deadline,' Ricky said, trying to be serious. 'So please put your pussy away until we reach Phoenix. Then I can give you what you really deserve.'

Later that afternoon she left him in Phoenix. In her possession was a mean-looking, old black Ford Camaro, bought for five hundred dollars from Ricky's brother-in-law, who happened to have a used car saleroom on the outskirts of the city. She had been persuaded after being shocked at the astronomical price of car hire, arguing to herself that she needed a car anyway, and that she might as well drive home rather than spend more money on flying. Then she headed north, into the wilds of Arizona. On the way she called an old friend, Sonia Lopez. Sonia had invited her countless times to visit her in Santa Fe but, until now, Daisy had never found the time. She called Sonia to say she would be arriving in a week with some good, juicy stories. Sonia had cackled lecherously down the phone at her and promised plenty of men to keep them both amused.

As she threw her bag in the back of the Camaro she felt a welling of freedom, but the feeling did not last. Wherever she went there was a vague feeling of dissatisfaction, and of time running out. For the next two days she was a tourist, chilling out amongst the soaring canyons and craters, but she kept moving forward. It was hard to admit, but she was getting lonely, and now she had time to reflect; she knew she was sub-consciously searching for something. Grow up, get real and enjoy what you see, she told herself severely, and most of the time it helped. But not always.

Near the Painted Desert she passed a place selling geodes. Thinking that she hadn't bought any souvenirs of her trip just yet, she stopped the car. The store was not much more than a shack amongst the large pastel dunes, with a large wooden crate full of round rocks, a little larger than a cricket ball. For five dollars, she could pick one out and have it cut in half by the surly Mexican standing behind an electric saw. She was just turning them over when a presence made itself felt beside her.

'Look for the light ones. If it feels light for its size, you've got a goodun.'

She turned and saw a tall man with a scrappy beard and a red bandanna around his head. His thickly muscled torso was bare under a leather waistcoat with 'The Real Outlaws – Houston Chapter' on the back. He looked mean and hungry, but his dark eyes were smiling. She thought she had seen him before at Meteor Crater.

She dropped a grey ball into his hand. 'What do you think of that one?'

He hefted it in his hand. 'A bit heavy. Try this.' He handed her another. It really was impossible to tell. One rock looked and felt much like another. The man smiled at her again and moved on. She decided on the one that he had picked out and paid for it.

The Mexican began to cut the geode. Daisy didn't know what to expect, so it was exciting seeing the sparks fly and the seemingly impenetrable stone being sliced like butter. Eventually it was done, and the Mexican held out the geode.

'You are lucky,' he said in broken English. Daisy gasped. It wasn't like the sparkling slivers she had seen in the souvenir shops, but for a five dollar lucky dip she had not done bad. The middle of the geode was hollow, encrusted with muddy crystals, surrounded by milky blue stripes of feldspar. The man sprayed varnish on it to enhance the colour even more. She thanked him, bought a Snapple from his cooler machine and headed back to the car, feeling very pleased. As she reached it she recognised the dull, throaty roar of a Harley Davidson, heading towards her.

'How did it turn out?' It was the man who had actually picked out the rock. She had forgotten all about him.

She showed the geode to him. 'You obviously know your rocks. Thanks.'

'You're welcome. I'm Tex, by the way.'

She looked at him, confidently astride the big bike, with the tall handle bars and laid back seat. He looked good, but just then she was happier on her own. Must be hormones, she thought as she smiled.

'Of course you are,' she said, and drove off in a cloud of dust.

She tied her unruly waves back into a loose ponytail and put her foot on the accelerator, breathing in the desiccating heat of the desert. Her skin was turning a deep caramel brown, the sun streaking her chestnut hair with strands of gold. She wore nothing more than her bikini top and cut away shorts and enjoyed the toots from passing cars when she stopped to drink her Snapple on the side of the road. The haunting wail of a distant train and invisible skylarks were the only sounds in the arid heat. She climbed on to the hood of the Camaro and flashed her breasts at the driver as the train rumbled past, a quarter of a mile away. He pulled the horn at her, a two-note hoot that was the train equivalent of a wolf whistle, as she laughed at her naughtiness. She watched it disappear into the heat haze, a freight train almost half a mile long, heading towards Chicago. She was feeling very horny again, thinking about sweet little Ricky and his whacking great dick. Or that biker with his dark, inviting eyes. Sometimes you can be such a twat, she scolded herself, running through the sensual possibilities. She had found her vibrator and it was inside her pussy, tucked neatly into her panties as she drove, a thick, solid presence that made her bite her lip every time she shifted on the seat. The road stretched endlessly in either direction, baked by the sun, a heat haze shimmering and obscuring the distant mountains. She put her foot down and flew along the empty silver ribbon of road, the feel of the vibrator inside her giving her a burst of fresh speed whenever she desired it. She was totally alone, with nothing but telegraph poles and tumbleweeds and crucifying heat for company.

On a particularly desolate stretch of road she noticed blue flashing lights and heard the whoop of a police siren. She had no idea how long he had been following her. Her music was loud and her attention had been on a dust devil whirling playfully along beside her. She certainly hadn't seen any police motorcycles lurking behind any rocks.

'Where the hell did you come from?' she muttered, slowing to a stop. The big blue and white motorcycle had Arizona State Trooper on the side, and more mirrors and lights than she could count. The man wandering slowly towards her looked like an alien being in his large helmet and dark uniform, bristling with all kinds of weaponry. She had no time to remove the vibrator but, with her shorts on, he wouldn't even know it was there, she thought wickedly. She climbed from the car so he could get the full benefit of her minimally clad body and grinned.

'You must be as hot as hell under all that,' she said, referring only in part to his uniform. She couldn't see his face but he had a hard, built-up body, with wide shoulders and slim hips.

'Did you realise what speed you were doing, ma'am?'

She bit her lip and looked guilty. 'Not really. I've been in England and they drive a lot faster over there. I guess I just forgot. Sorry.'

It was hard to tell whether or not he was moved by her apology. Under the black visor he could have been laughing his head off, but she doubted it. His lips, the only part of his face that she could see, remained stern. They were slim, slightly cruel lips, like . . .

'Let me see your papers, ma'am.' His voice rescued her from the brink of any dangerous thoughts. She knelt on the drivers seat and stretched over to the glove compartment, knowing that her short shorts were exposing a lot of pale, firm buttock flesh. It was the one part she had not exposed to the sun just yet. The vibe moved and she moaned softly, hesitating for a moment to let the wave of sensation pass before standing up again. Instinctively she knew he was staring.

'It's all here,' she said, handing him her licence documents. 'Was I really going that fast?'

'Fast enough for me to charge you, ma'am.' He looked dismissively through the papers and handed them back.

'But you're not going to, right? I mean, it's so beautiful out here. There's no one else around . . .' Three big Harleys went by at that moment, with priceless timing. The rider of one hollered at her. It was Tex, the feeler of good rocks. 'Except them, of course.' She stuffed her hands in the back pockets of her shorts, slyly thrusting her breasts out at him, and scuffed the dust with her shoe. He was watching her blankly, but beneath the tight, dark trousers she could see the unmistakable shape of something not quite as large as the nightstick at his hip, but getting close. With her sunglasses on, he had no idea that she was feasting on his burgeoning erection, but she hazarded an educated guess that he was transfixed by her breasts, bursting out of the small bronze bikini top, her nipples poking out like bullets. God, she loved being female.

'I really am sorry. In this heat it's easy to forget small details,' she said imploringly. 'Don't you find that?'

His tongue travelled slowly over his lips. 'I'd like you to step over to that rock, please.'

She hesitated. If he found the vibrator she would be humiliated big time.

'Are you resisting my orders, ma'am?' His voice was stern.

'No, officer.' She obligingly went to a large outcrop of sandstone and stood meekly. The State Trooper took her arm and led her around the back of it, where they would not be seen from the road.

'I don't want to embarrass you, ma'am, but I do need to search you.'

'That won't take long,' Daisy quipped, glancing down at her minimal dress. She braced herself for the ultimate embarrassment. The State Trooper turned her around and pushed her against the rock. He pushed her feet apart and began to run his hands all over her body.

'Are you frisking me, officer?' she asked playfully.

'Arizona can be a very violent place, ma'am. We can't be too careful.' The cop's voice was neutral but his hands were warm all over her body and legs. When his hand slipped up between her legs, she stiffened. He felt around, obviously realising that something was amiss, and pressed against the hard lump in her panties. The action pushed the vibrator deeper inside her, and she moaned with mortified pleasure. He did it again, and she sagged against the rock, weak with lust.

'Ma'am, I'm going to have to ask you to drop your shorts,' he said firmly.

She unbuttoned them and let them slide down her legs, her face flame red. His expression was still blank as he slipped his hand inside her panties and grasped the end of the large vibrator. He drew it out slowly, so slowly her legs trembled and she wanted to grab his hand and make him thrust it back in again, over and over until she came. But he didn't. In his hand the vibrator looked very fat and long, now glistening in the sun with her juices. Daisy didn't know whether to laugh or cry. The cop was staring at her, but what his expression was now she could not tell under that damned helmet.

'I could take you in for speeding, dangerous driving, resisting interrogation and possession of an offensive weapon,' he said severely.

Daisy saw the implications, and the involvement of her father, and knew she had no choice. She offered a small, helpless smile.

'Would you settle for a blowjob instead?'

For one horrible moment she thought he was going to

add bribery to his list of misdemeanours, but he just smiled cruelly.

'Put that back where you had it before.' He held out the vibrator, expecting her to put it inside herself again. He licked his lips, watching her pull her panties to one side and inch the large latex cock into her pussy. At first it wouldn't go. She had dried up with the embarrassment of having been found out. But looking at the bulge in his trousers and the half-open set to his lips, she could tell he was enjoying every moment of her trying to stuff that thick organ inside her. She drew it out and licked it, lavishly coating it with her saliva before trying again. She could hear his uneven breathing as her pussy lips squelched around the large glans. His trousers tented even more as the vibe slowly disappeared inside her. She gave a little whimper of pleasure as her panties snapped back, holding the vibrator firmly in place. He motioned to her to pull up her shorts.

'Now get on your knees,' he demanded, slightly huskier this time, unzipping his trousers to reveal a girthy penis that made her mouth water. It stuck obscenely out of his dark trousers like the stamen of a grotesque flower. She sank to the ground, sticking her bottom out so he could see her buttocks just protruding from the frayed shorts legs, like ripe peaches.

'That's some nightstick you have there,' she purred, curling her hand around his cock. He leaned back against the rock to let her suck at him.

'This is my nightstick.' He rubbed the heavy weapon along the crack of her buttocks as she swirled her tongue around his shaft. She sucked him all in, hearing his explosive sigh of pleasure, and began to fellate him properly, suck, pull, lick, over and over. He tapped her bottom in time with the nightstick, not hurting her, but enough for her to acknowledge its potential. He ran it between her legs, knocking it against the end of the vibrator. She pushed back against him, encouraging him to do it again. The cop panted above her, bouncing the nightstick against her stuffed pussy, forcing the vibe deeper inside her. It felt so good, almost like a real cock banging away at her, that her mumbles of pleasure vibrated against his shaft and his hips began to pump unevenly. He spurted all over her breasts, his semen thick and creamy and lots of it, as her own climax peaked, not as strong as she would have liked, but enough for that moment. Abruptly he tucked his sagging cock away and made himself decent.

'Thank you, ma'am,' he said with endearingly old-fashioned courtesy. Then he was stern again, as if remembering his role. 'If I have to pull you over again the punishment will be greater.'

'I'll remember that, officer,' she said meekly. He stared blankly at her from behind the great black visor for a moment before striding back to his motorbike, leaving her soaked with his sperm.

She wiped herself clean with her shorts and changed into a short, stretchy black dress. She also put the vibrator away as her pussy was getting sore with it inside her. It was tempting to lie back and give herself a much needed clitoral orgasm to finish what was started, but decided instead to see what lay ahead that night. Fifty miles further on there was a motel she could stay at that night. It had a bar and a store for provisions, and if it was a dump she could move on in the morning.

Ahead she could see the three Harleys, parked by the side of the road. When they heard her car they stood in the middle of the road so she was forced to stop. The tall one she had spoken to before wandered ever so casually over to her.

'Hey, chickadee. You have some trouble back there?'

'Nothing I couldn't handle.' He looked friendly enough behind mirrored sunshades, as did his companions, but she felt a little apprehensive, being in the middle of nowhere. Still, he was better looking that she remembered, and so were his friends. Her clit throbbed wickedly, in anticipation of an unexpected treat.

'You boys on vacation?'

He nodded. 'Doing the tour from the East Coast and back. We're setting up camp just up the road. Why don't you join us for a beer?'

She looked over at the two other men. They were all minimally dressed and very toned, their thick biceps adorned with tattoos. Despite her misgivings her sex was pulsing, still primed from her encounter with the randy State Trooper. Maybe all they wanted was to hang out and have a friendly chat but, if they wanted more, was she really going to complain?

'Sure. Why not?' She grinned.

She followed them off the highway, down a roughened road towards a bar that was more like a shack, in the middle nowhere. There were other people around, some with tents, others happy to sleep under the stars. Loud music rocked the shabby building, which had no name. Her new friends found a spot well away from the others and lay down their jackets, making a comfortable, if somewhat lumpy, nest for them to sit in.

'I'm Tex, if you remember,' the tall one with the feel for rocks said, handing her a cold beer.

'I remember. What about you two? Do you have rough, tough macho names as well?'

JD confirmed he had. Young Wayne looked sheepish, but he compensated by being the best looking of the bunch, with dirty blond hair and movie star good looks.

'What's yours?' he asked.

'Daisy Mae.'

'You're shitting us!' JD said, laughing in disbelief.

She put her hand on her heart. 'Nope. I've had it since the day I was born.'

'So what are you looking for out here, Daisy Mae?' Tex asked. His eyes held a familiar hungry look. She made the decision to up the stakes a little.

'A bit of fun,' she replied, holding his gaze over the beer bottle. Tex toasted her with his beer, flashing a piratical grin that left her in no doubt. Message received and understood.

They sat there all afternoon, drinking, talking, the men smoking joints. Sometimes people joined them for a while, but as night fell they were left on their own. The following day other bikers from different Chapters would come, and a hog roast was being held. The location was remote, to try and avoid attracting trouble from rival gangs.

'We'll protect you from any rough stuff,' JD said, squeezing her leg. He was the most dangerous looking of the three, with ropy hair, two-day-old stubble and a faded Kurt Cobain T-shirt, but his eyes were a piercing blue, and his features as sharp as a hawks. She found he was stirring her more than baby-faced Wayne, who looked no more than 23.

''I'm sure you will,' Daisy said, smiling at him. She no longer feared these husky men smelling of sweat and leather and motor oil, and by now she accepted she was going to get wasted. She was halfway there already, with the alcohol and the pot and the desert heat, replaced by the heat of a small camp fire as dusk fell, having a soporific affect on her senses. The sun had gone behind the hill and cicadas had started their nightsong, chirping softly in the tall grass behind them. Tex gave Daisy his jacket to put around her shoulders. She thought he had the most exquisite manners, far better than the stellar Mike Bradley, whom she had all but forgotten.

'I've never been on a bike before. Which of you boys would like to give me a ride?' Her eyes were on Wayne. He grinned slowly at her.

'I'll give you one,' he said suggestively, and held out his hand. He led her to his Harley which, in close up, looked absolutely huge.

'I've never had anything this big between my legs before,' she murmured.

'It's OK, hon. You put your arms around me and I'll take it nice and easy.' Wayne's voice was smooth as honey. He straddled the bike and waited for her to get on the back.

'You'd better.' She hitched up her dress until it was almost above her panties and sat on the seat, pressing herself close to Wayne's back. She put her arms around him and held him tight.

'Like that?'

'Yeah, that's it, doll. Hold on.' He fired up the bike. The roar of the engine ripped through her as he revved it up and took off into the night. Her hair flowed freely behind her as she held on for dear life, purely terrified. As she gradually became used to it she relaxed and began to enjoy the throb of the engine beneath her buttocks. Feeling daringly reckless, she boldly moved one of her hands down to Wayne's crotch and cupped it, holding on to the firm bulge between his legs. The bike wavered slightly as he unzipped his jeans, leaving her to draw out a long, firm piece of meat. She wondered how his cock felt, out in the open air with the wind flowing against it. Her hand curled around the shaft, wanking him into rampant tumescence. Not just satisfied with tormenting him that way, she pulled up her dress and his T-shirt and let him feel her warm naked flesh. His body jolted and the bike speeded up. Still she pumped him, he helpless to do anything but take what she was giving to him.

He slowed the bike to a stop and climbed off, his cock sticking out in front of him.

'You are a very nasty girl,' he admonished her, and

pulled her into his arms for a deep, wet kiss. 'You want to go for a real ride?'

She wasn't sure how it was possible, but she nodded. He pushed her along the seat so she was in front, and he climbed on behind her. She could feel his cock pressing warmly against her buttocks. Lifting her bottom, he pulled her panties to one side.

'On my cock,' he said.

'I don't know how this is going to work,' she said doubtfully, leaning forward slightly. She felt him guiding his cock into her pussy, all gaping and open from her straddled position on the bike. He filled her like a generous meat sandwich, throbbing strongly inside her as he guided her hands to the handlebars. It felt incredibly unsafe and exciting at the same time.

'Now you can't misbehave, pussycat. You just hold on and let me do the steering.' He kickstarted the Harley. The engine leapt to life, the noise seeming harsh enough to rip out her spine. Then the power was surging between her legs, through his cock, being pumped directly into her heart and soul as the bike roared forward. The wind lashing her face forced her eyes closed and her lips back against her teeth. His arms were a safety cage around hers, but she felt the same fear she had experienced under the bridge, with the tornado bearing down on her. Annihilation probable, exhilaration consummate, as she whooped with terrified glee and felt his flesh pulse deep inside hers. She squeezed him tight as his leg muscles bunched and shifted under hers, forcing him deeper and her legs wider. Now she was being fucked at fifty, no, seventy, shit! one hundred miles an hour! She held on, screaming with exquisite fear, concentrating on the swelling of his cock and the delicious throbbing of metal between her thighs. She wanted to come but dared not, lest she make him lose control of the speeding bike. He hit a ridge in the road, jolting them closer together. The bike surged forward as he came with a volcanic burst, shouting his triumph in her ear. At that moment she let go of fear and succumbed to her orgasm, feeling the wind beat against her exposed clitoris and nipples. The weakness in her limbs was absolute as she held on, screaming with pleasure and terror, sagging forward as wave upon voluptuous wave bore down upon her.

The road gradually slid back into focus as he slowed down, still pulsating inside her. When he slowed to a halt, they paused for a moment, heads hung down, regaining their breath. She climbed off first and he leaned back on the bike, his long cock still stuck arrogantly out in front of him. She felt a renewed lust so urgent it made her knees feel like jelly.

Tex and JD had joined them.

'That was a first for me,' she said breathlessly.

'But did you enjoy it?' Tex asked her.

'I did,' Wayne said, climbing off the bike. 'Don't be fooled, guys. This woman is evil.'

Daisy smiled angelically as JD led her back to where they had been sitting. She sat back down. The delicate hem of her dress had risen dangerously high up her thighs but she was too aroused to care. 'I need a drink,' she murmured, to no one in particular.

JD took a swig of Wild Turkey and kissed her mouth, trickling warm bourbon straight on to her tongue. The tepid liquor ran out of their mouths on to her skin, washing all of her inhibitions away. He did it again, and rivulets of hard liquor dripped down on to her breasts. The whisky glistened on her caramel skin, cooling her nipples to taut points, the smell of it intoxicating and sensual. Caught up in the intense pleasure, she let her legs fall apart, unconsciously inviting whomever to explore her. Her panties were puckered between her sex lips and sodden with Wayne's semen. Still kissing JD, she wriggled out of them, wiped the semen off her body and threw them away. JD had unzipped his jeans. His cock was sticking out: fat and solid, unwavering. Unhesitating, she sucked him into her mouth.

Tex scooped up a handful of desert sand and trickled it over her bare toes. She wriggled and giggled around JD's cock, a luscious, watery sound calculated to tease.

'Oh, my God, which heaven did you come from?' Tex murmured, feasting on her lubricious pussy pouting out from under the short dress. She crouched down and thrust her bottom out at him. He ran his fingers over her satiny skin and felt her move against him, inviting more of his touch. He stroked her backside, cupping a globe in his hand and tickling the crease underneath. JD had his eyes closed, whimpering softly as she sucked him in up to the root, the vibrations caused by her mumbling with satisfaction transferring right along the length of his cock.

She pulled away from him and sat back on her knees, considering her options. The men watched with expectant expressions as she eased the dress down over her shoulders, stopping to tease just before it revealed her breasts. Wayne licked his lips, his eyes glued to her chest as she inched the dress down, showing first one breast, then the other, the nipples tilted invitingly upwards, rosy pink with dark chocolate areolae. Her waist was curved, her stomach perfectly flat. Emerging from the black cocoon, she was a fertile goddess, coyly hiding her fruits from the men with her hair. She teased her nipples with her hair, making them crinkle in the cool night air as the men watched her raptly, daring not to move. She combed her fingers through her hair, letting it fall over her breasts in a chestnut wave. Her nipples poked through the silky dark curtain. She stretched her arms up over her head and gyrated her hips, awed by her own lasciviousness. She had been overtaken by a desire to be out of control, fucked out, stoned and reamed from head to toe by these lusty, dirty, hairy men. It made her behaviour with Mike

Bradley and Ricky seem positively prim, she laughed to herself, aware that she was drunk and stoned and loving every minute.

'Aren't any of you dumb fuckers going to touch me?' she murmured.

Tex moved first, pushing her hair aside and drawing her nipple into his mouth. Wayne took the other one and their hands slipped between her legs, fingers probing, kneading her inner thighs. She sighed happily as the tongues lapping at her nipples sent spikes of pleasure throughout her whole body. She put her arms around their necks so she would not fall over and pushed out her breasts, encouraging them to continue their worship. JD worked his head between her knees and drew her down to sit on his face. His tongue worked deeply up inside her as the other two men tugged on her nipples, letting her relax against them. When JD shifted to suck gently on her clit she moaned out loud.

'I'm going to come,' she groaned, gyrating her lower body against JD's mouth. He kept up the pressure on her clitoris, his tongue flicking hard against it, the other men sucking and blowing cold air on her nipples. The orgasm when it came sent wave upon wave of heat over her body, her lubricating juices flowing over JD's face. Through half-closed eyes she could see his hands pulling on his cock, his hips moving with every shockwave passing from her to him. As she came down to earth Wayne and Tex laid her down on the comforter. She felt two fingers slide into her molten opening, joined by a third. She was so turned on, she could imagine a whole hand in there, exploring her depths. She was more slippery than the men could believe, her whole body quivering as she felt two tongues licking her clean, up her inner thighs towards her cunt, probing, tangling, quivering against her clitoris. She held on to their hair and spread herself wide.

'I want some cock,' she whispered lecherously, drugged with need by their lavish attention on her body.

'Turn around, doll. I'll give you some,' JD said.

Daisy knelt on top of JD and he was immediately deep inside her, letting her move against him. Wayne was whipping her tongue with his semi-erect, rubbery cock, not letting her close enough to lick it. He rubbed the bulbous head around her lips, into her mouth, back out, all over her face, while she tried to capture him between her lips. When she finally succeeded he was once again solid as rock, his hand stroking her hair back from her face so he could see every movement of her lips stretched around his shaft.

Tex watched the proceedings, breathing unevenly. His fly was unbuttoned and his briefs bulged through the opening. Still sucking on Wayne, Daisy ran her finger along Tex's tightly encased cock, feeling it lift towards her hand. Tex pulled the briefs down to let his cock spring out. Daisy left Wayne and began sucking on Tex instead, smiling up at Wayne.

'If you're hungry, have a sandwich,' she said, winking saucily and thrusting her bottom out at him. JD grabbed her hips to keep her impaled on him and began to thrust up into her to remind her of his presence. Wayne knelt down and tenderly slipped his finger into her. She rubbed against JD's cock, making him moan and stop thrusting just to enjoy the feeling. Daisy mumbled around Tex's cock as well, as the thickness inside her suddenly grew.

'Can you take us both?' Wayne whispered hoarsely.

She had meant Wayne to take her up the ass, but this new suggestion lubricated her puss even more.

'I've never found out,' she gasped. 'Try it and see.'

Wayne soaked his fingers with his saliva and rubbed them all over her labia. Telling JD to keep still, he crouched down and positioned his cock. JD eased out slightly to give him more room. At first it seemed it wasn't going to happen, but Wayne prodded at her gently and persistently. Suddenly she widened enough to let him in.

'Oh, God,' she moaned, a low, debased, gurgling sound of pleasure as the two cocks rubbed up against each other inside her. They felt huge and punishing, the two men rasping hoarsely in her ears. She felt split in two, taking more cock than she ever had before, feeling them push against her pelvic bone, releasing flood after flood of honeyed juice. They were taking pleasure from each other as well as her, their cocks rubbing against each other, carefully so they did not damage her. She felt totally overcome, unable to do anything but sigh and moan and think that Clare should see her now and learn how it was really done. She tried to clench her internal muscles, eliciting a louder moan from the men.

'Yeah, doll, do that again,' Wayne said through gritted teeth. She did, trying to concentrate on squeezing her muscles in a regular rhythm, but all she wanted to do was be open and receptive to their cocks. She wondered how it felt, having another man's organ rubbing against one's own. This would be something to tell Chico, she thought dimly, drawing Tex's massive member greedily into her mouth again. Still pulling on him, she guided his hand round to her backside. Catching on immediately, he spat on his finger and probed her tight hole. His finger slipped in, up to the knuckle. She squeezed him hard as he drew it back and forth, picking up the rhythm of her sucking on his cock. She sighed prettily, a slender willow of a girl almost lost between the heaving mass of male flesh ravaging her body.

Tex's finger was delving deeper into her arse, dousing it all over with his saliva. She looked hazily up at him, knowing what he was thinking. It wasn't possible. She was too full of cock to take any more, but the thought of it made her cream up inside. Her inner muscles, stretched

as they were, managed another weak spasm of anticipation. Wayne leaned back to let Tex move in front of
him, holding on to Daisy's thighs so he did not slip out of
her by mistake.

'No!' Daisy cried out softly, thinking that Tex's cock
would do her damage she would not recover from, but
the two cocks still moving inside her kept her silent and
weak, drunk with the decadence of being stuffed with so
much male flesh. Even when the blunt tip of Tex's cock
threatened her puckered arse she did nothing but moan,
salivating at the thought of even more cock. Beneath her
JD tried to smile, but his features were too distorted with
depravity to even focus on her.

Too weak to resist, she opened up and Tex slid in with
a long, drawn-out grunt. She almost fainted with the
bestial intensity of having three men inside her at once.
The discomfort was great, but the pleasure even greater,
as they moved in one careful heaving mass, her rising
cries mingling with rasping breath and whispered
obscenities. Two fingers, from whom she did not know,
fluttered against her clitoris. Another hand teased her
nipple to an unbearable length. She felt herself swooning
into a deep dark pit of hedonistic pleasure, her body
unable to do anything but take. The men's urgency was
reaching its peak, Tex shooting first, unable to hold back
as her body gripped his so tightly. Triggered by his
pulsing orgasm, Wayne and JD exploded together, Wayne
giving out a prolonged howl, peaking with every spurt.

Tex quickly scrambled away and thrust his hand
between JD and Daisy's bodies, agitating her clit with
slippery fingers. With him gone again, she no longer felt
as full and she started to move faster against the other
mens' thrusts. Stimulated by Tex's hand on her clit she
came in deep, torpid bursts, her clitoris swelling against
Tex's fingers, her body jerking against JD. On and on it
went, sapping at her energy until she could take no more

and she was physically and mentally exhausted. She collapsed in a gelatinous heap on top of JD, almost sobbing with pleasure. The other two men lay next to her, soothing her with long, gentle strokes.

'Shit,' she whispered. 'That's another first.'

10

The next day she soaked up the sun, lying in a replete heap with the three men, talking about her adventures on the storm tour. There was a carnival atmosphere around the desolate motel as people converged around the two giant spits where whole hogs were being roasted. Harleys lined up next to Honda Goldwings, and bikers from five to eighty watched sword-eating and other reckless stunts being performed. The smell of roast pork mingled with smoke and exhaust from the many revving engines. As night fell, smaller camp fires were built again as the party split up into their own groups. Eventually the families and the older members dispersed, leaving the young and the rebel-rousers to some serious drinking.

Daisy's crowd had grown, including a tough-looking, dark-skinned beauty called Gina, who seemed to take an instant dislike to Daisy. It didn't take long to figure out way. Apparently, she and Tex were an item. After she learned that, Daisy kept away from Tex, not allowing him to put his arm around her or kiss her. She wasn't in the business of intentionally stealing someone else's man. She even felt a little guilty, thinking of what they had been doing the night before.

She wore a simple white dress with handkerchief points that showed off her tan. Her firm breasts pushed readily against the thin material as if resenting the constraint it put upon them. Even in the cool of the evening as she walked to the bar her nipples had started to stiffen. They looked fat and pornographic, the swell of her breast rising above the low neckline, enhanced by a white lace Gossard wonderbra. The dress flipped around her thighs as she walked and emphasised the length of her tanned legs. She had brushed her hair into a thick, glossy curtain and pinned one side back with a white lily barrette and critically assessed the result. With her deepening tan and dark hair she looked almost too feminine and exotic for a seedy roadhouse in the middle of the desert. She certainly didn't look as if she had been butt-plugged and doubly penetrated by three men only the day before. A slick of lip-gloss and mascara to enhance her long, fluffy lashes finished the effect. She felt good and ready for whatever the evening chose to throw at her.

Catcalls greeted her as she walked into the bar. Tex gave her a smacking kiss on the lips, to Gina's annoyance. Daisy felt sorry to be the cause of her displeasure. She looked like a lot of fun when she smiled, a real rock chick with gothic black straight hair hanging loosely around her shoulders. She had wide, bee-stung lips that dominated her small, heart-shaped face, and long-lashed eyes heavily rimmed with kohl. Her short black dress was leather, a snug-fitting halter neck that plunged low in front, leaving her back bare except for a series of leather laces in a criss-cross pattern. And she knew her stuff about Harleys, having one of her own. Tex was lucky to have her, Daisy thought. Maybe he should be reminded of that later on, when she had had enough bourbon to loosen her tongue.

The music had started up. It was a live band with a female vocalist belting out Shania Twain's 'Feel Like A Woman' with enough enthusiasm to disguise her lack of talent. People were already dancing under the red and green disco lights. JD motioned to a table in a dark corner that had just been vacated and they went to it, Wayne holding Daisy's hand. He was cute, she had decided, like an overgrown golden retriever and twice as soppy. He pulled her on to his lap.

'You don't mind, do you, Daisy?'

She squirmed on him. His Confederate flag belt buckle felt hard and lumpy. 'Maybe you should remove that. It's digging into me,' she complained, squirming again and feeling the undeniable pulse in his crotch. He let out a sharp breath. JD pulled her on to his lap instead.

'Am I any softer?' he asked.

She wriggled around on his lap, grinding her buttocks into his groin. He was already hard as rock.

'Hmm, not where it counts,' she whispered, 'but I like to consider all my options.'

'You just have,' Gina said, moving swiftly on to Tex's lap. Tex grinned. He obviously liked the idea of being scrapped over by two women. Daisy smiled peaceably at Gina to show she wasn't playing the game and went to find the restrooms.

When she came out of the cubicle, Gina was waiting for her, smoking a half-used spliff. She blew the smoke in Daisy's direction.

'Why are you here? You're not one of us.'

Daisy carried on re-applying her lipstick. 'No, I'm not. I'm just having a little fun that's all.'

'Tex is my man. If you want fun, have it somewhere else.'

'I didn't know he was your man until this morning. If you bothered to notice I haven't exactly been throwing myself at him since then.'

Gina couldn't argue with that. She smoked the spliff, looking Daisy up and down as if she were a prize cow.

'Do you mind?' Daisy said crossly. 'If it makes you feel happier I'll be gone in the morning.'

'I'd rather you went now.'

'Look, if you want a catfight about this I'll give you

one, but personally I'd rather not give Tex the satisfaction of enjoying it. If you think I'm the competition, you're wrong. In fact, I think we complement each other. That's a great dress by the way.'

Gina looked disconcerted by the unexpected compliment. 'Uh, thanks. Actually, I was thinking the same about yours.'

'Thanks. We could swap if you like. Give the boys a surprise?'

Gina laughed suddenly. 'Are you always this nice?'

'Believe me, I'm not, but I hate confrontation.' Daisy gave the peace sign. Gina handed her the dwindling spliff and took another one from a small tin tucked into her bag.

'OK, hippy chick, how are you not nice?'

It was a test, but as Daisy told her about Jason Cordell and Mike Bradley Gina's grin widened.

'And being triply penetrated has been pretty much the highlight of my vacation so far,' Daisy added lightly.

'Was that with Tex?'

'Er, yeah. And Wayne and JD. But as I said . . .'

'It's cool,' Gina shrugged. 'Some of the bitches here don't know their boundaries, do you know what I mean? But you seem to so, for tonight only, I'm willing to share. I don't make a habit of it.'

'Best not to.' Daisy drew on the ragged ends of the spliff, feeling mellowness seep into her bones. 'You want to swap clothes now?'

They dived into two cubicles and hurriedly stripped, tossing each garment over the partition. Daisy gave Gina her bra as well. It was way too small, but better than nothing.

Gina came out first. Her breasts challenged Daisy's C cup Wonderbra to its limits. She twisted and turned in front of the mirror.

'Oh, God, you can see my panties!' She wailed. Her black thong was very noticeable under the thin white cotton. It wasn't a good look, especially with Gina's rounded rump.

'You'll have to take them off,' Daisy said. 'They look awful.'

Gina hesitated, then said what the hell, and stripped them off, stuffing them in her small shoulder bag. Afterwards the result was far more pleasing, clinging to her curves and stretching over her unashamedly round little belly, which made her look even sexier. Daisy wasn't so pleased with Gina's dress. The supple leather, hot from her body, felt a little loose as she jiggled around inside it, pushing her breasts up so they fitted properly in the cups. Even so, they still didn't look quite as enhanced as she would like.

'Hold on,' Gina said behind her, and pulled the laces at the back so hard she was almost jerked off her feet. Gina tied the laces and reached around, putting her hands under Daisy's breasts and lifting until they almost tumbled out at the top. She let her hands linger longer than necessary, her eyes meeting Daisy's in the mirror.

'This looks so hot on you,' she murmured, pressing up against Daisy's back.

Daisy flushed, feeling slightly confused at the arousing feelings caused by Gina's hands. Even so, the transformation was staggering. The laces had pulled the whole dress together until it moulded to her body like a second skin, making her waist look tiny and her breasts like a Barbie doll's.

Without warning Gina kissed her on the mouth, her tongue probing and sensual. Daisy was shocked at her own response, her tongue sliding against Gina's as if it were the most natural thing in the world, any doubts smoothed out by the whisky and the spliff.

'I've never done that before,' she whispered after-wards, blushing like an idiot.

'You did great,' Gina reassured her. 'Let's go get laid.'

There was confusion on the men's faces as they walked back out, almost an hour after they had first gone in. They clapped and wolf-whistled as the girls paraded in front of them.

'We thought you'd killed each other,' Tex said, running admiring hands over Gina's shapely body. 'This looks great on you, babe.'

JD pulled Daisy on to his lap and placed her hand on his crotch. He was rock hard.

'Enough said,' she grinned, giving him a squeeze. Another man was with them, whom JD introduced as Flynn. He was cleaner cut than the others, smiling so knowingly at Daisy that she was sure they had met before. He had close-cropped blond hair and was bare-chested under a sleeveless denim waistcoat, with massive biceps so pumped she could see the veins pushing through them. She held out her hand, leaning forward so he could appreciate her cleavage. She guessed that Tex, JD and Wayne had been updating him on their exploits the evening before. He looked more lazily powerful than the three of them put together, and she shuddered deli-ciously at the thought of being overwhelmed by his buffed-up body.

'I hope you haven't been using that offensive weapon, Miss Lovell,' he said, winking at her. Suddenly she realised why he looked familiar. He was the State Trooper from the morning before. She blushed fiercely as they laughed at her, and she held up her hands in surrender.

'Guilty as charged,' she quipped, winking at Flynn.

They were talking about the diminishing likelihood of trouble. The enemy wouldn't pitch up now was the general opinion. It was too late, and the word on the ground was that the real ruckus had been up in Salt Lake City earlier that day. Every now and then Daisy nuzzled at JD's crotch with her buttocks and he pulsated back at her. Things were shaping up to be very interesting later on, especially as Gina knew the owner of the bar.

'Daisy, honey, can I have a kiss?' Flynn asked, holding out his arms to her. She removed herself from JD's lap and obediently sat on his, facing him this time, twining her arms around his neck. He had a body builder's physique that his police uniform had done no justice to, with a thick neck and a mile-wide chest that felt smooth and alive under her fingers. Boldly his tongue tasted hers as arms like steel hawsers enfolded her completely. He was a great kisser, deep and insistent, not too wet. His jeans were so tight that she could feel the thick outline of his prick clearly, pushing into her thigh. As her tongue tussled with his, she pressed against it, exciting him even more.

'Oh, baby, don't,' he groaned, pushing her off his lap. 'I've got to stand up.'

'I'm sorry, was I bending your nightstick?' Daisy asked innocently. The men fell about laughing, and she was immediately grabbed by Wayne.

'Hey, guys, Jed says we can use the other bar,' Gina was saying.

As the others rose from their chairs, Wayne held Daisy back for a moment, enjoying the depth of their kiss too much. When it ended he was bleary-eyed and soft-mouthed with lust.

'Come on, honey,' Daisy whispered, pulling him to his feet. Through his faded denims she could see a thick phallic ridge reaching down his thigh. She pattered her fingers against it and he held them there, for a moment too aroused to walk.

The other bar was very much like the main one, but

much smaller and with comfier chairs. When the door closed behind them, the atmosphere immediately became charged with sexual tension. There seemed to be some competition between JD and Wayne as they guided Daisy to the bar. Tex rubbed his hands and headed for the optics behind the counter.

'OK, now for the real party. More Wild Turkey, anyone?' He took two bottles from behind the bar and broke the seal of one of them, drinking straight from the bottle. Daisy stood on the railing and felt hands running all over her buttocks. Then her dress was lifted and hands were sliding between her legs. She parted them slightly and pushed her bottom out. It was a nice feeling, being fondled by lots of hands. A finger slid inside her receptive pussy, made hot and oozing by the feel of Wayne and Flynn's hard pricks earlier.

'She's as wet as Lake Michigan,' JD said as she moved against his hand, drinking her bourbon as if nothing was happening. Gina leaned on the bar next to her, and they looked like any other women just having a chat, except for the hands roaming over their private places.

Daisy licked her lips at Tex, who had climbed behind the bar and was kneeling on the counter in front of the two women. He unzipped and took out his respectably thick cock, presenting it to them. Daisy picked up her camera and took a picture from right up between his legs, capturing his huge hairy scrotum and rigid phallus, topped by eyes insolent with confidence. Then she took an ice cube from her drink and rubbed it along his cock from tip to root and back, whilst Gina followed the ice with her pointed tongue, before sucking in as much as she could reach. At the same time Daisy felt another tip, bigger than a finger, push against her receptive opening from behind. It was Wayne, rubbing up against her, pushing his long cock between her legs. Gina sank down to her knees and began to flick at it with a hot tongue from the front. Daisy almost fell over when she felt a sly lick over her clit. Looking down, she saw Gina looking up, a crafty expression on her pretty face. Never breaking eye contact, she snaked out her tongue again and lapped at the tiny nut of flesh, as Daisy's thighs trembled and she bit her lips to stop the gasp from escaping. She wanted to sag, to spread her legs and let Gina do whatever she wanted. Her sensible side said no, but then she reasoned, in the five seconds it took before lust swept her away completely, it hardly mattered. Fucking another woman was no different from fucking three men at once. They were experiences, not future agendas.

Gina began to lick at her with a strong, rhythmic tongue, lashing at Wayne's protruding cock head at the same time until he pulled away and found Daisy's soaking entrance instead. He began to alternate between her pussy and Gina's mouth until Daisy's need for release became too much to bear.

'Fuck me or suck me. Someone just do it,' she panted desperately, crying out as Wayne thrust back into her and Gina latched on to her clitoris. She grabbed hold of the bar to prevent herself from falling over as the first wave of orgasm began to hit. She thought she would never come standing up, but the tremors overtook her and she screamed, her body jolting as Gina held on to her legs and kept up her relentless attack on her clit, wringing out the last shockwaves from her body as Wayne pounded her from behind. His thrusts became harder, more urgent, as she thrashed her head around, mindless with pleasure. He came hard, throbbing wildly, his drawn out sigh of pleasure more like a hiss of triumph. He pulled out, still hard, and pushed between her thighs again so that Gina could suck him clean of come and Daisy's honeyed juices.

He had his hands on Daisy's hips, rocking slowly, his face in her hair, murmuring lewd endearments.

They sat down in the chairs. Gina was straddled on Tex's lap, and he was buried deep inside her. JD and Flynn eyed Daisy hungrily, waiting their turn. Wayne sprawled in another chair, eyes closed, stroking his already burgeoning erection. He should be a professional, Daisy thought, his golden body resplendent in its half-nakedness, his cock rearing from curly hair like spun gold.

'So what's it like having three at once?' Gina asked Daisy, her dark eyes vivid with curiosity. She was fucking Tex with undulating grace, and he looked like the happiest man on the planet.

Daisy considered her answer. 'It's like eating so much of your favourite food that you feel bloated but desperate for more, even though you know the consequences might be disastrous.'

Tex grinned at her. 'You're saying you could have taken four of us last night?'

Daisy smiled enigmatically and chose not to answer. She motioned to JD and Flynn, who were watching the show with glazed expressions, Flynn's hand on his cock, gently stroking the swollen red end with his thumb. It stuck out of his jeans like a fat salami as he staggered towards Daisy. She told him to take off his jeans, which he did. His body was completely hairless, even his balls, which felt velvety and supple between Daisy's lips. She and Gina began to lick them, combining long, slow laps around each pronounced globe with tonguing kisses of their own, while he braced his legs and groaned loudly with satisfaction.

'Hey, babe. What about me?' Tex said plaintively, still fucking up into Gina's hot little body.

Daisy wet her fingers with saliva and rubbed them all

around Gina's dark, hairy hole and Tex's red shaft. Then she motioned to JD and drew his cock into her mouth, getting him really hard again. He supported himself on her shoulder, rocking back and forth. Gina leaned forward as he knelt down, positioning his cock against Tex's. Her pussy was more open than Daisy's, and it did not seem such a struggle for her to yield to the second cock invading her body. Gina's mouth opened and her eyes closed as the overwhelming feelings swept over her. Her pink pointed tongue seemed stuck to her top lip. Daisy felt her own clit throb and burn, seeing Gina getting what she had enjoyed the night before. She went behind JD and fondled his balls, then Tex's, and the two men and Gina moaned so loudly it echoed around the room. Flynn was there, waiting in line, his narrow eyes eager and his cock like a rock. JD was really getting into it, fucking Gina with slow, arrogant strokes, his washboard stomach muscles rippling. But Flynn was more than ready to get his share. JD moved back so that he could position himself. Daisy spat on her fingers and massaged them around Gina's puckered anus. At the cool, slippery touch of her fingers it contracted and relaxed slightly, allowing Flynn's blunt penis to get slight purchase. He pushed into her with a low groan, his jaw clenching as she squeezed him tight. Daisy went around to Gina's front.

'Is that good?' she asked. Gina was panting like a dog, her eyes glazed.

'Yeah. I know what you mean now,' she said with difficulty as the men moved slowly and tensely behind her. 'I want to fuck the whole fucking world!' Her pretty features distorted with lust and pain as the reaming continued. Daisy motioned to Wayne. He walked over, his cock bouncing with each step. He pushed it against Gina's full-blooded, rosy lips. She instantly gobbled him in, eliciting another moan from Tex who was watching from below.

'Come on, Ginny, take what you can get,' he said, pushing up into her again. He licked his fingers and felt for her clitoris, squashed under all those bodies. When he found and began to agitate it she squealed around Wayne's cock, adding her animal sounds to those of the men. They were moving as one, drawing pleasure from every sensation of cock against cock against cock, separated by the thinnest of membranes. Daisy prowled around them, moistening her fingers again and giving pleasure where she thought it was due, on balls, on shaft, on clitoris, on nipples, like an artist flinging paint at a live canvas. Then she picked up her camera and captured them on film, knowing she would never get the opportunity again. Gina's eyes were like slits, her mouth stretched over Wayne's cock while the other men moved with increasing desperation. JD shot first, his back arched, setting off Flynn and then Tex. Daisy took more snaps of the orgasmic tableaux they were making before rubbing up against JD's firm body and grinding her pubic bone into his backside, driving him deeper into Gina's crowded cunt. It wasn't enough to make her come, but it felt damned good. He reached back, holding her to him, as he continued to spurt the final drops of his climax into Gina's overflowing body. Then it was Wayne's turn, a long drawn-out grunt at his sperm bubbled up over Gina's pretty face, all over her tongue, all around her lips. She licked it up hungrily, watched lovingly by Tex. Wayne's head dropped and he staggered back into another chair, his long cock having at last given up on him.

One by one the men fell away to recover, leaving Gina and Tex to kiss and caress and whisper to each other. Watching them, Daisy felt she was intruding on their intimate moment. Like a bright light, jealousy hit her, the ugliest emotion of all. Over the last few days she had been able to forget what it was she really wanted, her vision blurred by the likes of Mike, and Ricky and everyone else she had screwed. She wanted just one man, one intense relationship to nurture and treasure and call her own. She wanted to make love, not fuck, and she wanted it to mean something more than just one night's forgettable pleasure. Suddenly melancholy, not helped by the alcohol and drugs, she fought the urge to cry. The bar was smoky and smelly and dirty, not her scene at all. What was she doing here? Suddenly desperate for air, she stumbled towards the door.

'Hey, where are you going?' She heard Wayne ask.

The door burst open before she got there, halting her bleak thoughts in their tracks. At least six men piled in, rough-looking, rudely interrupting the others' post-coital bliss. The opposition, Daisy guessed, judging by the knives and knuckledusters. Her bowels felt horribly loose. There was no escape, and nowhere to hide. Tex and Gina were on their feet, the others fumbling for their clothes. The six men leered at Daisy and Gina.

'You want to give us some, honeys?'

'Fuck you,' Gina replied coldly.

Daisy heard two silver clicks. JD and Wayne also had knives. Flynn drew her back into the shadows and told her to stay put.

'We just want the bitches,' the ringleader said, and without provocation punched Tex solidly on the jaw. He fell back into the grasp of another two men who launched him through the window out into the night. The sound of breaking glass was deafening, drowning out Gina's scream. Outraged, she drove her fist into the nearest man's face. He staggered back amongst the chairs, scattering them, but before she could finish the job with an empty Wild Turkey bottle she was grabbed around the waist. Her assailant held her tight, despite her desperate wriggling, and dragged her out the door. He was three times her size, with a greasy ponytail and a long beard. Daisy shuddered in revulsion. She had no chance.

All hell broke loose. JD and Wayne waded in, fists and feet flying. Daisy could tell they had done it before, by the way they were skillfully evading the slashing knives. Flynn was grappling with two of the others and doing quite well. One was soon draped over the counter like a Dali watch and the other was on the floor, but Daisy saw he had a small triangular blade in his hand.

'Watch out!' She screamed as he plunged it into Flynn's leg. Flynn collapsed on the floor, clutching at his calf. As his attacker gave him a stunning butt to the head Daisy cast around for a weapon and found another empty bottle. She smashed it over the man's thick shaven head. He dropped the insensible Flynn and turned to her instead.

'Come here, pretty. Papa's gonna show you who's boss.' He backed her into a corner, the blade an inch from her throat. Behind him were three of his friends, bloodied but unbeaten. Wayne had joined Tex in the parking lot. JD was out cold on the floor, blood from a shoulder wound oozing between his fingers. Flynn was comatose on the floor. The bald man grinned nastily at her as she assessed her situation. It wasn't good.

'That's right. No help for you, pretty. We're gonna give your pussy a pounding.'

She tried to think. He was too close to enable her to knee him in the groin. His fat hands were pawing at her dress, pulling it up. His friends were smirking at her, waiting their turn.

That's when the miracle happened. She did not recognise the metallic click of a safety catch being withdrawn, but they did. Their faces changed, and as one they turned to see a man aiming a semi-automatic at their heads.

'Ditch the bitch and leave. Now.'

She sent a silent prayer skywards. Max Decker had

proved his worth at last. It didn't alter the fact that he was one against four, but she had never been so glad to see anyone before in her life.

There was much contemptuous laughter. The bald man sneered at Decker.

'So you think you can take us all out before we rip out your spine?' He grabbed Daisy and held her in an arm lock around the neck. She could feel cold, sharp metal, tickling her ribs. 'Or hers?' he added.

'You really don't want to do that,' Decker said mildly.

'OK, why don't we break her windpipe so she can't scream, fuck her until she bleeds and leave her for the coyotes? You can have a front row seat before we do the same to you.'

The huge, hairy man who had taken Gina outside was back, waiting in the doorway out of Decker's vision, but with her voice stifled by the beefy forearm around her neck, Daisy could do nothing to warn him. Frantically she tried to convey the danger with her eyes and with the one hand trapped down by her side, pointing desperately. Decker showed no sign of understanding her.

'She's the daughter of one of the richest men in New York,' he said in the same calm voice. 'When he finds you, and he will, he'll rip your balls off and make you eat them for breakfast. By the time you get to lunch, you'll be begging him to kill you.'

Another derisory laugh from her captor. 'But he won't find any of us. We're outlaws, on the run. Who's to know where we are?'

Decker smiled for the first time. It was a terrible, sick smile that made Daisy's bladder weaken. She was beginning to understand why her father had employed him.

'You're right, of course. Who's to know?' Decker pulled the trigger, one, two, three and four times, then spun on his heel and took the fifth man out with the knife hidden up his shirt sleeve. In less than five seconds the five quiet thumps had a devastating effect. The man behind him fell backwards, the ivory handle of the switchblade protruding between his eyes. The four men surrounding Daisy dropped from her like felled logs, the arm around her throat slipping away like a dead snake. She stood there, surrounded by corpses with neat holes in their foreheads, choking back the desire to scream her head off.

Decker grabbed her hand, pulling her over the heap of bodies. She stepped on a flabby hand and its owner groaned. Decker immediately had the gun in the man's face.

'Wait! He's friendly.' She knelt beside Flynn. 'Are you OK?'

'Sure. I'll sort this out. Just ... get the hell out of here.' He was white with pain, but she knew he would live. 'And keep to the speed limit this time,' he added with a weak smile.

'Will do. Thanks, Flynn.' She leaned over to kiss him, but Decker was already pulling her to her feet.

'Let's get out of here before anyone else sees us.' He retrieved his knife from the fifth corpse without even breaking his stride and dragged her out of the bar, into the cool, black night. People were running towards them, shouting and screaming. Amongst them were Gina, Tex and Wayne. Decker ducked into the shadows before they could be seen and let the crowd pass. Swift as shadows, they ran to where his SL500 was parked next to the Camaro. Her skin felt sticky and dirty and she was shivering with cold, as well as the shock of having seen five men put down like sick dogs.

'Can you drive?' he demanded.

'I think I'm over the limit but ...'

'Do it. Follow me and keep your lights off.'

'What about my stuff?' She had left her clothes back at the motel, not thinking that she would be doing a moon-lit flit with a homicidal hitman.

'I've cleared your room already. Get in and ask questions later.'

She climbed in her car, thanking her presence of mind for grabbing her handbag and camera and feeling absolutely sober despite the copious amount of bourbon she had consumed that evening. Quietly they stole out of the parking lot, unseen and unheard. In her rearview mirror people were running around like rats leaving a sinking ship, but no one pursued them. In the blazing light of the bar she could see Gina silhouetted with Tex, obviously wondering where she had gone. Silently she murmured goodbye.

11

She followed Decker along a roughened road, the new moon lighting their way. It seemed like hours before he stopped and got out. They were still in the middle of the wilderness, with nothing but the very faint orange glow of some far-off town over the horizon. He told her to get out of the car and he climbed behind the wheel. It felt very lonely, listening to invisible chirping insects and the wind rustling through the grass. She shivered, watching him drive to a nearby outcrop of rock and park it in the shadows. Too cold to stand still, she ran after him, wondering what he was doing. He had the bonnet up and was scraping away at something underneath. When he took a screwdriver to the front number plate she began to realise what he was up to.

'We're not leaving it here! I paid five hundred dollars for that car!'

He did not reply, making short work of the back number plate. A quick check inside revealed that none of her personal possessions were still there. Finally he took a can of petrol that she had not noticed before, and doused the seats with it. He held out a tab of matches to her.

'Five hundred dollars or a stay in San Quentin? It's up to you.'

'Flynn's a cop. I trust him.'

Decker laughed bitterly. 'Never trust a cop, Daisy. He might forget we ever existed, but for my own piece of mind I'd rather cover my own tracks.' He took the matches from her, lit one, and threw it through the car window. There was a solid *whump* as the petrol caught alight. She bade a sad farewell to the old Camaro as he led her back to his car.

It seemed like forever before they hit the main highway. In the dead of night there was no one else around. Looking back, she could not even see any orange stain on the night where her car had gone up in flames. She did not ask him where they were going. The wall was back, so high between them that words could not breach it.

'I can't believe you were bitching over five hundred dollars. I thought you rich girls spent that on a pair of shoes each week,' he said suddenly.

She blinked at him, the scales falling from her eyes. 'So that's what all this has been about! You're sore because you've been sent to babysit a spoilt little rich girl, which isn't as exciting as murdering five people in cold blood! Well, just to set the record straight, I've worked my ass off for the last three years without a break, just to see my job go down the pan, so I decide to blow some of my hard-earned severance on a vacation, only to have it ruined by one miserable asshole who makes Rambo look articulate. And, just for your information, I've never asked my father for anything. I learned to live on twenty-five quid a week when I was in England, just so that I could have fun at the weekends and I'll repay my Mastercard without his help as well. I'll buy my own house and my own car with my own hard-earned cash, and even if he wants to help I won't let him, because my life belongs to me, no one else.'

'How much do I have to pay you to shut the fuck up?' he muttered when she drew breath.

She couldn't be bothered to retaliate, even though he had had the last word yet again. Silently she stewed, wondering what was next on the agenda.

'So what now?' she asked, when the need to find out became unbearable. She had told her father she would be back the following Saturday, five days from then, and despite all that had happened, she still wasn't ready to go home just yet. She needed another vacation just to get over this one.

'I need a vacation even if you don't,' Decker replied tersely, echoing her thoughts. 'Just try and keep it a little less eventful for the next few days, if you don't mind.'

His prickliness made her smile in the dark. She only realised she had fallen asleep when she felt him shake her gently. The car had stopped.

'Come on, let's get you into bed.' He hauled her out of the car into the cold, deep night. Blinking, she leaned on him as he took her bag out of the car. Her watch said just past midnight. It felt like four in the morning.

'Where are we?' She asked. Then she saw the sign.

The Chieftain's Rest was tucked into a crescent-shaped blind valley. Big warning signs to avoid later litigation claims were everywhere: Not For the Infirm or Physically Challenged; Not For Those Persons Intimidated By Heights; and, the real cruncher, which woke and sobered her up completely, This Establishment Bears No (underlined three times) Responsibility for Those Under The Influence Of Alcohol, Drugs, Prescribed Medication or Those Indulging in Horse Play.

There was one long, low building on the cliff edge, no doubt the reception area, although it was in darkness, a fence and a gate leading to a narrow path with a handrail between her and a stomach-dropping two-hundred-foot chasm. At the end of the path was a fifteen-foot rope ladder.

'Great,' Daisy muttered to herself. Nothing like a little mountaineering after witnessing mass murder to get a girl in a good mood. She was very conscious of her bottom in the tight leather dress, inches away from Decker's face. She arrived on *terra firma* sooner than she anticipated, and found herself in the circle of his arms. There was an awkward pause before they disentangled themselves, not looking each other in the eye.

A very tiny, ancient Indian woman greeted Decker like a son and smiled knowingly at Daisy when she was introduced. Daisy wondered what Decker had told her. She lit the way with a hurricane lamp, and Daisy had the fleeting impression of adobe walls and the smell of oil lamps. The old woman showed them to their room. It was a cool, dark cave, softly lit with an oil lamp above each bed, and the walls were the slightly damp stone of the mountain. Daisy immediately fell on to the first bed. Decker dumped the bags by the other one.

'I need a drink,' he said shortly, and left her alone.

She stripped off Gina's dress and lay back amongst the cool sheets. She stank of sex and booze, her body sticky with bodily fluids, but she was too tired to care. Her muscles felt as if she had been in the saddle for three days solid, and she dared not look in the mirror, lest she discover she looked like a child's drawing with a triangular body and a leg at each corner.

She heard Decker come back barely an hour later, bringing with him a strong smell of whisky. She heard him cursing under his breath and crawling about on the floor. When he saw her sitting up and watching him he lifted his head as though it were a ton weight and gave her a dissolute stare.

'Fancy a fuck?' He hauled himself on to her bed and put his hand on her bare stomach. 'I don't see why not. You've fucked everyone else.'

Incensed, she slapped him hard across the face. 'In your state you couldn't even get it up anyway!'

'I could for you,' he said, before passing out. He landed across her legs, on his back.

'Oh, that's great,' she said, wriggling out from under him. She thought about rolling him unceremoniously off the bed and letting him sleep on the floor, but something about his comatose form stopped her from doing it.

Now fully awake, she wondered what to do. Then she remembered an old piece of feline wisdom. If in doubt, wash. The bathroom attached to the bedroom was minute, with just enough room for a toilet, a basin and a shower, the water draining directly into a gully that lead into the mountain wall. She took a refreshing shower, removing all evidence of her excesses earlier that evening, dried herself quickly and slipped on a clean T-shirt and panties. Decker had not shifted, so she lifted his feet on the bed to make him more comfortable. Then she undid one shirt button, thinking he would wake and move away, but he didn't. She undid all of them, opened his shirt and stared.

The reason why he had kept so covered up was running in a slim line down his satin-smooth chest to his navel. The scar was of the old-fashioned railway track variety, a slightly raised ridge of tissue with faint, evenly spaced horizontal marks where the stitches had been. And, in the middle, above his nipples, there was a bumpy, ugly patch of distorted flesh that looked more raw than the creamy skin around it. At some time in the not too distant past, somebody had tried to rip him apart.

'Oh, my God,' she murmured, running her fingers over the disfigured skin. It felt bumpy and warm, not repulsive at all. He mumbled and his hand came up, as if to ward her off, but dropped down again before he was even close. This new evidence of his vulnerability awakened a sympathy in her so sharp it hurt, and she found herself pressing her lips to the damaged skin, knowing how mad he would be if he woke just then.

But he showed no signs of waking up, long, dark lashes feathering high cheekbones, his jaw relaxed, making him look younger and less aggressive than he did when he was awake. She lifted his arm and dropped it again. He was out cold. That little tingle of devilment was rising in her again and, although she knew she shouldn't, the opportunity just couldn't be missed.

'You are mine, Max Decker,' she whispered with a gleeful grin.

She swiftly unfastened his trousers. He shifted and mumbled as she removed them but still did not wake up. For a while she gloated over his body, his muscles well-defined but not over-developed. He looked pretty fit in all senses, she thought. The scar only added to his appeal. It showed he had fought great odds and had been strong enough to win. In fact, if the large bulge in his boxers wasn't enough to advertise his maleness, that piece of damaged skin definitely was.

She paused, staring longingly at his crotch. Her fingers itched to remove the boxers so she could take a good, long look at his cock. How deep in the shit would she be if she removed them as well?

She could not resist cupping her hand over the bulge and feeling its weight and heft. As she did so, it thickened against the palm of her hand. How bad she was being now, she thought, fondling him gently and voyeuristically watching his cock tent the silk as his unconscious mind filled with some nameless fantasy. He grew harder in her hand, though he still showed no sign of waking up. Daringly she peeled the boxers down past his pelvis. His pubic hair was the same dark red as the hair on his head, and silky and soft. When she saw the size of his cock and the meaty balls that fed it her sex pulsed in appreciation.

'No hang-ups there,' she murmured, and before she could stop herself, she pressed her lips against the bulbous glans. It quivered under her touch, releasing a tiny sparkle of moisture at the very tip. She looked at his face for any signs that he had woken up and was faking it.

Nothing except deep, peaceful breathing. Knowing that she was playing with fire, she continued to fondle his cock. He started to moan, his pelvis moving against her hand. Emboldened, she ran her tongue up his shaft, from musky smelling root to salty tip. It tasted and felt so good that she did it again, enjoying the flickering feelings darting over his face like minnows in shallow water. Again, alternating each lick with each smooth hand movement as he rose towards the surface of consciousness again. She was rapidly reaching the point of no return, the desire to make him come overwhelming the potential for trouble when he found out what she was doing to him. Suddenly his cock tensed and released a spurt of creamy white semen over his chest. She scrambled back to her bed, pulling the sheet up over herself before he had a chance to open his eyes. Tense and breathless, she listened to him as he woke up.

'What the fuck? Jesus, not again.' Wiping sounds and a long, drawn out sigh. 'Get a grip, Max, you're losing it,' he muttered. Daisy bit her lips to stop herself giggling as she heard him go outside, deliciously fearful of what he would do if he heard her. Presently the faint smell of cigarettes permeated through her cotton shield. She dared to move and get more comfortable. Wicked, wicked, wicked, she thought, inhaling his feral, spicy scent on her fingers.

Ten minutes later he was back, standing over her bed as if to check that she really was asleep. She tried to breathe deeply, wishing she had the courage to open her eyes and smile at him. He went back to bed, but she knew he wasn't asleep. Through half-closed eyes she could see him lying on his back, shimmering with tension. He covered his face with his hands and groaned softly. Further down the bed, she could see the sheet that covered him was lifting slightly.

'Get a grip. What a fucking joke,' he said very quietly

to himself, blissfully unaware of his audience. She could see his hand, travelling down to his cock and massaging it with his fingertips. She had never witnessed a man masturbating before, and was fascinated by the rough yet tender way he handled himself, his hand now wrapped around the shaft, his thumb stroking the swollen red end. As he really got into it he looked as if he were in the midst of a violent dream, the bed sheets bunched and draped half on the floor. Keeping as still as sleep, she could see the outline of his cock, impressively thick and heavy, and the spurt of semen shoot way up over his chest. He bit his other hand to stifle deep felt grunts of pleasure, and in the indistinct light she saw his cock pulsate and beat against his belly.

Her wicked side urged her to be cruel. 'Deck? You OK?' she whispered drowsily, as if she had woken just then.

'Huh? Yeah. Go to sleep.' He scrambled for the sheet and covered himself. She kept her eyes shut and listened to him go outside for another smoke. So the big question was, what had he been thinking, masturbating in front of the boss's daughter? Maybe it was the frustration of having her so close and so untouchable to him after he had seen so many erotic images of her. She counted them all. That first encounter behind the pub, the free show she had unwittingly given him and the sounds of her and Mike Bradley screwing inches away from him on the other side of the motel wall. Oh, and she could only guess at how much he had seen at the biker's bar before he had waded in and massacred half the clientele.

Eventually he came back in and presumably went back to sleep judging by his deep, even breathing, but she lay awake, hotly aroused at what she had witnessed. Getting her vibrator out would make too much noise, so she worked with her skilled fingers, knowing that if she didn't bring herself off then sleep would not come. Under the sheet her nipples were stiff and tingling. They tightened even more as she stroked them over the sheet, enjoying the added frisson of cotton against her sensitive flesh. For a while she played with them, until the answering plea from her clit became too loud to ignore. She licked the fingers of one hand and began to stroke herself. She was soaking wet, her body still responding to the sight of Decker pleasuring himself, and the memory of his body, so hard and capable-looking. How had he felt when he had watched that first time? He had never mentioned catching her in such a compromising position, but it could not have failed to excite him. Had he been thinking about it, imagining her naked before him, pussy so open and wet and he not being able to do a damned thing about it? Her fingers flew over her clitoris, out of control, as she imagined him restrained, whilst she stood inches from him, touching herself, making herself come, perhaps playing with his cock and torturing him to the brink of orgasm again and again, like she had with Mike Bradley, only this time she would let him go and take whatever punishment he chose to give her.

'Oh, oh, oh!' she hissed, as she peaked, biting her lips hard as the secondary spikes followed. Struggling to regulate her breath, she looked over at his recumbent body. No movement.

'You snooze, you lose, Deck,' she murmured, before curling up under the sheet and falling asleep almost immediately.

When she woke up again it was nearly noon the next morning. Decker was obviously a heavy sleeper. His naked body was only half covered by the thin sheet, exposing his hip but not the dark shadow between his legs. One leg hung over the bed, his foot brushing the floor. As she accidentally kicked her bag he curled into a foetal position, exposing his buttocks. They looked smooth and tactile, and she feasted visually on them for a few moments before leaving him in peace.

The small woman immediately appeared outside her door, almost as if she had been waiting, and asked Daisy if she wanted coffee. She had the walnut brown, wrinkled complexion of the ancient Navajo, and coal black, knowing eyes that made Daisy feel strangely uneasy.

She followed the woman up towards the main hub of activity. She could see the picnic tables on a huge veranda situated on a natural balcony of stone up above her. Her impressions of early that morning had been correct. The Chieftain's Rest was a cliff dwelling, albeit a relatively modern one. The rooms were more like caves, decorated as simply as they would have been hundreds of years before. Daisy felt only mildly cheated when the woman explained that the place had been built in 1910, and had running water and electricity. The hub of activity was in a kiva, traditionally a ceremonial meeting place, although if it were for real, the woman explained, it would have been underground and no white person would have been allowed near it.

At night a huge fire was lit in a pit for the guests to gather round and eat. There was a simple menu on offer, cooked as one watched. It seemed to revolve around every permutation of chili con carne and not much else, owing to the logistical difficulties of transporting supplies, but there seemed to be plenty of alcohol on offer. Breakfast was continental, which meant coffee and pastries. Daisy had experienced some gruesome variations on the theme, and she wondered if it would be any different here. Still, she accepted the woman's offer of coffee and headed for the stone balcony.

It was a serendipitous moment, because she knew without doubt that this was the special place she had been looking for. A strange thickness rose in her throat and hot tears welled up that she hastily dashed away.

Luckily the balcony was deserted, apart from chattering blue jays in the trees below. Further down lay the green valley filled with pine and oak and juniper. And in front of her was the vast desert, filled with otherworldly rock formations and plunging arroyos, showing every hue of ochre and salmon and burnt gold. Facing South, her vantage point had a full 180 degree view with the sunset staged dead centre, and over five hundred miles of uninterrupted wilderness. From the balcony a narrow, hazardous path led to the forest below, hiding nature trails and walkers. Their shouts occasionally bounced off the yellow rock like ping pong balls.

The old woman came back with richly scented fresh coffee and a plate of sticky cinnamon rolls that looked freshly baked. Manna from heaven, Daisy thought, thanking her gratefully.

The woman seemed happy to pass the time, telling Daisy about how she and her late husband had bought the place in the 1970s and had been running it ever since, living a charmed existence amongst the adobe walls until his death just the year before. Now she was thinking of selling up and moving to Lake Havasu, where they had built their retirement home. Up until now she could not bear to go there, but her eyesight was failing and her bones were weakening, and she knew the time was coming when she would have to leave.

They were in Colorado, on the verge of the Mesa Verde national park, looking out towards New Mexico. The bikers' bar had been left over a hundred miles back west. No wonder Decker had needed a drink the night before.

Talking of whom, he appeared at their table and sat down heavily, as if the effort of walking from the room had been too much. He was buttoned up, washed and shaved, but ever so slightly hung over. The old woman looked guileless as she rose painfully to her feet.

'You don't need me now you have each other.'

'Oh no, it's OK, you can stay!' Daisy said, more desperately than she intended.

'I have work to do and so do you,' she replied, with that same gleam in her eye. Decker seemed oblivious to her blatant attempt at matchmaking. He curtly ordered black coffee and she went away.

'You're not in New York now, Deck,' Daisy chided him gently. 'People out here like to be nice.'

The woman came back with the coffee and more cinnamon rolls. Wordlessly she slammed a packet of paracetemol on the table in front of him, winked craftily at Daisy and left again. Daisy laughed disbelievingly, wondering how that old prune had him so pegged. He popped three of the white and red capsules with the coffee.

'Sleep well?' she asked innocently.

He stopped in mid-chew and nodded curtly. 'And you?'

'A little restless. It's amazing what one hears in one's sleep.'

He swallowed. 'What did you hear?'

She captured his gaze over her coffee cup. 'You.'

'That's the damnedest thing, because I could have sworn I heard you as well.'

'I guess that makes us quits then.' She mopped up the coffee she had spilt and cursed the redness that had suddenly bloomed on her cheeks. 'You don't look like the rope ladder type, Decker. How come you know about this place?'

'Looks can be deceiving,' Decker replied. She searched his face for any hint of suggestiveness, but there was none. 'I mean, look at you. Gang-banging all evening and now you look as fresh as the proverbial. What is it with you?'

Daisy toyed with her coffee cup, fighting annoyance at his persistence in putting her down.

'You're just jealous because there's no way a guy can

walk into a bar, snap his fingers and have four women willing to suck his dick just like that.'

'I just don't get why you do it, that's all.'

'That's understandable. You don't seem to know the first thing about wanting to give pleasure.'

A bleak look passed over his face. She remembered the scar, and knew that she had hit too far below the belt.

'What happened to you?' she asked carefully.

'In what way?' The question was equally guarded.

'I mean your scar.' She noticed he flinched at the word. 'Did someone . . .?'

'I don't want to talk about it.'

She sighed resignedly. 'Fair enough, for now. We'll talk about your problem with me instead. Like what makes it so wrong for me to enjoy myself? It's no different from you going to a two bit hooker, only I don't have to pay for it. Is that your problem?'

'My only problem is getting you back in one piece to your father. I don't care who you fuck.'

'So why are we having this conversation?'

He stared moodily away from her and drank his coffee.

'If we're going to survive together you're going to have to lighten up a bit,' she sighed.

'Fine! I'll lighten up if you grow up. Deal?'

'I don't make deals with self-righteous pricks,' she said coldly. As she stood up to go, his hand stopped hers.

'I'm sorry. Just don't ask me difficult questions when I've got a fucking hangover, OK? Sit down.'

She sat. He nodded at the glorious view. 'You like this place?'

'It beats a Days Inn,' she said lightly, unwilling to give away how enraptured she was. She could get a job in Durango, use her savings to buy a place. Then what? A bed and breakfast? No, that wasn't quite her style. How about a studio for local artists, photographers? Her mind chased through endless avenues of possibility, searching the maze of her thoughts for an elusive centre that she could focus on.

'Someone's going to get it good later,' he said, making her jump. For the first time that morning she noticed how attractive he looked, in a cream linen long-sleeved shirt, casually rolled to the elbows, showing more than a hint of a golden tan. At his suggestive words, she suddenly felt all of aquiver.

'I'm sorry?'

He lit a Chesterfield and nodded at the towering white thunderhead in the distance.

'The storm over there. Looks pretty severe.'

'Yes, it does.' She had been so involved in her thoughts she hadn't really registered it. His expression was closed off, hidden from view by the cigarette. It would make a great picture, she thought, in black and white with the ethereal smoke veiling his face, against the backdrop of the sheer cliff face.

'What are you looking at?'

His slightly impatient voice hauled her back to reality.

'I'd like to take your photograph,' she replied. Then she mentally kicked herself for being insensitive. Having his photograph taken was probably the last thing he wanted. 'You never did answer my question,' she said, hurriedly to change the subject. 'How come you know about this place?'

He drew leisurely on the cigarette. 'When I was a kid, the church had a charity for city kids to go on vacation for a month in the summer, somewhere healthy. One year it was my turn. We stayed in a dude ranch just outside Cortez. I was twelve and it was the only vacation I had ever had. As soon as I could afford it, I came back. I've been coming every couple of years or so since.'

She was about to make some comment about it being the most he had ever said to her, but she bit it back, realising that they were on the verge of having a proper conversation.

'So what's the appeal?'

He gestured to the far-reaching landscape. 'Do you really have to ask?'

'I know why it appeals to me, but not to you. People see beauty in different things. I know some people who would think this is hell on earth.'

He nodded. 'Fair enough. Minnie, that's the old woman who runs this place, and I are good friends. She taught me how to read the weather and appreciate the land. And it's a kind of cleansing process. It gets rid of that Manhattan filth from my mind.' He laughed self-consciously and plucked at a blade of grass growing out of the wall. Daisy remembered something that seemed to have happened years, not days ago.

'So that's why you knew about the tornado. You probably know more about the weather than Keith, Karen and Mike put together.'

'Hardly,' he replied mildly. 'I'm not a scientist. I just know what I feel.'

I wonder what you're feeling now, she thought. 'I wish I could say the same,' she said out loud.

He looked at her with an expression that could have been mistaken for pity. 'Life's pretty confusing for you at the moment, I guess.'

'Not confusing, just purposeless, but I'm working on it.' She contemplated the scrubby grasses below them and the vivid orange mesas casting strange silhouettes against the relentless sun, aware that he was watching her curiously.

After breakfast she walked with him up to the top of the cliff, so he could give her some idea of her bearings. He pointed out the monolithic lump of the Sleeping Ute mountain in the west, and huge turkey vultures cruising around in the sky above. Over to the north there were white topped, craggy mountains where the aspens grew and the river water ran as clear and hard as diamonds. Her eagerness to know about the land triggered an equal eagerness in him to share his knowledge. For the first time, she felt they were actually communicating on an equal level.

But she needed time on her own to think, so she asked to borrow the car so she could explore the Mesa Verde national park. To her surprise, he seemed happy to let her go. He was going to help Minnie that morning, he said, as a fence had blown down in a storm the previous week. He even gave her advice on the best trails to follow, and seemed to possess as much information as a Park Ranger.

She drove to the park, feeling curiously refreshed after her minimal sleep the night before. Everything that had happened at the bikers' bar seemed as unreal as a Tarantino movie. Even Decker seemed different that morning, like Manhattan's answer to Grizzly Adams. Certainly not like the stiff, unwilling bodyguard he had been for the last two weeks, or a man who had just shot five people in cold blood.

She had packed a small rucksack with mineral water, crisps, fresh peaches and pastries from Minnie. On the short route to the park she passed a store selling Native American crafts and western fashions. Bearing in mind that the prairie girl look would hit New York like a tornado that summer, she went in. She browsed for a long time before buying an unusual buff suede arm cuff, adorned with turquoise beads and feathers, and a short, swingy denim skirt, the hem edged with red embroidery and a tiny scrap of white lace, which she teamed with a white cotton gypsy top, also edged with broderie Anglaise. The skirt, if she were very incautious, would give anyone close by an unsolicited glimpse of her panties if she bent over. That would amuse Chico when he next took her clubbing, she thought. If he ever did. She had begun to feel that he was evading her. Regretfully she had to walk away from a turquoise and hand-carved silver necklace, the centerpiece fashioned as an Anazasi bear claw, even though she would never get anything as good for that price on the Eastern seaboard. Later she regretted her decision, but reminded herself that she now needed to make money, not spend it.

At the park she tried to call Chico, with no success. She called his office but he was away on business, they said. Daisy didn't believe them. His mobile was also switched off. Something was going on. She wanted to call Enrico, but was reluctant to, just in case it put Chico in an awkward position. He might have been away with one of his lovers, and said he was with her. She did not bother sending him any more messages. If he wanted to ignore her, fine. She wasn't going to let it spoil the remainder of her vacation.

In the shadow of an outcrop of rock, well away from the tourists and out of the blistering afternoon sun, she settled to read her book for while. With only pretty collared lizards for company, it was so peaceful that she did not notice another presence until she glanced over and saw a man on a rock nearby, silhouetted against the sun. He had his back to her, and she assumed he had not seen her, as he began going through a series of graceful moves that she recognised as t'ai chi.

She was transfixed. He seemed to be standing on the edge of the world, his balance perfect, his feet bare on the scalding rock. Sweat glistened on his golden shoulder blades, soaking into the small sleeveless vest he wore as a token and the black bandanna around his neck. His khaki fatigues were also stained with sweat, rolled up at the ankles to reveal slender ankles and prehensile feet. Occasionally she could hear his sharp intake of breath, and the slow outward expelling of carbon dioxide from the depths of his body. The book forgotten, she was happy to watch him, thinking idly that he reminded her of someone . . .

Shit! She scrambled for cover further under the rock so he wouldn't spot her, and cautiously peered round it. He was poised, one leg behind and ninety degrees to the other, his back as straight as a table. And so still, his arms reaching out to the wilderness, before standing tall again, taking his leg up, higher than she would ever manage it in her Pilates class, holding it, then back down. He was as supple as a dancer, suggesting a steely inner strength to match the steel in his mind.

She shifted, noting the dampness between her legs. It would be so easy to call him over and attempt to seduce him beneath her rock, to peel away his clothes and let his body bathe hers in its sweat, to feel him spear her against the unforgiving sandstone. Her lips parted in a silent gasp, so enraptured was she by the mental picture, that when he turned and stared directly at her from behind dusky Aviators the unmistakable look of lust was still written all over her face. For a breathtaking moment they were joined, an invisible bolt of energy flowing fast between them. Then he approached her.

Her first instinct was to grab her bag and run, but he was as swift and surefooted as a cougar, catching her easily and spinning her around to accept his kiss. His fingers tangled in her hair, preventing escape. For an endless moment they were joined by a breathy tangle of tongues, their limbs slick with sweat, before he ended it, violently, as if she had scalded him. But before he could pull away with a limp excuse she kissed him with equal intensity, at once angry and fearfully excited at the emotions he was arousing in her. Their breath was loud and shallow in the punishing heat. Somehow, she didn't notice it happen, they were down on the ground, and the ice cool, unemotional Max Decker was ravaging her mouth, her throat, her neck with superheated kisses that spoke of much pent-up tension. She guided his hand to her breast and let him mash it against her rib cage. He dispatched her tiny bikini top with awesome efficiency and continued his hectic exploration of her breasts as she thrust her hand into his trousers and squeezed his buttocks. Too desperate for finesse, he seemed to want to feel every inch of her body before the opportunity was snatched away. His tongue was hot and slippery in her mouth, still tasting of peach juice, saliva mixing like the sweat glistening on their bodies. Daisy could feel it oozing from every pore, responding to her racing heart and the blood pumping through her veins. She pushed up against him, needing the fingers that were now working up towards the edge of the frayed shorts and underneath. His mouth was soft and bruised as he finally stopped the kiss to look at her properly, his eyes changing, becoming sleepy-looking with arousal as he discovered pubic fluff and her damp slit, her sex lips already swollen and supersensitive. Under his cotton khakis there was no mistaking now how hard he was, thrusting out the soft material. She felt him fumbling between them for his zip, and readied herself for the hard pounding he was about to give her.

'Hi there!'

They scrambled to rearrange their clothing. Silhouetted against the sun was a tall, slim figure in a ten-gallon hat. He wore a green shirt with 'Park Ranger' marked clearly on the pocket.

'You folks having a good time?' he asked amiably, in a soft southern drawl.

'We were,' Decker replied darkly.

'That's good to hear but this is a public place, sir, ma'am. I have to ask you to have your good time somewhere private.'

Daisy saw Decker's jaw tighten, and for one moment

she thought he was going to take exception to the Ranger's request. Actually, not a request, but a friendly demand, not to be disobeyed. Daisy didn't meet the Ranger's eyes. She knew he was copping a free look at her breasts.

As they walked back to the viewpoint an awkward silence fell between them. What they did hadn't exactly been planned, and there didn't seem to be any natural way of finishing what had been started. There was no sign that the previous heady few minutes had moved him in any way whatever, and his stance was an unapproachable as his manner. Why couldn't he be as assertive as he had been ten minutes earlier, she thought angrily. She didn't want to make the first move, because she didn't want him thinking she was an easy conquest. What had happened was more than just a meaningless fumble amongst the rocks, but conveying that message seemed an insurmountable task.

'Did you enjoy what we just did or were you just scratching an itch?' she asked when the tension became too much to bear.

He suddenly sat down on the next lump of rock and looked up at her.

'I'm sorry.' He said it wearily, as if the admission had drained him.

She stared at him, furious at his sudden weakness. 'Is this for groping me or the whole damned vacation?'

'It isn't easy for me to grovel so take it any way you want!'

'Grovel? I thought you were attempting to apologise. If you want to grovel, do it to my father. It cuts no ice with me.'

'Give me a break, will you?' His hands were massaging his temples, blocking her out, but nothing was going to stop her now.

'In England you ran out on me like a coward. Then you

say you work for my father but won't say why you're following me around like a bad stink. You've just attempted to seduce me for the second time and, if I'm not mistaken, are you asking now if we can be friends?'

'Don't, Daisy . . .'

'Don't what? Don't totally annihilate what you're saying because it's bullshit? You know what I think? I think the real scar isn't on your body, it's up here.' She tapped the side of her head. 'I don't know what your problem is, Deck, but before you even think about touching me again, sort yourself out!'

He did not reply. His attention was on the haunting shadows cast by the distant mesas, and the golden sunset turning the desert to burnt gold.

'I'm going back,' she said, loading as much disgust into those short words as she could muster.

'Wait. There are . . . things you don't know about me. Would you have dinner with me tonight and give me a chance to explain?'

She stopped and looked at him. The mask was back in place, but behind it she could see regret. Feeling suddenly ripped apart by the prospect of rejection, she nodded mutely. It was better than nothing. Keep saying it and it might become believable.

Back at the cliff dwelling she took a long, warm shower, washing away the memories of Decker's hands all over her body, if not the great big dent he had left in her mind. Eight o'clock would be confession time. What would it be? He was married, a cross-dresser, or had herpes? Maybe he was a convicted criminal, or a serial killer. As she was musing these last two possibilities he came back from the shower room. The awkwardness was palpable between them. He told her to go ahead while he made a couple of calls.

She left him to it and went out to the veranda. Strings

of lanterns were hung about the balcony, imparting a festive air. She could hear two men tending the fire pit, and the shrill instructions of the old woman in a strange tongue. Small groups sat at some of the tables, talking, drinking beer. The breeze had freshened, and the starlit sky had sucked all the warmth away, leaving a blanket of freshness that raised goosebumps on her arms and legs. She went back to the room to change into sweatshirt and jeans. As she was leaving again she heard Decker's voice from above. He had climbed up the rock where there was a better signal, and was talking on his mobile. From where he was, he could not see her listening to him.

'Are you sure she's OK? Yeah, I know, but you know I'm crazy about her. I miss her like hell.'

A short pause and then:

'What? Thanks, you always told me pussy would bring me down.' Then a laugh and, 'yeah, yeah. Just shut the fuck up and put her on. I want to hear her voice.' Then:

'Hey, sweetmeat, are you missing me?'

Daisy had heard enough. She ran back to the sanctity of the room. The affection in his voice made her feel nauseous. He was a callous, cold-hearted womaniser, and she had been too starry-eyed to see it coming. It shouldn't have surprised her. His hostility towards her had made it clear that his interests lay elsewhere. He was just an opportunist, grabbing the chance for an easy lay because he thought she would be game. Stupid, stupid, stupid. Without thinking she began stuffing her belongings frantically into her bag. She was running away again, something she despised herself for, but there was no other choice. She couldn't sit through his justifications and his pity and the inevitable excuses, knowing he was lying though his teeth.

No one tried to stop her as she scrambled up the slope and ran to the Mercedes. He could find his own way home, the heartless freak, she thought, her hand trembling as she fumbled for the ignition. As she turned the key a figure appeared in the headlights. She felt sick with apprehension.

It wasn't Decker, but the old woman. She looked stern and stronger than her 83 years.

'The Arapahoe had a warrior they called Powder Face. He took a vow to never give up on a fight. Remember that.'

'Thanks for the tip,' Daisy muttered, and sped away. When she hit the highway she headed towards Santa Fe.

12

Sonia greeted her like a beloved sister and pressed a Bacardi Breezer into her hand before she had even got through the door. Daisy's timing was perfect, as a big party was being thrown the following night for a family friend, she said excitedly, dragging her into a large, messy ranch house that seemed full of people. She stepped over empty beer bottles and pizza boxes, being introduced to Col, Juanita and Tony, Col's brother, as muscled and chunky as a prime Texas bull; it was Col's birthday they would be celebrating the following night. There were several others, but Daisy didn't have a hope of remembering all of them. It seemed that every night was party night in Sonia's house.

'I can't believe you're actually here!' Sonia had a loud, penetrating voice despite being a doll-like four foot nine. She habitually tossed her long, straight black hair and shimmied her magnificent breasts, which were entirely out of proportion to the rest of her. As more alcohol was consumed, the party seemed to be getting hotter, but Daisy was too emotionally and physically exhausted to appreciate it. She made her excuses, promising to be better company in the morning, and went up to bed, feeling like an old woman.

The next day she rolled out of bed for brunch at eleven, then spent the remainder of the day lounging around the open-air pool, talking about the party that night. After a day in Sonia's brash, relentlessly cheerful company, Daisy actually felt like hanging loose a little. Besides, she desperately needed something to exorcise the dangerous feelings she was unwillingly cultivating for Max Decker. She shook her new Western outfit out of its bag. Sonia surveyed it critically. 'This is great, but you need some heels, honey.' She threw open her wardrobe. In a heap at the bottom were at least fifty pairs of shoes, most of them breakneck stilettos, in every colour under the sun. She pulled out a pair of blue denim covered espadrilles with a curved high heel and laces that tied around the ankle. Daisy was sceptical, but with the short swingy denim skirt they made her legs look endless.

'Hey, that's better,' Sonia said, from far below. She was stuffing her breasts into a crossover red jersey top. Her cleavage was like the Grand Canyon, her rounded rump tightly encased in black leather. She adjusted her fishnet stockings and slipped on red patent heels. Then she laughed fruitily in the mirror. 'We look like a couple of hookers!'

'Good. Tonight I feel like being one!' The words sounded hollow to Daisy but she didn't want to be a party pooper. She toasted Sonia with the white wine they had started earlier that evening. They had just about finished the bottle, and it was only seven o'clock.

'Be happy then. There'll be lots good-looking men and they all want to get laid.' Sonia stretched luxuriously, straining her tight top to its limit. 'Young, dumb and full of come. You want to see how many we can bag tonight?'

'Don't try and stop me!' Daisy replied, laughing. They high fived each other and left the house.

The bar was lively, festooned with colourful lanterns and a piñata for later, shaped like an enormous pair of breasts. 'Modelled on mine,' Sonia said cheerfully. She was proud of her bosoms, and used them indiscriminately to get her own way.

Tony came towards them, stocky in a black sleeveless vest to show off his muscles and tastelessly chunky gold jewellery. He gave Daisy a strawberry marguerita, holding it out to her like a love token. The edge of the glass was prettily encrusted with pink salt crystals. The thick, fruity cocktail tasted divine and insidiously non-alcoholic. Sonia laughed knowingly, and Daisy felt her blues begin to lift.

In between margueritas she danced with most of the men, but it was Tony who kept coming back for more. As the party hotted up so did he, his dark skin glistening under the multi-coloured lights. She was happy to press close to him, enjoying his hard-on rubbing against her thighs, and the compliments he was whispering in her ear. After Decker's veiled sarcasm it was comforting to know that she had eyes like the desert after rain, and hair as soft as mink.

In the end, however, even his company began to pall, and she escaped outside. A dry lightning storm was in progress, shooting almost continuous trails of white heat across the sky, lighting up the Los Alomos mountains. Eventually Sonia found her.

'There's a crowd coming back to my place.' She sat on the chair next to Daisy's. 'You OK?'

Daisy sighed heavily. She had tried to drink herself happy, but sneaky thoughts of that overhead conversation of Decker's were bugging her yet again.

'What would you do if you like someone you shouldn't, and they think they don't like you but really they do, and you can't stop thinking about them?'

'I'd stop waiting around for him to make up his mind and enjoy every big fat dick that aimed in my direction, that's what I'd do.'

'Yeah, but what if he disapproves of you enjoying that dick?'

'Honey, if you want to behave like a hooker, then behave like a fucking hooker! If he loves you good he'll be cool about waiting until these other dicks are out of your system. You get it?'

Daisy laughed finally. 'Not really, but it sounds good.'

'Good. Come on! Shake that ass a little, huh?' Sonia pulled her to her feet.

Back at Sonia's house ten or so hardened partygoers opened more bottles of wine. The house was open plan throughout the ground floor, the living space and kitchen and dining area all merging into one sprawling mass of archways and Aztec rugs on a slate floor. Large couches and chairs were scattered throughout, every one occupied with at least one couple, drinking and making out.

Daisy sprawled on a couch with Sonia, opposite Col and Tony. Sonia's arm was around her neck as they exchanged flirtatious chat with the men, who in turn were enjoying the sight of two nubile women draped so easily over each other. Daisy had removed her bra and pulled the top down from her slim brown shoulders. She had also borrowed some of Sonia's vivid red lipstick and had put her hair up in a high, messy ponytail. Her new look was wanton and somehow a lot more sexy than it was earlier that evening, which lifted her mood immeasurably.

Someone had ordered pizza. Large flat boxes lay everywhere amongst beer bottles and overturned glasses. Sonia shrugged at the mess, saying she had all the next day to clear up. It was after midnight and Daisy felt strangely languorous, as if her inner self were disembodied from her physical being. The sparkling wine had something to do with it, and the potent scent of patchouli oil incense. One couple were kissing on another couch, getting really carried away, his hand up her skirt and hers in his trousers.

'Hey, Birthday Boy,' Sonia said in her sultry low-pitched voice. 'If you could have any woman in the room, who would it be?'

Col was slumped in a chair, his dark eyes brooding. Juanita had gone home, complaining of a headache.

'Her,' he said immediately, pointing at Daisy.

Daisy laughed disbelievingly. She felt like a sow compared to the dainty Juanita, but Col was staring thirstily at her breasts, dangerously displayed in the gypsy top, *à la* Jane Russell. She smiled slowly at Col, liking the way his look was making her feel.

'What would you like me to do?'

There was expectant silence as Col stood up, unzipped his trousers and took them off. He rested back again, his tanned, hairless body magnificent in its smoothness, revealing rippling abdominals, tense thighs and a thick piece of meat just waiting to be unleashed from black bikini briefs. Very sensuously he palmed it and moved his hand slowly up and down, his dark brown eyes boring deep into hers.

'Go on, Daisy,' Sonia urged softly. 'Suck it. Show us how the New York City girls do it.'

Daisy's mouth watered and she felt sticky between her thighs, but she wasn't sure how Col's brother would react. She looked at Tony, but he was grinning.

'He's my baby brother. We share everything.'

She drained the remainder of her wine to kick-start her courage. Tony rubbed his hands eagerly.

'Suck it, baby. Give my bro a present he won't forget.'

Daisy took a deep breath and knelt next to Col's legs. She willed saliva into her dry mouth as she grasped the elastic of the bikinis and pulled it down. His cock unfurled, straight and true and up to his navel. His balls were also hairless, with a narrow seam running straight up the dark, supple skin of his scrotum. He smelt of Kouros aftershave. She ran the tip of her tongue up the seam, up his cock, to the thick glans and back, over and over, as he watched every move, his breathing becoming shallower with every lick. When Sonia flipped up her skirt so that they could observe Daisy's behind as well, she did not protest. She was already being carried away by the sensual turn the evening had taken. As she sucked at Col's cock she moved her body in a sinuous dance, following the hands that trailed over her skin. Then she felt a tongue probing her slit, blowing on it to cool it down and lapping at it again. The moisture was all over her inner thighs. She spread her legs so the unseen mouth could gain better access, but instead a cock pushed rudely into her soaking pussy. With her mouth filled with Col's cock she could only grunt in protest; it wasn't that she minded but she liked to be asked first. But as the cock withdrew and plunged deep again she weakened with wanting. Col was moaning as another woman poured ice-cold wine on his chest and licked it off, sucking at his stiff little nipples. She poured more on his cock and Daisy licked it off with her hot tongue. Then she felt a cold trickle between her buttocks and another tongue deep in her ass, lapping, probing, making her moan louder as the cock continued to dip in and out of her smouldering cunt.

Col tapped her on the shoulder and told her to get on his lap, but he wanted her on her back, lying along his chest. As the birthday boy, he wasn't expected to do anything but take, so she lay on her back on top of him, and Sonia guided his cock into Daisy's swollen, receptive hole. The fact that she could do this in a room full of strangers was testament to how drunk she was. At the bikers' bar it had been far more intimate, as though she were part of a closed society. Knowing she should stop, but not wanting to, she gratefully drank the chilled white wine held to her lips as Sonia got on her knees between their legs and began to tongue Col's balls, making him pump up into Daisy. He covered her mouth with wet kisses as she whispered how big he was, how good he felt. It was all true, and the butterfly touch of Sonia's tongue on her clit almost made her pass out. She skewered herself on Col's cock with every ounce of her meagre strength as Sonia pleasured them both, giving Daisy a quivering climax that soaked Col's cock with feminine honey. Reeling with orgasmic pleasure, she let the other two men remove her from Col and lay her on a nearby sofa whilst Sonia had her turn on Col, riding him and pushing her plump breasts into his mouth to suck. Daisy watched them, sleepy with post-orgasmic bliss, until Tony came over and rolled her half off the sofa so that she was kneeling on the floor. Pulling her hips back towards his, he started to screw her, but in her heated imagination it was Max Decker, fucking her hard and true as he had in England, and she wished that he was there, doing it again.

Then she was dreaming. In that dream Decker was approaching her, his face white with anger. He was screaming at her, 'what the fuck is wrong with you?' Lashing out at people with his fists, flooring them and grabbing her by the shoulders. Then he was shaking her, tearing her from the womb of her hedonistic pleasure and delivering her shocked and shaking on the hard floor. As Tony rose up to attack, he was punched solidly on the jaw, sending him sprawling across the table, spilling drinks into everyone's lap. The women leapt up, screaming. Col launched at Decker but was shrugged off like an irritating fly. The other man tipped the table over with a mighty roar, intending to trip Decker with it but he was too quick, leaping over it as it fell with a deafening crash. The man was dispatched with a crunching kick to the stomach. He collapsed, wheezing, on to the floor.

Decker armed himself with a broken chair leg and was holding it like a baseball bat. He was breathing heavily, eyes staring like a madman. He fielded a flung bottle with an accuracy that would have made Babe Ruth proud. It hit the wall and shattered.

'What the hell are you doing?' Daisy shrieked. Her arousal had left her breathless and weak. Decker whirled round to face her.

'Why did you run from me?'

'I didn't! I . . .' What was she saying? Of course she had.

He swung the bat, knocking over the remaining table with a loud smash.

'You ran from me,' he said tightly. His voice was dangerously quiet but she wasn't fooled. He was fighting drunk and she was the sole reason. What did he intend to do? Grab her by the hair and carry her away to stake his claim to her body under another rock? The erotic possibilities poured into her veins like cocaine, and suddenly she was more turned on than at any other time that evening.

'So you do want me,' she said softly. 'Is that why you came?' It was a rhetorical question, because the answer was written all over his face. She pushed her blouse down over one brown shoulder, then the other, her slim hands tantalising, not allowing him to see any more of her breasts though they ached for his tongue. With her eyes goading him, her hips started to move in a slow, lewdly graceful dance. She felt as wild and wanton as a gypsy, running her hands down her body, through the folds of her skirt. His eyes followed them, then quickly focused on her face again. He was breathing heavily, and not because of the fight. 'Come on,' she whispered, her body still keeping its slow, rolling rhythm. The whole room was transfixed, suddenly under her spell. Decker was still in the same position, chair leg raised, his eyes all over her body yet he was tense, waiting for attack from any corner.

'Why else would you follow me here, Deck? Why did you jerk off the other night, and drink yourself crazy tonight? I know you want me, just as much as I want you.' She ran her hands up her body, catching her skirt between her fingers. It rose with her hands, exposing her moist slit before falling back down, her hands continuing up, over her breasts, the nipples so prominent that he could see them clearly under the thin white cotton between her fingers. Her hands ran up through her hair, gathering it up to fall wildly again around her shoulders as her hips continued to move. By this time he was concentrating solely on her, on the private dance she was doing just for him. She extended her hands towards him, pressing her breasts together in a valley as deep as a siren's pool.

'I'm yours, Deck. Do the right thing and take me.'

For one sickening moment she thought he would just walk away, but he stumbled towards her and planted a deep, bruising kiss on her lips, the chair leg forgotten. It clattered to the floor and his hand was instantly on her cunt, soaking his fingers as one by one they slipped inside her. She was drunk with heady feelings, tenderness, raging lust, triumph, feeling his cock so hard against her hip and his other arm possessively around her waist. They were oblivious to the strangers around them, to the wreckage of the party, as she relished the liquor-stained depth of his kiss.

Distantly she heard an enraged roar, then Tony's voice, bellowing 'that's my woman!' Decker falling away from her, too stunned by what had just happened to defend himself. As Tony bore him to the ground the other men joined in, some throwing punches at each other. Sonia started shouting in Spanish, imploring her brothers to leave the crazy man alone. But this was now a matter of male pride. Daisy dived for cover and crawled through the crowd, intending to get help, though where from she had no idea. Someone trod on her hair.

'Ow!' She crawled faster and made it to the other side. Looking back, there was a maelstrom of brawling men, their women slapping them, shrieking at them, hitting them with their bags and pointed shoes. Bottles were being thrown. One smashed quite close to Daisy and she found the energy to get to her feet. She stumbled in her too-high shoes and headed for the door into cool, sweet night air. Someone flew past her and was deposited in the street. The man body-rolled, stood up, and dived back in. Blue flashing lights arrived, and three weighty police officers with nightsticks. A shot was fired, and then there was silence.

A one-room jail in a small New Mexican town is no great place to spend a night. The bed had iron springs. There was a bucket to shit in. And because there was no door, just a small entrance cut into the thick bars separating the cell from the outer office, there was no privacy. The harsh overhead strip lighting hurt Decker's eyes and added to the discomfort he was already feeling. He had been one kick away from unconsciousness, and at least two ribs creaked ominously, as if fractured at least.

The guard outside the jail belched and farted almost continuously through the night, adding to the noxious odour already permeating from his unwashed body. Decker lay on the bed and covered himself with the blanket to block out both the sickly light and the fumes, only to find that underneath it was hotter than hell itself.

He must have dozed off, because when he woke the light was different, and there were voices behind the metallic clanking of locks. Then he was prodded impolitely.

'Hey, sleeping beauty, beat it. This isn't a hotel.'

Decker blinked and blearily assessed the company around his hellish bed. There was the fat guard, a police officer and someone else. Someone brown and slim, in a short white dress. His nostrils flared at a familiar rose perfume.

'Get up, Decker. I'm bailing you out.'

Daisy drove along an empty highway, all windows open to relieve the stifling heat in the car. It was late the following morning and she was putting some miles between them and Santa Fe. Quitting town in a hurry was becoming something of a habit.

'Jesus, you stink,' she muttered, looking back at Decker. He was sprawled on the back seat of his Mercedes, filthy and sweaty like a work-stained horse.

"How much did you have to pay?' His voice was reed thin.

'Ten thousand. No questions asked.' It had wiped out her UK severance money, but there was no way she wanted to involve her father just yet. Now she only had her savings to survive on. Sonia had been a true friend, negotiating Decker's release even though he had all but trashed her house. Apparently she knew the officer in charge. It didn't use up too many brain cells to figure how she had persuaded him to let Decker go. Besides, the paperwork for reprimanding a drunken partygoer was more trouble that it was worth. Daisy had wired the money into the appropriate account and had taken Decker away with the promise that they would never darken the city again.

'A thank you would be nice,' she said pointedly.

'Like the one you gave me when I saved your ass?' His voice dripped with acid. They did not speak again for the next forty miles. Then she realised he had fallen asleep.

Eventually exhaustion caught up with her. She stopped at the next motel and pulled in. A large neon sign flashed sporadically above the tatty, low buildings. It was a total cliché of a place, as curiously soulless as her mood. She swung the big car into the forecourt with a flourish, leaving a plume of red dust spiralling in the air. As she walked into the office the bovine woman behind the counter looked at her suspiciously. Daisy didn't blame her. She and Decker looked like extras from a bad road trip movie. The woman sat scratching absently at a sparsely haired armpit with her splintered, yellow thumbnail. She was dressed in a truly horrid housecoat, covered in purple and yellow flowers. It looked tatty and stained.

'Arne!' she screeched, 'we've got guests!', as if it were a rare occurrence, which it probably was. Her husband was a picture of Western excess, in a stained vest straining to contain an enormous belly that hung ominously over his Wranglers. A curl of greasy, black hair was plastered right in the middle. He gave Daisy a leery, gap-toothed smile and the key to her room.

Inside, she surveyed the threadbare red carpet and obligatory wobbly lamp beside one vast, neatly made bed with a brown bedspread. Hectic wallpaper, with big, vulgar brown flowers on a cream background, covered three walls. A faint watermark where rain had leaked in lurked near the adjoining smoked-stained wall. The furniture was all 1960s and putrid brown, built for function, not looks.

Daisy inspected the bathroom. Requisite white china glared at her under painfully bright light. It wasn't spotless, but far from dirty. Lack-lustre towels hung on the rail, which despite the heat was burning hot.

Decker lay on the bed, his eyes closed, but she nudged him and pulled him to a sitting position.

'Come on, Deck, help me out and get in that bath. You smell like a goat.'

Just then the air-conditioning kicked in, shattering the peace. The horrible clanking settled to a smooth hum, just loud enough to be intrusive. Every so often a crunching buzz would announce the death of some unfortunate insect. Decker heaved his body off the bed and staggered into the bathroom.

'Get your kit off,' Daisy said shortly.

His shirt had been glued to his chest with dried blood.

Someone had given him a slug to the nose, but it didn't look broken. Her attempts to remove the stiff cotton were met with feeble yelps of pain.

'Don't be such a baby. Just wait until it soaks off.'

He sat pathetically in the bath, his head resting on his knees, while she shimmied the shower over him. Carefully she peeled away the sodden material and exclaimed at the unbroken but mottled skin underneath. The red water around his feet gradually turned pink and then clear again. He stepped out again, using her for support while she ran hot water and splashed in a liberal capful of disinfectant. The smell filled the room, making him grimace. Dark bruises were already beginning to form on the golden skin covering his ribs and back. Bubbles loomed ominously over the top of the tub. Quickly she turned off the taps, averting her eyes as he dropped his trousers.

'Don't you wear underpants?'

'Not as a rule. Aaah!' He lowered himself into the bath, wincing theatrically as his tender spots made contact with hot water. 'Turn that light off.' His voice was thick, ragged with pain. The brightness of the overhead neon bulb was making his eyes ache. She turned it off and used the light from the bedroom to wash him by. A couple of times he shied away from her. In the end she threw the sponge at him in exasperation.

'You do it then! You know where it hurts!' She handed him three tablets. He took them from her and swallowed painfully. He lay back, eyes closed, while she poured whisky into a glass and curled his hand around it. As the liquor hit his belly he sighed gratefully.

'I don't think anything's been broken,' he said, feeling around his ribs with careful fingers.

'You should know.' She was still dabbing at him with the sponge, tenderly getting him clean. Steam rose around them. He closed his eyes and relaxed. Under the clear water his body was pale and damaged, but she shivered with sensual remembrance. In England he had satisfied her more in five heated minutes than a whole week of hedonistic orgies had. What would he be like if he really took his time? She shivered again, wondering if she would ever find out. His eyes flickered open and caught her staring. She flushed guiltily.

'I was just wondering about that scar.'

He looked down at his flaccid cock, floating in the water. 'It doesn't go right down there.'

Irritated that he sought to mock her, even in his vulnerable position, she left him to it and went back to the bedroom. In truth, she was feeling pretty jaded after helping Sonia clean her house whilst fighting off a magarita-induced hangover. The headache had gone but her body did insist on reminding her that she hadn't slept for nearly 24 hours.

Decker staggered in from the bathroom, naked and several shades of blue.

'You should see a doctor,' she said. 'You might have ruptured something.'

'I've been in a worse state than this and walked away from it.' He pulled the sheets down and eased into bed whilst she fought the desire to be all nursy and tuck him in. 'You look like you need some sleep as well.'

'Sleep? What's that?' she said yawning widely. 'I need a shower first.'

He was still awake when she went back in to the room. She was glad of the small chemise she had slipped on before going back in. It wasn't much, but it covered the essentials. She hovered awkwardly, not really knowing where she was supposed to go. He flipped the sheet down.

'Get in, shut up, and get some rest. I'm hardly going to jump you right now, am I?'

She didn't hesitate, though she should have done, just

for a moment to show him she was not to be taken for granted.

'At least you smell better,' she muttered, lying like a virgin with the sheet up to her neck. But tiredness soon overcame primness and she fell into a dreamless sleep.

13

When Decker woke it was late afternoon. Daisy was still asleep, curled away from him in a foetal ball. Her breathing was deep and contented, whilst he had been woken by a killing headache, his whole body cold and aching. He slugged back two more painkillers with tepid water and climbed back into bed. Her warmth radiated temptingly in his direction, luring him towards her. Carefully he edged towards the middle of the bed, minding his sore ribs, and curled around her back. She mumbled and nestled more comfortably against him. He relaxed, gradually descending into a drug-ridden haze filled with half-realised fantasies until he was at last asleep.

When he woke again it was dark and she was still asleep beside him. Moving carefully so as not to disturb her, he washed down another two painkillers and found a bottle of Jack Daniels. The liquor made him feel mildly better, but also incredibly horny, especially looking at her curled so innocently on the bed. Her chemise had ridden up to her waist, and her bare bottom was thrust invitingly towards him. He moved back on to the bed, unable to resist gently stroking her thighs, moving to the crease under her buttocks. From there it seemed natural to progress to the soft, plump lips enclosing her sex. Slipping his middle finger inside her was like dipping into a honey pot. Slowly, deeply, he finger-fucked her sleeping body, until she began to stir and move against his hand. It would be so easy to slip inside her, to take his pleasure from her until she rolled sleepily over and invited him into her deliciously warm, soft body, but he also wanted her to make the decision that it was him she wanted, not Chico Mendoza or any other anonymous stud. And he wanted her to look him in the eye and know what she was taking on. With monumental self-control in place he left her and went outside for a smoke.

As Daisy started out of her slumber, she wondered if Decker was still in the bath. He obviously wasn't, but he wasn't in the room with her either. His clothes were still on the chair, though, and his bag by the bed. The room was airless and smelt of stale cigarettes, so she went outside, taking one of Decker's shirts to wrap around her shoulders. All around her was an aura of supernatural calm, like that before a storm.

'Can't sleep?'

The voice startled her. She turned and saw him leaning against the wall, his face half lit by the glow of far off street lights. He joined her on the rickety seat.

'How are you feeling now?' she asked.

'Better. I'm a fast healer. Thank you, by the way.'

'Yeah. Thank you as well.' There was no need to say more. He was very close, their skin sharing the same warmth. A cicada chirped seductively somewhere close by. He lit another cigarette and they sat in companionable silence.

'Why did you never get married?' she asked eventually.

'I was married once. We divorced a few years back,' he answered shortly.

'Why?'

He glanced at her. 'That's personal.'

'Oh come on, Deck. I think we've gone past the secrets stage.'

He sighed heavily, as if resigned to the inevitable of having to explain himself. 'I was a cop. That turns some women on. Unfortunately I married one of them. Should have just fucked her instead.' He crushed his smoke out in the dust and lit up another. Daisy waited, sensing there was more.

'She didn't realise until too late that a cop's pay wouldn't finance the lifestyle she wanted. She blamed me. It's crazy because I was honest with her from the start. "We won't be rich," I said. A cop is supposed to love the job for the glory, not the cash. It was fine for a couple of years and then she said, "OK Max, what's next?" She wanted me to get promoted. More money, less street involvement. I didn't want that. I was happy amongst the scumbags, keeping a lid on them. Not that it ever happens. They're like mushrooms sprouting in a mound of shit. She didn't understand the appeal. Then some low down punk jumped me and spilt my guts on the floor. I spent three months in hospital, and went back to a desk job. Suddenly I was a loser with no fucking career, and I didn't see her for dust. The real irony is that, six months after we divorced, I quit the NYPD and moved into security. I've been there ever since. And that, Miss Lovell, is my life.'

'So when the guy cut you, is that . . .?' She motioned to his chest.

'Yeah, it's that.'

She could feel him closing off from her, but she held her breath and reached out to touch the scar, feeling how silky the damaged skin felt beneath her fingers. He instinctively moved away, and she had the strangest sensation that he was a wild animal on the verge of being tamed.

'You must have been hurt pretty bad,' she said softly.

He shrugged. 'Whatever. As I said, I'm a good healer.'

'I think that's open to debate.' She reached out again, ready to draw back rapidly if he moved to strike her away. This time he did not move, letting her run her fingers down the thick, smooth scar tissue to where it disappeared beneath his trousers. In the moonlight it gleamed as if it were one white, pulsating vein giving life to the difficult man it belonged to. He smelt hot and fresh and very male as she moved closer to press her lips against the smooth tissue at the base of his throat. He was as tense as a high wire, unaware that she had already familiarised herself with his body. With her lips against his skin she felt with her tongue how utterly smooth the scar was, a thick ridge of flesh that felt intensely sensual as she ran her tongue along it. As she moved lower he sharply drew in his breath. She looked up, suddenly self-conscious.

'Is it . . . sore?'

The look in his eyes was full of regret. 'I'm not what you want, Daisy.'

'How do you know what I want? You've never asked me.'

'I know you don't want a man whose scarred, divorced and carrying a lot of emotional baggage. You said so yourself in the bar in England.'

She blinked at him. Words so carelessly said, she had all but forgotten them.

'But they didn't stop you from . . .' She didn't quite know what the word was. Seduce, ravish? 'Touching me,' she finished, colouring slightly. 'What's so different now?'

'I was just a face in a bar. You didn't know me then.'

'I hardly know you now, thanks to that wall you've built around yourself.' Her eyes searched his face. 'What would it take to break it down?'

'For a start you could stop running away from me.'

At his words she remembered the conversation she had overheard at the Chieftain's Rest.

'If you already have someone,' she said carefully, 'I'm not going to interfere with that. It isn't what I'm about.'

He looked uncomprehending. 'Someone? What are you talking about?'

'I overheard you talking to her on the phone. You're crazy about her, remember? You miss her like hell?'

He looked bewildered, then his face cleared and he started to laugh. It was a deep, rich, alien sound that she had never heard before. She smartly stood up, ready with a retort that she didn't know what was so damned funny, but he grabbed her hand and pulled her on to his lap, holding her tight to prevent escape.

You mean Delilah?' he asked.

'I don't know! How many do you have?'

'Just the one. She's all I can cope with just now,' he said, still laughing. She could see a strange sparkle in his green eyes. It made her heart ache.

'Thanks for being so honest!' Again she tried to move off his lap. His embrace tightened.

'She's my cat.'

She blinked, struck dumb.

'I rescued her. She didn't have anyone to look after her after I . . .' He halted, seeing her amazed expression.

'A cat? As in pussy, purr, purr, kitty chow and fur balls?'

Decker had stopped laughing. He pushed his cigarette butt around on the dusty ground with his toe. 'Yeah. Pretty damned funny, isn't it?'

Daisy was feeling too relieved to find it funny. 'What . . . kind of cat is she?'

Decker looked at her closely, as if trying to decide whether or not she was laughing at him. 'A Siamese, I think.'

'One of those long, slinky ones, coffee-coloured and very vocal?'

He seemed to relax a little. 'That's right. She purrs down the telephone at me. No one's ever done that before.'

'I would,' she said softly. Immediately she thought it sounded as frank as an admission of love, and she turned her face away so he would not see it burning. He turned it back.

'Is that why you ran from me, because you thought I had another woman?'

'I didn't know what to think. You're one of the most complicated men I've ever met.'

'That's another discussion we'll have later. For now, I want to talk about you. Do you have someone waiting for you at home?'

She smiled slowly. 'Not yet.'

He made her face him. He looked very serious. 'You may be beautiful, rich, the best fuck in the world, but if you're not honest with me, I'm not interested. Understand?'

'I understand,' she said gently, not understanding why he was so vehement. Maybe he had made lousy choices in his women, but he did not look the kind of man to make the same mistake more than once. The cicada had moved. It was now very close to the chair, unseen in the dark. The silence lengthened as they both realised how far off the original subject they had strayed.

'Why do you wear this?' She ran a finger underneath the flat gold chain he always wore. It fitted snugly against his skin. As the back of her finger caressed his neck he swallowed, causing the gold to tense and release.

'It pleases me,' he said finally, not looking her in the eye.

'And what else pleases you, Max Decker?'

'This.' He tilted her chin and planted an assertive kiss on her lips, following it with his tongue. She could feel him trembling as they continued the kiss with tentatively exploring tongues, his fingers seeking out her breast and teasing out her nipple. Quite naturally her fingers began to caress him. The arrogant outline of his penis pushed against soft cotton khaki, unencumbered by underwear.

It felt thick and hard and very, very good, and her knees parted slightly in a subliminal message of wanting as they continued to feel their way back to each other.

No one could see them making out in the shadows like horny teenagers, with only the soft, protesting creak of the old seat to give them away. She was warm and squirmy and temptingly accessible, her short chemise riding up under the loose shirt. With his mouth still locked on to hers Decker hooked her leg over his, straddling her on his lap and freeing her special woman scent. He continued the kiss, ravishing her mouth with a deep, penetrating tongue. She responded joyfully, pleasuring herself against him with voluptuous grace. When he worked the chemise up above her breasts she did not stop him. Next to his cool, naked skin they were as warm and soft as clouds in heaven, with mouth-wateringly large, rigid nipples catching against his own. Sensing what he wanted, she proffered them to his lips, leaning back on his legs like a limbo dancer, her thighs firmly around his waist. She was as supple as young wood, showing off to him as her back arched and her hair brushed the ground. He lapped at one of her breasts, responding to her body's desires as though he had written the blueprint himself. As his hot saliva mingled with cool air she cried out softly and offered him the other. In the distance there were voices, getting louder. As scuffling footsteps drew near he drew her upright and kissed her mouth again, showing with his tongue what he urgently wanted to do to her body. The large shirt kept her decent as two truckers, bleary-eyed from a night's heavy drinking, paused to let themselves into the room next to Decker's.

'Hey, bud, give her one for me,' one muttered. After the longest time they went inside. Daisy was enjoying the depth of his kiss too much to let the idiotic comment spoil the moment. She could smell her own excitement, growing stronger by the second. He broke their kiss and cupped her face in his hands.

'This is going to sound crazy but it's only ten o'clock. Why don't we go back to Mesa Verde?'

'What, right now?'

'Right now. It's only fifty miles away.' He picked up her hand and kissed the soft palm inside. 'Some things are worth waiting for. I've just about reached my limit of patience, but I'll be damned before I bed you in shithole like this.'

He drove, one arm slung around her shoulders. She rested her head in the crook of his arm, too content to sleep. On the way he called the Chieftain's Rest. There was a double room waiting for them. He said they would be there just before midnight.

'So is Delilah missing you?' she murmured sleepily.

'Probably not. Warmth, food and somewhere to sleep, that's all cats are after, isn't it?'

'And a big, strong alpha-male to take care of business.' Daisy slipped her arm around his waist. The feel of his hard body next to hers felt so good she wanted to cry. She squeezed him again, and felt his answering hard hug, his mouth against her hair.

The old woman greeted them as they climbed carefully down the ladder. Speaking in hushed tones as to not disturb anyone else, she showed them to their room. It was much larger than the other one they had stayed in. The bed was huge, draped in soft wolf fur throws. A cowhide rug in the shape of the animal it had belonged to lay on the bleached wooden floor. Dream catchers hung by the window, and candles in earthenware pots decorated with Anasazi designs flickered softly, giving the room a soft, shifting light and casting long shadows on the cave walls.

'It's beautiful,' Daisy exclaimed softly. The old woman sparkled knowingly at her.

'I told you he wouldn't give up,' she said, and left them to it.

Alone again with him, Daisy felt stupidly awkward, like a teenage bride on her wedding night.

'I should wash,' she muttered, heading back towards the door. He caught her arm and pushed her back on to the bed.

Their lovemaking was slow, sweet, crashing over her like rolling Atlantic waves. After the first awkward fumbling to remove their clothes he began to worship her body with his mouth, from the hollow in her throat to the tips of her toes. He opened her legs, feasting on her salty warmth, her female scent strong after their journey. At first she was self-conscious but he brushed her shy comments aside, making her sigh as his tongue slid deep into her cunt and explored as far as it could go. A heartfelt, shuddering orgasm bubbled up from her very soul like a refreshing spring, washing away all memories of what had gone on before, drenching him with her nectar. And while the aftershocks shook her body he kissed her mouth, sharing her juices, at the same time entering her so unexpectedly she gave a sharp, virginal cry.

'Daisy,' he whispered as he plunged into her again and again. 'What have you done to me?' And again, his breath hot against her lips, that same plea dropping words into her mouth. She did not attempt to answer, instead grasping his buttocks and driving him deeper. There was a fearful bubbling up of words she dared not say, of feelings that could not be ignored. She mouthed them against his ear, silently so he could not hear. He stopped moving against her and looked down at her face.

'Do you mean that?'

She was startled, unaware that she had spoken out

loud. His cock pulsed deep inside her, playing havoc with her concentration, but the words had been true. Not just said in the heat of the moment, but true. She really did love him. God only knew why, but there was no escaping it any more, even though saying so had probably ruined everything.

He kissed her, so hard it hurt. 'Do you realise how crazy you've been making me? Being with all those men, fucking them, loving it, driving them wild. And watching you touching yourself was one of the most beautiful things I've ever seen. You've been telling me I don't have any feelings but by God you're going to see how wrong you are. Starting from now.' And he kissed her again, so deeply he seemed to be reaching into her very soul.

The next morning she sneaked out for a shower before he was awake. The journey in the heat of the night before and their energetic lovemaking had left her aware of the aroma of her own body, and she wanted him to wake to find her fresh and looking her best.

When she came back he was sitting with his back to her on the bed, his shirt on. He jumped when he heard her, as if she had interrupted something he did not want her to know about. He began to button his shirt.

'Hey, let me do that,' she said, sitting beside him. But instead of doing up the small buttons, she began to unfasten them again. His hand closed over hers.

'Don't,' he said firmly.

'Why not? Didn't you want to put this on?' She retrieved a small pot of cream that had been concealed under his hand. He looked away as if she were defiling him as she opened up the shirt and saw the scar in the cold light of day. She heard his sharp intake of breath as she pressed her lips against the ugly twist of skin and licked it gently.

'Doesn't look any worse than it did last night,' she said casually. Or the other night, she would have added, but it was still too soon to confess that particular piece of wrongdoing as he was still so sensitive about his disfigurement. She unscrewed the lid from the pot of cream. 'This is going to happen, whether you like it or not, so you might as well enjoy it.'

He acquiescently sat back against the pillows and watched her dip her fingers into the cool white cream, smelling faintly of healing lavender. She gently rubbed it into his chest, concentrating on the main centre of damage first before methodically working it into the long ridge of tissue that lead to the base of his throat.

'You look like you've done this before,' he said lightly. She could feel him relax gradually, his eyes growing sleepy. He seemed to melt back into the pillows, the look on his face increasingly mellow, as she had rarely seen it before. Another dip into the pot, and this time she warmed the cream on her fingers before applying it to his stomach, working it into his skin, feeling his muscles tense and soften, then tense again as she moved further down, the concentration of that tension massing at his groin. More than once she accidentally brushed against a warm, rising lump in his boxers. His breathing had turned shallow, expectant, but he did not move, turned to rock by the tender touch of her hands.

Finally she looked up at him, sitting back amongst the pillows, the expression on his face unreadable. With his shirt undone and the scar fully visible, one long, elegant leg slightly bent and the merest hint of his growing erection, she decided he had never looked so good. Wordlessly she picked up her camera. He did not move, staring at her with those impenetrable almond eyes, a half-smile on his face as she took his photograph.

'Thank you,' she said softly.

'No. Thank you.' He reached for her and pulled her across the bed.

On their last night at the Chieftain's Rest they watched the fiery red orb of the sun sink down behind distant violet tinged storm clouds. For the last two days they had talked for hours between making love, strengthening the bond between them before other people got in the way. Other people, like her father, whose reaction she could guess quite accurately would not be favourable.

The future was the only thing they did not discuss. She sensed that he was holding back, but that was fine because so was she. Maybe there were things they would never know or understand about each other. It was too soon to let them get in the way of their new-found tranquility. It would end soon enough anyway.

That evening they ate at a small Mexican bar, which served the best tacos she had ever eaten, and washed them down with San Miguel beer. Halfway through the evening she went to the restroom and removed her bra. Their mood had been somewhat subdued, knowing they were to leave early next morning for Phoenix for their flight back to New York. She had decided it was time to heat things up a bit, so she tucked her bra into her bag and fondled her nipples to make them erect. They felt good rubbing against the tight white vest top she had changed into earlier, and looked irresistible.

Back at the bar Decker had ordered two more beers. As she rubbed her breasts up against his bare arm, his eyes immediately zeroed in on them, although he made valiant attempts to hide it.

'You don't look like the kind of guy that screws a girl in a pub car park and runs off before she's had time to pull up her knickers,' she said teasingly, licking the rim of her beer bottle.

He grinned self-consciously. 'And you don't look the

kind of girl that gets routinely fucked by four bikers at once.'

She ran her finger lightly over the top of the hand resting on his knee. 'What is that saying? Two negatives make a positive?'

'That makes a hell of a lot of sense to me,' he said thickly.

'Though it does depend whether you're thinking with your brain or your dick,' she continued, salaciously licking the condensation up from the side of her beer bottle.

'That is also true,' he conceded, but the heat was still there in his voice.

'So tell me, Max Decker, what is your brain telling your dick right now?'

He cupped his hand around the back of her head and drew her to him for a smouldering kiss so deep she forgot they were in the middle of a public place.

'I want to fuck you like a coyote,' he replied.

On the way back to the cliff dwelling they stopped the convertible at a viewpoint where the vista was so big it touched the star-splattered night. The distant mesas were mere haunting shadows, punctuated by tiny clusters of dwellings like lonely galaxies in an endless earthbound universe.

'This is a very pleasant way to end a vacation,' she said as they lowered their seats until they were almost horizontal. For a while they just lay back, finding each constellation, arguing over the names of some. Eventually she unzipped him, notch by notch over the straining cock fighting to get free. She could just see it, fat and greedy and musky, making her pussy contract with anticipation.

'Oh, mother,' he moaned as her tongue made a wet trail from root to tip. It beat against her lips as she fluttered her tongue around the glans, licking the musk of the day from him, tracing every vein and ridge. He grunted and squirmed, saying 'oh yeah', over and over, his hand buried in her hair. He stroked the silky strands between his fingers, not guiding her head but letting her do as she wanted. She tongued his balls, tugged gently at them with her teeth, soaked them with her saliva and drank it back in. She kneeled up on the seat and stuck her bottom in the air, encouraging him to fondle the soft globes of her buttocks, barely covered by her short skirt. His touch spurred her on, finally drawing him all into her mouth until her lips ached. There was barely room for her tongue to manouvre around the warm, wet cave of her mouth so she manipulated her muscles instead to squeeze and torment his cock. His finger had worked underneath her panties and was probing at her pussy. She squirmed, encouraging the finger to go deeper, at the same time burying her finger between his buttocks and finding the tight little hole of his anus.

'Oh, Christ,' he gasped, almost gagging with pleasure. 'Stop it. I don't want to come like this. I want to fuck you.' But she continued to suck at him until she felt his cock tense, thrusting her finger deep into his backside as he came. She drank down the sweet, viscous liquid, sucking him dry as his shouts floated out into the night. His spasms forced her finger deeper into his backside, prolonging his pleasure until he was gasping, pleading with her to stop. She did, removing her finger carefully and kissing his cock, which looked as flaccid and exhausted as the rest of him. They lay, Daisy with her head on his lap, as he recovered.

'That was cruel,' he said eventually. She felt him tug her hair to make her look at him. He was grinning. 'But you haven't gotten away with it. I'm still going to fuck you like a coyote.'

At his suggestion they drove back to the pueblo and carefully negotiated the narrow path. It was late and people were sleeping. They felt like bad kids playing truant at night, giggling softly in the dark. In their room he turned her around to face the mirror.

'Close your eyes,' he said firmly. She obeyed, shimmering with excitement, wondering at the awesome need his commanding voice aroused in her. She felt him move behind her and place something around her neck. It felt big, heavy and cold. He cursed softly, fiddling with some kind of clasp, then he brushed her hair away so it fell down her back.

'Now open them.'

She opened her eyes, and gasped. The necklace was a spread eagle, fashioned out of turquoise and hand-carved silver, like the one she had coveted in the craft shop, but far more detail had gone into it. She tentatively touched it, tears in her eyes. The large turquoise stone at its centre felt alive under her fingers.

'It's beautiful,' she whispered. 'How did you know ...?'

'Because I went into the shop after you and asked what you had spent so much time looking at, and then I went to find the real McCoy, because I won't accept anything less and neither should you.' He kissed her neck, a hot, moist kiss full of desire. She turned and twined her arms around his neck.

'Thank you.' She pressed a kiss on his lips. 'Thank you.' Another one on his cheek, repeating the words and the kisses until his whole face was a patchwork of soft, tingling imprints of love. They collapsed back on the bed, their mood changing and becoming more urgent. He peeled the clothes from her body until the necklace was the only thing she had left on. Working his way down, he set her senses on fire with each touch of his lips. Finally he thrust his hands under her buttocks and lifted her pelvis, exploring every secret crevice as she ran her fingers through his hair and whispered his name, over and over again. His tongue found the tiny seed of her clit and strummed the tune of ecstasy to such a perfect pitch that she could not hold on. Her cries became incoherent, peaking with every orgasmic jolt that racked her body. Finally he spread her wide and entered her with such brutal force that her voice was nothing more than a raw whisper as she dug her nails into his buttocks, driving him on and up, deeper and deeper into her pliant, willing body. Clawing up that rough path to ecstasy together, they reached the top with unashamed screams of triumph, teeth bared in savage snarls of pure, feral joy.

14

Felix Lovell had tears in his eyes when she finally embraced him after more than three years apart. It was a good five minutes before she managed to extricate herself from his bear-like arms.

'It's so wonderful to have you back!'

'It's good to be back, Dad.' And she meant it, as long as he agreed to the plan she had formulated. Not that she would mention it just yet. There was a time and a place, and right now wasn't it.

Within five minutes he had presented her with her coming home present, a bright blue Mercedes SLK, tied with a large silver bow. She gave him another breathtaking hug.

'Dad, you shouldn't have.' Seriously, she wished he hadn't. It was just another thing for her to feel guilty about, but she pushed the ungracious thought down where it belonged and kissed her father again.

'Of course I should! Anything for my little girl. Anyway, you needed some wheels.' He led her to the veranda, ordering Perdita, his maid, to bring mint juleps. She brought them in frosted cocktail glasses, adorned with a crisp mint leaf.

'Tell me everything. I want to know it all,' he said eagerly.

No, you don't, she thought. As she gave a condensed version of her escapades she saw his mood change and become pensive, as if something was troubling him. In the end she asked him what it was.

'There's someone coming tonight that I want you to meet,' he said reluctantly.

'You're not trying to fix me up with a husband already, are you? I've only been here five minutes!'

'Christ, no!' Lovell shuddered as if repulsed by the thought. 'I'll tell you more later.'

When she finally went upstairs to her old bedroom she saw that Perdita, her father's housemaid, had already unpacked her travel-stained clothes. The white Chloe dress was hung up in the wardrobe, freshly pressed. The sense of not having to lift a finger to do anything made her feel slightly claustrophobic. In spite of all the luxury, her heart was still back in Colorado.

The sound of a car crunching on gravel deterred her half-formed, wistful thoughts. It was a sleek-nosed 8 Series BMW, dark green, obviously cosseted by a loving owner. The windows were darkened to screen whoever was inside.

He climbed out and looked up at her as if knowing she was waiting for him. After two weeks of khaki fatigues she had forgotten how devastating he looked in a suit. It was a dove grey Valentino, softly tailored, with a white shirt to show off his tan. She knew it was silk even from that distance, just as she could read the heat in his eyes under his graduated Aviators. There was an immediate answering heat in her sex, moist and heavy with desire.

Felix came into view, breaking the palpable electric bond between them. She moved sharply away from the window, taking care not to make the drape twitch. She did not want her father to start suspecting that something was going on even before they were in the same room.

She dressed carefully, choosing a white lace Elle bra and panties to go under the flimsy dress. The bodice was as first glance modest, but with one tug of the laces that held her breasts in place they would fall out of it, exposing her to the world. She had fallen in love with its dreamy eroticism, the flower girl hiding the rock chick beneath its floaty skirts. At six o'clock, Perdita came up and told her Felix was waiting on the veranda for her. She slipped her feet, with silver-painted toenails, into high wedged white leather espadrilles and sprayed herself with Yves St Laurent's Baby Doll, and went downstairs.

Felix looked highly displeased at the news that Decker had just given him. It meant that Chico Mendoza was out of reach, at least for the time being. As for Enrico, all the investigative skills Manhattan had to offer had failed to come up with anything juicy in his company accounts. The man was clean, apart from one unpaid parking ticket two years before. Even the IRS weren't interested in him. And Daisy was still determined to move to New Jersey on Monday morning.

'Why New Jersey, for fuck's sake? It isn't even the right side of the river!'

Decker didn't answer. He knew when to keep quiet. Felix paced the veranda, his hands stuck deep in his pockets. 'Well, she can't move out, not with Mendoza threatening to do Christ knows what!'

'But the alternative is to keep her a prisoner here, and that's hardly practical either, is it?'

Felix turned sharply at Decker's exasperated tone. He wasn't used to hearing dissent from his minions. His eyes narrowed.

'Has she said anything to you about this?'

'Not in so many words, but she's a very independent young woman. She's set her heart on doing her own thing. If you try to push her to stay you'll only drive her away, probably for good.'

'So what do you suggest I do? Let her go and send a fax to Mendoza with her address on it?'

'You could do two things. One, let her go to New Jersey and say nothing, or two, tell her the truth about the threat from Mendoza and let her make her own choice. Either way, she'll have me to keep her safe.'

'I want to keep her safe!' Felix snapped, then looked guiltily around to see if Daisy had materialised in the doorway. He lowered his voice. 'Goddamnit, how am I going to convince her to stay here?'

'You won't,' Decker said calmly.

'And what the hell makes you so sure? I've known her for 33 years and you've only known her two weeks!'

'Yes, but have you ever really talked to her? She isn't a little girl any more, Felix. If you get heavy with her now you'll lose her, believe me.'

Felix's eyes narrowed. 'You seem to know one hell of a lot about it.'

Decker's eyes moved past Felix's shoulder to the doorway. Just in time, Daisy had come to save him.

Felix Lovell's thick brows drew together at the sight of Daisy's curvaceous body, so subtly but obviously displayed. The warm evening sun glowed through the thin white cotton of her dress, accentuating every womanly curve. He practically stood in front of her in an attempt to shield Decker's view.

'Daisy, I want you to meet Max Decker, Lovell's executive director of security,' he said in a tone that meant that he obviously didn't. 'I believe you already know each other.'

Daisy brushed her father aside and held out her hand to Decker. Their fingers touched for the briefest of moments, but it was enough to make her shiver.

'Executive Director? I had no idea I was in such high-powered company,' she said playfully. Felix was watching her closely.

'I know what you're going to say, but it was obviously necessary. Max says it got pretty heavy out there.'

'Yes, it did get heavy.' Her thoughts were on his body, mashing hers to hot rock. She shook herself and smiled dazzlingly at Decker. 'Thank you for being so dedicated to your job.'

'You're welcome.' Decker smiled fleetingly, playing it cool.

They had dinner in the Orangery, which was cosier than the austere dining room, surrounded by standard shaped orange and lemon trees, a legacy from Daisy's green-fingered mother. Perdita served one of Daisy's favourite supper dishes: roasted salmon with a cous-cous crust, and angel hair noodles with julianned broccoli stalks and fennel. Felix talked of business mostly, but Daisy sensed he was holding something back. It didn't unduly worry her, because he was always wheeling and dealing. During the meal Decker tried not to watch her too closely, though his foot was almost constantly in contact with hers, within inches of Felix's Gucci loafers. Felix was blissfully unaware of the potent sexual messages being passed between them. Daisy eased off on the champagne, because it always made her languorous and flirty, but her sex ran hot and cold every time she and Decker made eye contact.

'Daisy, are you still set on moving to New Jersey?'

Here we go, she thought. 'Yes, Dad. I'm moving in on Monday. I told you that over two weeks ago.'

'Well, that's fine but Max is going to check the place out first. You know, make sure the front door is still on its hinges, that kind of thing.' He laughed falsely. 'If necessary we'll have to make some changes to the security system.'

Daisy looked at Decker with dismay. 'Dad, I'm only

renting it for the summer. It isn't even a formal agreement. Anyway, their security is fine. A whole new system was fitted just before Christmas.'

'Even so, I want it checked out.'

She felt Decker's feet squeeze hers under the table. Humour him, his eyes said.

She sighed and threw down her napkin. 'Fine, if it makes you feel happier, but I won't have anyone banging nails in the walls or putting sensors down the toilet. What's the big deal, anyway? You've never been this paranoid before.'

'It's a minor issue, Miss Lovell,' Decker said smoothly. 'One of the businesses your father is acquiring owes money to some unpleasant people. There have been talk of threats, but nothing substantiated. Security for all Lovell personnel has been reviewed as a result. You, as Mr Lovell's daughter, get preferential treatment.'

'Which means I get personal attention from the executive director of security?' she asked lightly.

'Absolutely,' he replied, dropping his guard just enough for her to see the lustful gleam in his eye.

'How reassuring,' she said, and smiled winningly at her father. 'Don't worry, Dad. I won't give Mr Decker here a hard time.'

'He might give you one,' he retorted. Out of the corner of her eye she saw Decker choke on his champagne and hide his laugh with his napkin. 'Well, now that's sorted out you can leave us, Max. Daisy and I have a lot to catch up on.'

Daisy was shocked at Decker being so arbitrarily dismissed, but he seemed to be used to it.

'I'll be back on Monday afternoon to assist you with your move, Miss Lovell. Two of my men will check out the house. Don't worry, they'll be very discreet. You'll hardly know they're there.' He shook hands briefly with Felix and left them.

Later that night, Daisy pleaded tiredness and went upstairs. She undressed and lay on the bed, breathing in the heady scent of the jasmine outside her open window. She was willing Decker to come through it, like a thief in the night. When her fingers brushed against her pussy lips they were engorged and open, ready for her secret lover. The sex she had indulged in over the past two weeks was nothing to the illicit excitement she was feeling now. She lay on the bed, fully dressed, and stimulated her nipples through the fine cotton. How was she going to last until Monday?

She was woken up by his lips, crushing hers to prevent her screaming. His hand was needy on her breast, seeking out her nipple as the kiss continued, breathy, silent, fast and furious.

'God, you looked fabulous tonight,' he groaned, tugging on the ribbons of her bodice. She pushed him away and sat up, then slowly pulled the ribbon loose, letting the weight of her breasts push the two halves of the bodice apart. He swallowed hard and pushed his face between them, inhaling their sweet fragrance.

'If Dad finds you here he'll remove your internal organs,' she whispered as he removed his clothes and slipped into her large bed. He was already erect, urgently nudging against her thighs. She opened them and let him in. Their coupling was intensified by the hazard of being found out.

'I could happily die fucking you,' Decker whispered into her hair.

'Please don't. I've only just got to like you,' she replied, and dug her fingernails into his buttocks. He wriggled down, under the duvet, and started eating her out with such finesse that she had to stifle a sob of pleasure. She toyed with his hair, gripping it hard when she heard Felix's footfall in the corridor.

After a moment she felt Decker's sly tongue flicker

against her inner thighs. He found her clit and fluttered delicately against it, his finger now working into her sodden pussy. Her hips began to churn again as he found the right spot and stayed there, building on her orgasm, wave upon wave, until she had to come with tiny pants of pleasure. As she jolted with the aftershocks he plunged inside her, smearing pussy-juiced-up kisses all over her mouth.

'Daisy,' he whispered hoarsely, measuring each thrust so the bedhead did not bang against the wall. 'Daisy, my love, my sweet little sex-bomb.' And he came with a low, animalistic groan, filling her up so much she thought she could taste him.

Afterwards they lay, still joined, while he found the energy to sneak back out of the window. He knew how to evade the security cameras, having overseen their installation, he explained, when she asked how he had the nerve to break in. When he left she felt bereft, but Monday would soon come around, and then they could lie together all night. With that pleasant thought she fell asleep.

It was late on Monday afternoon. Felix had skilfully delayed her departure, inviting friends for lunch so she could regale them with her adventures. And even as Decker was waiting to take her to New Jersey, he was still trying to persuade her to stay.

'But what's wrong with living here?' he asked, almost plaintively.

'For a start, within a week I'll want to kill you, and you know it as well as I do. Besides, you're set in your ways and having a female around again will only make you miserable.' She kissed him tenderly on the cheek. 'I'll call you tonight.'

Felix glanced into the car where Max Decker was

waiting. 'I want you back here this evening, Max. We've got things to discuss.'

Decker nodded and looked regretfully at Daisy. Daisy wondered whether her father was doing it on purpose, just to make sure he didn't stay at the house any longer than necessary. She wouldn't put it past him.

He drew Daisy out of Decker's earshot. 'One thing, honey, and I want you to answer truthfully. Max didn't . . . I mean, I trust him but . . .'

'Did he try to get into my pants?' Daisy suggested helpfully. 'No, Dad, he didn't.'

'Oh, good. Just checking.'

At the house, she sat on the porch and waited while the three men checked the house. Decker came out minutes later, looking grim.

'Holy mother, I should tell Felix this place is detrimental to your eyesight.'

'You don't like cows then?' She laughed.

'And what's with all the frills and shit in the bedroom? It looks like Tammy Fay Bakker did a real number in there. Oh, I also found these.' He held up a pair of handcuffs. 'They were under the bed, along with a whole lot of other stuff. Does Felix know your landlords are fudgies?'

'Of course he doesn't, and don't be rude. Phil and Paul are sweet people.'

Decker edged closer to her. 'Sweet people who like whips and chains and butt plugs the size of the Empire State Building. One of them even had a fur tail stuck on the end. I think it was sable.'

Daisy giggled quietly. 'And do you consider that a threat to my security?'

'The only threat I can think of right now is this damned great hard-on I've got, thinking of fucking you in that damned great bed.' He moved to sit more comfortably and lit a Chesterfield. 'They had a black mink mitten in the bedroom drawer. Tomorrow night I'm going to use it on you.' His voice was casual but the suggestion made her sex steam up. She had been thinking about the handcuffs, and how he would like being on the other end of them. She told him about her father's question earlier.

'Don't worry. Tomorrow is my night off. Nothing on this planet is going to keep me away from you,' he said quietly.

The two men appeared in the front doorway before he could enquire what the surprise was.

'Is it safe for me to enter?' she asked facetiously. Their bland faces did not change.

'We're all done here,' one said. 'You know the drill, Miss Lovell. Report any hoax calls, don't, under any circumstances, give out this address or telephone number. Your post will be delivered to a box number in town. And don't follow any routines which might alert someone to the fact that the house is empty, even for the shortest time.'

'And don't talk to strangers,' Daisy added. 'Mr Decker, can you come inside for a moment, please?' She drew him into the house and looked for the other two men. They were casing the outside of the house. 'This is really weirding me out, Deck. Are you sure there's nothing going on I should know about?'

'He's paranoid about security. Why do you think he pays me two hundred thousand a year to go storm chasing?'

'But all this . . . just doesn't add up. It's like he's really afraid of something.'

Decker hesitated, as if he were trying to decide what to say next. Out of the kitchen window they could see the two security guards lurking conspicuously in the front yard. 'Like I said on Saturday, he's doing a deal. Nothing heavy, but in his usual bull-headed way he's got some people really pissed. Now he's expecting the worst. You know what he's like, Daisy. Either full on or flat line, that's the way it goes.'

It seemed feasible, but she wasn't convinced. It must have shown in her face because he suddenly drew her away from the window and pushed her against the kitchen wall.

'Look, he's getting old, eccentric, and he loves you to pieces. Rather like me, apart from the old and eccentric.' He kissed her deeply to stall any more arguments. She twisted her head away.

'You would tell me, wouldn't you?'

He was kissing her again, her neck, her throat, sinking slowly to his knees and gathering up her skirt. Her delicate silk panties were all puckered up between her pussy lips and she gasped as he eased them out with one finger and pulled them to one side. His hot breath on the smooth skin on her inner thighs made her shudder as it was replaced by cool moist air. He was licking and blowing gently on the dampened flesh, making her want to forget everything else and just spread herself wider to him. When his tongue found her clit and curled gently around it she sagged, supporting herself with her hands on his shoulders. The erotic moment was ruined by footfall on the wooden porch.

'Someone's coming,' she gasped softly. He rose to his feet again and gave her a deep, sticky, musky kiss.

'I'll come back tomorrow,' he whispered hotly, licking her essence from his lips. Then in a loud voice, hard enough to truncate any lingering sensual need, 'call us if anything concerns you, Miss Lovell. We're on duty twenty-four seven.'

'Will do,' she replied shakily.

The following morning she drove to Manhattan. It was time to find out where the hell Chico had disappeared to.

In the heated passion of the last few days she had forgotten all about him, but now there was to be no more hedging or playing of telephone tag. She was going straight to the top.

Enrico Mendoza was at his desk as she was ushered in. He stood up and held out both his hands to capture hers.

'Daisy, it's so good to see you again!' He kissed her on both cheeks and stood back to look at her. 'More beautiful than ever. Some coffee?'

'Thank you, Enrico.' She wanted to burst into the explanation of why she was there straightaway, but knew from past experience that he would not be pushed. So she drank the coffee and answered his questions about her life in England. He was still a very handsome man, with a lean, unlined face and dark hair greying only at the temples. When they were lovers a few years before, he had wanted to take her as his mistress, and to buy her an apartment in Manhattan in return for her company on business trips and vacations abroad. She had been tempted, but knew that, in the long run, it would make her a glorified whore. She had gently turned him down, and he had taken her refusal with dignity.

'So you're looking for a job? Is that why you're here? I could easily accommodate you.' In more ways than one, his eyes read.

'That's generous of you, Rico, but no. I'm here because I'm worried about Chico.'

He rose to his feet and wandered to the window. 'Of course, Chico. My staff were under strict confidentiality orders regarding my son.'

'Which they obeyed. What's going on? Is he all right?'

Enrico held out his arm. 'Let's walk in the Park.'

She agreed, forcing down her frustration. He insisted she take his arm as they strolled down Fifth Avenue towards Central Park. They looked like any other well-heeled couple, the older smartly suited man with his young, beautiful companion. When he did not speak she asked him again. He looked so bleak that she felt instantly nauseous.

'He's alive, but not well. He's in a clinic on Mount Sinai. He's been there for over a week.'

Her grip tightened on his arm. 'What happened?'

He gestured helplessly. 'Some kind of overdose. Not deliberate, just the result of some drunken orgy, apparently. In his apartment!' His face grew hard. 'I go there because of complaints from the people above, and he's still in bed, filthy, drugged up. His apartment's been stripped. He'd been robbed while he slept. Holy Mother!' He couldn't go on. She squeezed him closer, wanting to give some kind of comfort.

'Why didn't you call me? You must have seen all the messages I left!'

'I did, *querida*, but I did not want to spoil your vacation. I knew it would bring you home, and he is in the best possible care.' He suddenly grasped her hand like a lifeline. 'What possessed him, Daisy? You know him better than I, maybe better than anyone. I was so glad when he said you were coming back. Not just for him, but for me also.' He kissed her hand, his dark eyes boring into hers, then he moved closer to kiss her mouth. She pressed her fingers over his lips and led him to a park bench.

'I'm going to tell you something, and you're not going to like it, Enrico but you must hear it. Chico isn't responsible for his problems. They've been brought on by you.' She felt him stiffen, but she carried on. 'You obviously love him, but you have to accept him for what he is. There is no other Chico. What he is, is what you've got, whether you like it or not. This is the 21st century, for heaven's sake! You could advertise that he was gay from Times Square but would anyone care? No. It isn't going to make a blind bit of difference to your stock prices, or to your rivals. Let me ask you something. Why did you employ Piers Molyneaux?'

'He's good at his job,' Enrico said promptly, with a hint of defiance.

'But he's gay. Chico is also good at his job, and he's gay. What's the difference?'

'He's my son.'

She threw up her hands in despair. 'Not for much longer if you insist on being so blinkered! You're as bad as these bloody horses!' She motioned to the skinny animals pulling tourist carriages around the park. 'The difference is that those poor beasts don't have a choice, but you do. Take the blinkers off, Rico. You're going to lose him if you don't. Love is so similar to hate, and he's right on that line.'

He turned sharply away from her and stared up at the soaring buildings. She waited, sensing his inner struggle. He lit a slim cigar and smoked it, and still she waited. Finally he returned to her and took her face in his hands. The kiss he planted on her lips was gentle, but she could feel the need for something more behind it.

'Chico is very lucky,' he said softly. 'You're beautiful, and a wise and loyal friend.' He bent to kiss her again, and this time she felt his tongue slide against her lips. She returned the kiss for the briefest of moments before pulling away. He looked saddened, but not surprised.

'What are you going to do?' she asked.

'Can I persuade you to have dinner with me?' he asked, avoiding the question.

'I can't, Rico. I'm seeing someone.'

'And you obviously feel a great deal for him. Too much to let me persuade you to give me one night for old time's sake?' He kissed the back of her hand. He looked so suave and devilishly handsome that for a moment she was tempted. Then she remembered Max Decker, her new lover, her love. It was time to put casual flings and opportunistic encounters behind her.

'No, Rico. It has to be no.'

'You know where I am if you change your mind.'

It wasn't until after he had left her that she realised he hadn't answered her question.

That afternoon she went to see Chico. The clinic was cool and decorated in white and green. The nurses seemed to float on cushions of air as they passed silently by. Chico was in bed, looking wan and very young and vulnerable. She went in, slightly apprehensive.

'I've come to bore you with some holiday snaps,' she said.

Chico pulled a face. 'I don't know what's worse. That or you saying "I told you so."'

'I wouldn't do that and you know it. How are you feeling, anyway?'

'Like I've had too many drugs. And why are all the nurses female?'

'Don't worry, have a look at these.' She handed him the first batch of photos. He flicked uninterestedly through them.

'Rocks, rock, rocks. No shit, those are real rocks!' He laughed weakly when he saw the pictures of Ricky and his massive phallus. 'Can I keep this one?'

'No you can't!' she said with a laugh, snatching it from him. He carried on looking through the heap of photographs, laying out the sexy ones she knew would interest him. Gradually she saw his face change and become truly animated, she guessed for the first time in weeks.

'These are good, Daisy. They capture the moment exquisitely. You've been holding out on me.'

'I just shot what I saw,' she said, but thought he had a point. They were better than she had anticipated.

'They've certainly had an affect on me.' He pointed to his crotch. There was a slight tenting of the bed sheets. 'I think you could have a new career on your hands. You really have the eye for capturing someone and making them look good, even this ugly bastard.' He motioned to a head shot of Mike Bradley. 'Don't tell me he was Mr Pussy Magnet?'

'Actually he was, but after he nearly killed me I shaved all his pubes off.'

Chico laughed so hard a nurse rushed into the room. Daisy hastily scooped the photos up but not before the nurse had seen them. She turned pink and compressed her lips.

'I think you should go now. Mr Mendoza needs a lot of rest.'

'Five minutes, Arnie,' Chico said, turning pleading dark eyes on to the nurse's stern face. 'Please?' To Daisy's amazement her lips softened.

'Five minutes. I'll be back.'

She disappeared. Chico chuckled to Daisy. 'She always says that. That's why I call her Arnie. Okay, now show me the photo you've been hiding from me.'

Daisy blushed. 'How did you know that!'

'Because I have enough female chromosomes to know when a woman is lying. Come on, give it to me.'

She sighed and delved into the envelope, drawing out the intimate photograph of Max Decker. She had not wanted to show it because it felt like betrayal, reducing her relationship with Max to coffee table gossip. Chico seemed to sense it, because he did not snatch the photo from her reluctant fingers, but took it gently. She explained what she knew about their unfolding relationship, and about Decker's past, and the tenacious way he had pursued her. Chico handed the photograph back.

'Whatever you've got with that guy, hold on to it,' he said softly.

'I'll try,' she said, only realising just then how much she meant it.

The nurse's appearance prevented them from talking more. 'I really must ask you to leave now,' she said, more kindly than she had before.

'No problem.' Daisy kissed Chico's forehead. 'Take care, toots. I'll come by tomorrow.'

15

Back at the house she had a long, fragrant bath and thought about what Chico had said. She had never thought of being a professional photographer before, but she had to admit it appealed. She could do private shoots for couples wanting to have a portfolio of themselves in their most intimate moments. Gay, straight, it didn't matter, as long as she could capture the tenderness as well as the eroticism between them.

She towelled herself dry and opened her wardrobe. Decker was taking her out that night to an intimate Italian restaurant in Clinton, but there would be enough time for some sensual foreplay before they went. He was due in half an hour, which just about gave her time to figure out what to wear. What would it be? The Chloe dress, so that he could slowly undo the ribbons and feel her breasts yield to his touch? Or the little bronze silk dress that looked more like a chemise, with spaghetti straps and a scrap of lace around the hem of the very short skirt? Then she had an even better idea, one that made her go hot and cold with naughty anticipation.

Twenty minutes later the doorbell buzzed. She opened the fly screen and he was there, looking stunning in a black Prada suit with an aubergine silk shirt. Behind him, parked on the driveway, was the shark-nosed BMW. A real pussy puller, she thought hungrily. It was certainly pulling at hers. The thought of making out on the beautiful cream leather back seats had already made her wet.

'You're not ready,' he said, looking at her innocent

white silk robe. She sensed tension in him that had not been there for the last few days.

'What's wrong?' She didn't like the hard look in his eyes and the sharpness of his tone but, just as unexpectedly, he kissed her, carrying her away with his passion. He broke away again so suddenly she stumbled.

'I'm sorry. It's been a shit day,' he said with a tight smile.

She caressed the back of his neck and pressed her cheek to his. 'Why don't you come upstairs? I'll make you feel better.'

Again a strange stiffness in his body, and then it was gone. He let her lead him up the stairs to the bedroom. The chair was waiting, an innocuous-looking instrument of sensual delight. It looked like a specialist posture stool. The back was slim enough that the person's arms could be pulled back and tied comfortably at the wrists and also fastened to their ankles, drawn back behind a secondary support cushion for their knees. Once attached, there was no chance of escape. With their genitalia and buttocks totally exposed, they were totally at the mercy of their captors.

But Decker didn't know this. She guessed that he had given it only a cursory glance during his inspection of the house. Now he was looking curiously at it, no doubt wondering what it was for.

'It's a feng shui massage chair. Why don't you sit down?' She suggested. 'I'll give you a shoulder rub.'

He looked sceptical but with a humouring look he sat and waited. Rapidly she put the handcuffs on his wrists.

'Oh, very funny,' he said, but his smile was sinister. It said, get me out of this *now*. She rewarded him with a light smack on the cheek, her face serious.

'Shut up,' she said imperiously, unzipping his trousers and pulling them down and off. No underwear, bad boy.

When she bent to cuff his ankles, passing the second cuff over the wrist cuffs, he was totally unable to move.

'This isn't funny, Daisy. Let me go.' His voice warned her he wasn't in the mood. She didn't answer, but unbuttoned his shirt and removed his tie. Then she gave him a long, loving kiss.

'I'll be back,' she whispered.

In the second bedroom she stripped off her robe and pulled on the thigh-high leather boots she had found in the closet. They looked stunning next to her stringy black thong and black bra that tied in the front with a single bow. She painted Carmen red on her lips and pulled her hair up into a high ponytail, making her look a lot more aggressive than she usually did. Finally she picked up a soft leather switch and the black mink mitt, then walked back in to the bedroom.

'Holy shit,' Decker said when he saw her. She couldn't tell if he was dismayed or not. She nudged the switch up under his chin and forced his head up.

'If I were you, I'd keep quiet,' she snarled, thoroughly enjoying the ambivalent look in his eyes. She could tell he hated not being in control, but when she slipped her hand, encased in the mink mitt, down his body it undulated with pleasure. When she was sure the whole surface of his skin was shimmering she picked up the switch and flicked it lightly across his stomach, making it contract. Then harder, leaving a slight red mark across his taut flesh. He drew in his breath and snarled silently at her, determined not to give her the satisfaction of showing his pain.

She stepped back and let her attention fall to his groin. His cock was ramrod straight and bobbing gently under her scrutiny. Seeing him so hard and so helpless aroused her to the point of weakness, but she ran the switch lightly along his cock, the same severe expression on her face, then tapped it very gently from side to side, playing with it, enjoying Decker's humiliation.

'You insult me with that pathetic little prick,' she hissed, and slapped the switch across his exposed buttocks.

'You'll pay for this,' he growled, and received another lash for his insubordination. 'Fuck you,' he retorted. And another lash. Another retort, and another blow, until she suspected that he was pleasuring himself by making her hit him. The control had shifted, and it was time to claw it back. She slapped him hard on the face then thrust her tongue down his throat, smearing the red lipstick all over his mouth. Then she gagged him, using one of her white silk scarves between his teeth like a bit. He was still powerfully erect, even more so after the whipping she had given him. She knelt down before him and toyed with his cock, wrapping her hand around the shaft and watching how the foreskin wrinkled and tightened around the large, bulbous glans. Above her his eyes were slitted with arousal, and he was unable to hold back from pushing his hips towards her. She bent her head and licked his cock daintily from root to tip, holding back from doing what he really wanted until he was least expecting it. He bit back a groan as she finally enclosed him in her hot mouth, pulling on him, really getting into it as he tried not to buck against his chains.

She decided he was enjoying himself a little too much, so she stopped, removed her panties and sat in a chair that she had positioned opposite his. It was so close that when she spread her legs wide, her juicy, pink centre was only inches away from his cock. She hooked her legs over the chair arms to give him an uninterrupted view up her darkly glistening slit, the plump lips slightly apart and engorged with arousal. She picked up her favourite vibrator and lubricated it with her saliva before pushing the large round end between her sex lips.

'You've seen me do this before,' she said, her voice catching as her inner muscles tensed against the thick tool. 'You could have fucked me right then, but you didn't. You were too afraid. You're a coward and this is your punishment.' She drew the vibe out again and held it against his nose, letting him smell her scent. Then to his lips, pulling the gag down just enough to force the end of the vibrator between his lips.

'Suck it,' she demanded. He didn't want to, she could tell by the humiliated anger in his eyes. It was against his macho nature to take something so similar to another man's organ in his mouth.

'Lick it, you low down piece of shit,' she commanded again, and this time he obeyed her, tentatively at first, then hungrily as he tasted her essence. She slid the vibrator inside her again and gave him more translucent juice to suck at. It smeared across his face, making it glisten. She climbed off his lap and grabbed his hair, forcing him to look in the mirror at his wrecked image, the lipstick all over his face, smudged with glossy pussy juice. His semi-tumescent cock hung down as if in supplication. She went behind him and replaced the gag. She tweaked at his nipples, twiddling them like the knobs on an ancient radio until they were hard and crinkled. His cock began to rise once more.

'You just can't help yourself, can you?' she said contemptuously, flicking at his cock with the switch. It rose further, adding to his silent humiliation. He glared at her as she held the vibe against his balls, letting the buzzing sensation shimmy up his body. Then it was inside her again, switched to Pump, her hand holding it in place to stop it falling out. Her eyes glazed as the fat vibe moved up and down inside her. Her other hand sought out her clit, a fat pink pearl amidst her cloud of pubic fluff. Her gentle strokes became rapid as the pleasure intensified, heightened by the dark look in Decker's eyes. She could feel his steaming anger, his frustration and shame at being so blatantly weak with desire. His cock strained to reach her, but he was thwarted by the cuffs. She came in a series of delicious shudders, feasting her eyes on his cock, jamming the vibe violently inside herself. After recovering for a few seconds she moved forwards, almost sitting on his lap, rubbing her breasts all over his face and chest, her pussy less than an inch away from the tip of his cock. She toyed with the bow on her bra, tugging it with infinite slowness, then a final flourish, letting her breasts slap against his face. He tried to nuzzle into them, but she slapped him again, feeling almost drunk with power. She sank down on his cock, riding it like a rodeo horse in slow motion. His eyes drooped closed as he was overcome by her nearness. She slapped him again.

'Look at me, damn it!' He looked at her, and she saw blatant, raw need in their very depths. The tension in his body told her that he wanted her to go faster, to really grind herself on to him, but she fucked him selfishly, uncaring of his need, concentrating on her own.

'I could get used to having my own, personal sex slave,' she mused, twining her arms around his neck. She closed her eyes, losing herself in the joy of having him totally at her mercy.

'I could get used to spanking you raw,' he growled.

Her eyes flew open. He had removed the gag, and was holding up one hand to show her that the cuffs were no longer doing their job.

'How did you . . . ?'

He flicked his wrist, and too late she remembered his trick with the knife that she had seen once before, when he had pulled it on Mike Bradley.

'My party piece,' he said with a shark-like smile.

She suddenly realised that her situation was hazardous at best. He had been toying with her all along, knowing he could get free but choosing not to. At once she was both angry and in awe of his self-control, which he hadn't lost at all, damn him.

He picked her up and slammed her against the wall, and started fucking her with such raw power she felt weak with the need to come. Then he threw her on the bed, flipping her over on to her front and fastening the cuffs around her wrists. She tried to jab at him with the heels of her boots but he swatted her away and gave her buttocks a healthy smack that resounded around the room. In the mirror she could see him stripping off his shirt. The profile of his cock looked massive and, despite her sudden apprehension, a rush of moisture made the inside of her thighs very sticky. He told her to kneel up and then held her down with a firm hand between her shoulder blades, so her bottom stuck high in the air. In the mirror she saw his cock disappearing into her body and god, did she feel it. He gave her the same selfish treatment, arrogantly screwing her at his own pace, despite her muffled pleading.

'I'm sorry, Miss Lovell but I seem to recall that you don't think I'm man enough for you,' he said evenly, picking up the vibrator. He spat on her rosy arse hole and lubricated it, stretching her buttocks wide apart. With his cock still deep inside her she held her breath and waited. The brutish round end of the vibe pushed against her rectal muscles, reminding her of Tex, JD and Wayne. Then she had had two cocks fighting for territory inside her. The memory was so erotic that she relaxed, letting the thick vibe in. It was larger than Tex had been and, when Decker turned the control on to Pump, she could not help a base, animal sound of pleasure. He switched the control again, this time to make the vibe squirm inside her.

'No! Oh, God, not that,' she moaned, her lust suddenly spiked with fear that it could actually do some damage.

'How about this?' The vibe began to buzz. 'And this as well? Come on, Daisy, give it like you gave it to those biker boys.' She could hear the edge of anger to his voice as he began to thrust into her as well, ignoring her pitiful moaning. He was drawing pleasure from the vibe as well as from her, his other hand on the cuffs around her wrists, using them to ride her hard. He came quickly, cursing and swearing, his cock jumping against the throbbing vibe in her backside. After a moment's respite he pulled out of her, leaving the vibe in place but switching it off. He slapped her buttocks.

'You deserve to be left like that all night,' he said sternly.

Daisy lay limply on the bed, still stuffed with latex cock, semen oozing wetly between her thighs. She heard him go downstairs, and for one horrible moment she thought he had left the house.

Minutes later he was back, unfastening the cuffs. He removed the vibe and pulled her to her feet, leading her into the second bedroom.

'We're going out to dinner. Get dressed,' he said, motioning to the garments on the bed.

Obediently she put on the Lejaby black and cream lace bra and panties he had laid out for her. She was relieved they weren't red latex or cheap black lace. The bra was cut to hold her breasts high and out-in-front, creating an impressive valley between them. The panties were frothy and delicate, with a tiny lacing detail fastened by a bow just above her buttocks.

'OK, now what?' she asked. He held out the next item, a short black trench coat that tied at the waist. She looked at it. 'Shouldn't I, like, put a dress on first?'

He slowly shook his head. She hesitated, but the glacial look in his eyes was enough to make her realise it wasn't worth arguing. She put the coat on. It swung around her thighs as she turned, just above her lace stocking tops. Finally he gave her a pair of black patent stilettos with very spiky heels. She looked like a high-class tart, and her backside felt very cold and exposed. She did not like his smile as she took his arm, but the thought of him being so aroused in public by her appearance overrode any lingering shame.

His driving was aggressive, like the music he was playing at high volume. Nickleback, 'How You Remind Me', a coarse, embittered anthem that both excited and worried her. His mood was dangerous, but she could not work out how or why. Before they reached the restaurant he took a detour off the highway to one of the viewpoints overlooking Warren Plains. Parking in a dark spot under some low lying trees, he told her in no uncertain terms to get in the back of the car. He straddled her on his lap, stroking her inner thighs casually with his thumbs. Outside, steady rain was falling, drumming against the car roof, making the silence inside the car even more potent.

'What did you do today?' He asked, so unexpectedly that she was completely thrown.

'I . . . visited an old friend. In New York.' It sounded like a lie, although it was true. She didn't want to say it was Chico Mendoza, because they had not talked about him yet, and he wouldn't understand their relationship. And right then, Chico wasn't the person she was concerned about. In the almost total darkness she could barely see Decker's face, but what she could see was not the man she had been with for the past week.

A loud bang on the window made them both jump like startled rabbits. Then dazzling light, accentuated by the raindrops rolling down the windows, splintered into a thousand blinding fragments. Daisy wrapped her arms around Decker, trembling with shock.

The car was locked, so whoever was outside would not be able to get in. They readjusted their clothing with lightning speed as the window was pounded again. Bright torchlight pushed against the glass, hurting their eyes.

'Who are they?' Daisy's eyes were wide and frightened. 'Cops? Surely not cops.'

'No, it's Enrico Mendoza.' Decker reached into the central console and found his gun, a compact automatic Berreta. His face had changed to anger, directly solely at her. 'Why did you have to go to him today, you stupid bitch? You've led him right to us!'

Daisy stopped fiddling with her coat and stared. 'What the hell do you mean?'

Then a familiar voice. 'Come on, Decker, show your face you treacherous fuck!'

'Shit, it's Dad!' Daisy's eyes widened in horror. Decker went for the door but her hand stopped him. 'You're going out there? Are you crazy? He'll kill you!'

There was a vicious kick on the BMW's expensive paintwork.

'Hey, watch my car!' Decker shouted.

'Max, you cocksucking bastard!' Something heavy thudded against the passenger door. 'Come out, damn you!' Another kick. And another. The car rocked.

'Just mind my fucking car!' Decker snarled through the glass.

'Let my daughter out of there, you sonofabitch!'

Daisy had scrambled into the driver's seat. The keys were in the ignition.

'Leave it!' Decker hissed. 'I can talk us out of this!'

'Like hell I will. He's gone stark raving mad!' The seat was too far away for her to reach the pedals. Feverishly she surveyed the vast array of buttons, looking for ways to move the seat forward. There was another hard thump, this time on the windshield. Her father now had a baseball bat.

'Come out, Decker! Get your cowardly ass out here!'

'Don't you dare go out there,' Daisy shot back at him. She had located the seat adjustment and started the engine. When she found reverse and stamped on the accelerator the force almost threw Decker into the dashboard as she slewed backwards. He dropped the gun and it landed between her legs. Screaming as if he had thrown a poisonous reptile down there she swerved, brushing the gun to the floor. She fumbled for wipers so she could at least see, found indicators instead, then hit lucky. As the rain was wiped away she saw pinned in the blinding beam of the BMW's lights two lean silhouettes and the unmistakable bulk of her father, his hands shielding his eyes. She thrust forward, scattering them to the four winds, and fish-tailed out of the entrance. She hit the highway sideways, spraying assorted vehicles into the outer lanes. The speedometer quivered at ninety. She forced herself to slow down before they aquaplaned into a wall. Her whole body was trembling.

'How the fuck did he find us?' She was shrieking at him, but could not control it. He had picked himself up from the rear footwell and was perching on the seat, holding on to the headrests with white-knuckled hands.

'Slow down! They won't follow us. Just mind ... the car.'

'Fuck the car! How did they find us?' She sounded shrill. She took deep breaths to calm down. 'And what the hell were you saying about Enrico Mendoza? What has he got to do with anything?'

'Turn off here. Find somewhere we can talk.' He motioned to an exit rushing towards them. They drove through New Jersey suburbs, glowing with sodium lighting. Eventually she found a small, silent shopping mall and parked so they could see potential danger approaching. For a moment they just sat, listening to the rain, letting calm seep back into the confines of the car.

'What the hell has this got to do with Enrico Mendoza?' she demanded again.

Decker lit a cigarette and blew the smoke out into the night. 'Why don't you tell me?'

'No word play, Decker, I'm sick of it. Just tell me what's going on.'

Decker drew moodily on the cigarette. 'Felix had you watched when you lost your job. He wanted to know what you would do next, and he didn't like it when you didn't go straight back home. That's how this whole damned thing started, because he suspected that you and Chico were seeing each other again.'

'That was imaginative of him,' Daisy said acidly.

'When he confronted Enrico Mendoza, he alluded that you and he had been lovers, so Felix threatened to ruin him. Then Enrico made some comment about you which Felix took as a counter-threat.' He lit a fresh smoke with the stubby remains of the old one and flipped the butt out of the window. 'I was sent all the way to frigging Arizona to protect your spoilt little hide from getting hurt. But, as it turns out, it's all been a waste of my time, because you've been screwing both father and son behind everyone's back. So now it's your turn to start talking.'

She resented the sarcasm in his voice. It took her back a week, when he was judging every move she made and finding fault with it. 'My father and Enrico have been bitching at each other for years. What's new?'

Decker laughed mirthlessly. 'Only the photographs some slimy dick took of you, Chico and one large Afro-American. I've seen them, Daisy, so don't try and bullshit your way out of it.'

'I wasn't going to,' she said quietly. The acid in his voice made her feel sick. 'Enrico wouldn't hurt me. What-ever thing he has going with my father, it's nothing to do with me. We're friends.'

'Yeah, friends. Like you were looking pretty friendly this morning in Central Park.'

She glared at him. 'So that's been your problem. You followed me! Thanks a lot.'

'It's my job.'

'The hell it is! You didn't trust me, did you? You were checking up on me!'

'Good job I did,' he said bitterly.

'Whatever you're thinking, it isn't like that! We were lovers a long time ago. Not any more.'

'I saw you kissing him!'

'He was kissing me! He wants me to go back to him but I said no, because I have you. That's before I find out what a hypocritical bastard you are. All that bullshit about being honest, and all along you were lying through your teeth to me! I've never been anything but honest to you, Max. What you see is what you get.'

'And Chico Mendoza? Do I get him as well?'

'Oh, for God's sake, Chico is gay!'

It was his turn to stare. 'You expect me to believe that? What about the other guy?'

'Gay as well. Not interested in me.'

'He seemed pretty interested,' Decker muttered sulkily.

'I was their lapdog for the night, that's all. Believe me, you've seen worse since.'

'Yeah, I have.' He sucked savagely on the cigarette. 'Better run back to Daddy. Tell him your personal lapdog has just quit. Why don't I call you a cab?'

She felt hot tears pricking the backs of her eyes. Focus, she thought angrily to herself. She didn't want to see her father right then, nor did she want to go back to the house and risk him confronting her there. And she definitely didn't want to be with Decker, now that he had decided she was worthless to him. Her heel brushed against something in the footwell. It was the gun. She offered up a silent prayer and picked it up.

He glanced over, then did a double-take. The gun was aimed unwaveringly in his direction.

'Get out.'

He laughed at her. 'Excuse me?'

'You heard. Remove your presence from this vehicle. Right now.'

'Don't be fucking stupid.' He grabbed for the gun and she pulled the trigger. The sound was deafening in the confined space. A small hole had pierced the upholstery above his head. He uncurled like a wary hedgehog.

'Jesus Christ! You could have killed me!'

'No, Decker. Before I do that I want to do you serious bodily harm. Don't tempt me, just get out of the fucking car.' She released the safety catch again, and this time the gun was pointed unflinchingly towards his groin. He finally saw the shimmering anger in her eyes.

'Daisy . . .'

'Get out before I do my father a big fat favour.'

He obviously decided that she was serious, because he resignedly got out of the car and slammed the door. She threw two quarters contemptuously on to the tarmac by his feet.

'Why don't you call a cab?'

She drove on, fighting back tears. Rain still spiked the windscreen, hindering her visibility further. She did not know where she was going, or whether she should just turn around and get him back in the car. As she decided to do just that she came to a T-junction. Behind her headlights were approaching fast. Too fast. As she stopped, the other car didn't. It ploughed into her back end as she ducked down to avoid the coming whiplash. When she looked up again, she was being pushed further on to the highway. She jammed on the brakes, but the other car kept pushing and pushing. Horribly aware of the eighteen-wheeler bearing down on top of her, she fumbled for the gear stick. Automatic, not manual, fuck-wit. As the monster truck threatened to crush her into oblivion she hit Drive and stamped on the accelerator.

The wheels span for a horrible split second before the car flew forward, its screaming engine almost drowned out by the truck's blaring horn. In the rearview mirror she could see her pursuers start the chase again.

Survival was her main focus now. The men were her father's heavies, and they thought she was Max Decker. If they got too close they would shoot first and ask questions later. There was nowhere to hide at this time of night. The towns were all too small. There was only one place she could run to, and to get there she had to get to the main highway.

As they hurtled down the hill towards a small village she remembered a short cut. The left turn was hidden and very tight and she nearly missed it. A solid little maple bounced her back on the tarmac with an expensive sounding thud as she stamped her foot on the accelerator, forcing the BMW up the steep slope. It could have been a bad mistake. The hill was notorious for grounding, its surface buckled by potholes that grew worse every winter. Dense forest grew up on either side, and the highway was still three endless miles away.

'Come on, baby, come on,' she muttered, pressing on and upward. The V8 engine responded eagerly to her touch, launching her up each extreme bump, but the long chassis was not built for off-roading and bitched about it every time they landed belly-down. Two men in a dark Lincoln were stubbornly behind her, headlights swaying crazily in her vision, disorientating her.

It seemed to last forever, but then they were on smooth ground, like calm waters after a rough sea, taking corners with frightening speed. She crooned to the beast at her feet, telling herself to keep calm, keep her wits. The rain had eased slightly, although the road was slick and deep puddles hid crater-like potholes that made her teeth rattle. The comforting ribbon of lights that marked

Interstate 78 grew nearer, but she wondered what the hell to do once she hit New York.

Once on the fast road they were still behind her, her nemesis on cruise control. She could lose them easily in the BMW but the last thing she needed was to be pulled over for speeding. This time a blowjob would definitely not get her out of trouble. In the dark she had the impression of a bullet-shaped head on thick shoulders, but his face was in shadow.

'Well it won't be Dad. He drives too fucking slow.' She spoke out loud, drawing comfort from her own voice. It crackled with barely supressed hysteria.

She remembered the hands-free phone. She would be in Manhattan before she worked out how to use the memory to find her father's number, so she hoped that the number she was clawing back from the recesses of her mind was accurate. She was told by a mechanical voice to leave a message, which she did in no uncertain terms. She told him to call off his dogs and leave Max Decker alone, and how dare he break her trust yet again, keeping her under surveillance just so he could keep tabs on her love life. The more she talked, the angrier she became, until she realised she had used up all the message space and had been cut off. She threw the phone down in disgust and checked the mirror.

The men were still there, doggedly tailing her. Her foot pressed down on the accelerator as she saw the Manhattan skyline appear over the brow of the hill. Through the Turnpike, she slowed just enough to toss in a quarter before merging with the other traffic. As she raced through the Tunnel they were still there, attached to her tail like a guided missile.

A vertical sign advertising a small parking lot gave her the idea she was searching for, and a gridlock caused by late night theatre-goers on their way home helped her achieve it. Soon she was surrounded by cars, and not one of them was the one she was trying to escape from. The lights changed and the mass pushed forward. As they were about to change back to red she saw a small opening and took it. The car jolted with a bump on its left side, but she ignored the angrily blaring horn and pressed on. She took the next turning and found herself on 42nd Street.

There were any number of small parking lots to choose from, marked by vertical neon. With a final all-round glance that revealed no gun-toting men she eased through one of the narrow entrances.

Parking the car in the darkest, most easily escapable slot possible, she tried her father again. He picked up almost immediately and sandblasted her ear with obscenities.

'I'm gonna flay you alive, you cocksucking sonofabitch!'

'If you do, you'll never see me again,' she said coldly.

She heard him strangle back the next vituperative outpouring. 'Daisy? Where the hell are you?'

'Keeping away from your heavies. They tried to kill me! I meant what I said, Dad. You won't see me for dust after this if you do anything to hurt Max Decker, or Chico or Enrico Mendoza. What the hell do I have to do to get through to you?'

There was a short silence. When he next spoke he sounded as if he had had enough of the whole thing. 'Where is Decker?' he asked wearily.

'Gone. I fired him on your behalf. And, just for your information, it's over. I seduced him, enjoyed him for a bit and dumped him. End of story.' She swallowed the catch in her voice. Felix cursed softly at the other end of the line.

'It's OK, honey, I'm not mad at you. Just come on home.'

'You've no right to be mad at me! I'm the one angry with you, remember?'

'Yes ... that's right, I'm sorry, honey. Just come home.'

'No. I'll call you when I can face it without feeling sick. Remember I am this close to doing something no daughter should ever consider doing to their father. Don't make me do it.' She cut the connection before he could ask her what that thing was, which was just as well, because she didn't know the answer herself.

Before leaving the car she made sure she hid the gun under the passenger seat and rescued all the loose change she could find. It amounted to two dollars and a dime. She had no bag, no phone, no credit cards, nothing except for the short trenchcoat that barely covered her ass and the memory of an apartment address in the Upper West Side. She had no option but to walk, as the fee for the parking lot was five dollars that she didn't have just yet. On reflection, going in there hadn't been her smartest of moves, but under the circumstances she had greater things to worry about.

Once out in the street she began to regret her impetuousness. The wind sliced through the thin coat with cruel ease. She expected to be challenged at any moment as she flitted through the emptying streets towards her destination. Eventually she found the address she was looking for. The doorman raised nothing more than a faint smile at her risqué attire. No doubt he had seen worse. Inside, the foyer was hushed. At the reception desk she was asked whom she wanted to see. After a slight hesitation he picked up the phone and spoke quietly. Five minutes after that, the elevator door opened with a soft ping and a small woman stepped out.

'Come this way, please.' She seemed to see nothing odd with Daisy's minimal dress either. They ascended in silence to the penthouse suite. On the other side of the door, Enrico Mendoza was waiting for her. A tall, very beautiful woman was with him. She gave Daisy a haughty glare and took her place in the elevator.

Enrico led her into his palatial apartment. On the dining table were the remains of a sumptuous meal, softly flickering candles and champagne.

'You didn't have to send her away,' Daisy said immediately, but Enrico hushed her.

'She doesn't care. I've already paid her. Champagne?'

The small woman materialized with a slender flute filled with Bollinger. As if in a dream state Daisy took it from her and she disappeared again.

'This is an unexpected pleasure,' Enrico said.

'Not for me it isn't.' Daisy realised how ambiguous the words sounded. 'What I mean is, I wouldn't have come, but I need your help. I don't have anyone else. I'm sorry.' Why she added the last bit, she did not know. Enrico watched her with impenetrable dark eyes.

'Why don't I take your coat?' he asked.

Daisy clutched it tighter around her body. 'No! It's fine, honest.'

'It obviously isn't, otherwise you wouldn't be here. You said so yourself.' He drew very close to her and undid the belt. She looked away as he opened the coat and saw her stunning black and cream lace underwear.

'It isn't what you think,' she said, pulling away from him. He stood behind her and massaged her tense shoulders.

'You come to me, asking for my help, dressed like that. What am I supposed to think?' He pushed her hair to one side and kissed the back of her neck, a superheated, moist kiss full of passion. She closed her eyes, thinking of Decker, of his contempt, his stupid jealousy. She would never get through to him. Their relationship seemed destined to be blighted by misunderstanding, however hard she tried. Enrico Mendoza was easing the trenchcoat from her shoulders, letting it fall to the floor. Ever the consummate Casanova, he did not grab at her breasts immediately. Instead he slipped his hands around her waist and let their warmth seep into her womb. She could feel him, warm and hard against her buttocks. Despite her misery she could sense the tremors of answering lust, triggered by memories of sensual night past, her sex growing full and steamy with need.

'Will you help me?' she whispered.

'That depends on you.' His fingers walked down to her thigh, stroking tiny circles on her skin, finding the soft crease at the top of her leg, lingering there for a moment before seeking out the fluffy curls underneath her panties. When his fingertip found her cleft and stroked the soft skin inside, she caught her breath, leaning back against him. The buttons on his waistcoat pressed into her back. She could smell exotic, fruity aftershave with the undertones of cigars and the fine cashmere of his jacket. Breathing him in, her pussy creamed up at his expensive scent. There was a wet, sticky sound in the silence as his fingers sank into her molten flesh.

'Oh yes,' he whispered hotly. 'I think we may be able to help each other.'

Turning around, she met his kiss. He tasted of spices and champagne, his lips much softer than Decker's. She mustn't keep thinking of him, she thought angrily to herself as she liberated Enrico from his jacket and started on his waistcoat, their lips still locked. His clothes were soon scattered over the carpet as he bore her down to a white fox fur rug by the softly flickering fire. By flame light alone he reacquainted himself with her body, every shadow and crevice, and she remembered his, as hard and toned as he had been five years before. The smattering of silky hair on his chest was still dark with only the occasional hint of silver, matching that on his temples. He stroked her with an artist's touch, as if trying to commit her to permanent memory. She sensed his feeling of bittersweet joy and resolved to make the memory good for him. He made no attempt to enter her just yet. He was a man who liked to take his time.

'So what do you need me to do?' he asked, as they lay entwined together.

She stroked his smooth jaw. 'How did this feud with my father start? What did you do to him?'

Enrico traced a slow circle on her shoulder. 'Actually I saved him from ruin, but he didn't see it like that. I could see that the business we were investing in wasn't going to make it and I pulled out, knowing that it would force him to do the same. I think he resented the fact that I saw the pitfalls first. Who knows?'

'Didn't you try to explain to him?'

'You know Felix. He shoots first, asks questions later. After he accused me of dishonesty and insulted my country, I had no intention of trying to justify myself to a bigot and a racist.'

Daisy nuzzled at his nut-brown nipple, sucking it gently between her lips. 'So you're saying that male pride has kept you enemies all this time. His and yours.'

'If you're asking me to apologise to him then you're wasting your time. I have nothing to be sorry for.'

'What about threatening to harm me?'

'I didn't. He misunderstood me, as he always has.'

'You were just winding him up?'

Enrico laughed softly. 'In a word, yes. I wanted to see him squirm for all the insults he has thrown at me.'

Daisy sat up, irritated at his lazy smile. 'When are you two going to grow up? I've had my vacation ruined by a twisted freak of a bodyguard because of your desire to see my father squirm!'

Enrico drew her back into his arms. 'Is that the twisted freak you're in love with?'

Daisy didn't answer. She lay her cheek against Enrico's lazily pumping heart and let him stroke her.

'Would you come with me to see Dad tomorrow?' she asked finally. 'I told him he'd never see me again if he hurt Decker, or you or Chico, but I don't trust him to listen to me. He never has before. The whole thing is one big fucking mess and I want to sort it out once and for all. Maybe if you're willing to compromise . . .'

Enrico pushed her back on to the rug and began pressing kisses over her face, soothing her with each one. Holding her hands together above her head, he ran his fingers lightly over her body until her whole skin surface was shimmering with the desire to be touched.

'Please,' she whispered. 'I'll do anything.'

'You don't have to whore yourself to me, Daisy,' he said gently, continuing his worship of her body.

She laughed softly. 'You could have said that two hours ago.'

'I'm not a saint, my love.'

He continued to kiss her, working his way down her body leaving velvet imprints of passion that made her greedy for more. He licked at her nipples with the relish of a connoisseur, admiring the way they crinkled and grew under his touch. She mewed softly and arched her back as he tugged at them very gently with his teeth, batting his tongue against them, then gathered her breasts together and tongue-teased them until her legs opened wide and she was pleading for him to eat her. Obeying her ragged command, he plunged his face into her dewy cleft. His tongue was wickedly skilled, drawing her juices out of her until she could feel the dampness on the rug. She gripped his thick, silky hair, riding his tongue as the first waves of orgasm washed over her. More and more, faster and faster, the tip of his tongue fluttering so frustratingly over her clitoris that she ground herself upon him, screaming for more. As she was jolting from the aftershocks he reared up and speared her deep with his cock, his eyes feverish. Their mouths locked in a musky kiss, seasoned with her juices, as she wrapped her legs around his waist and rode his passion with equal fervour. He came with two huge spasms, his cry long and drawn-out, ending on a whispered gasp. His eyes widened, grew hazy, and then he collapsed on top of her.

After a moment his weight was too much, so she tried to nudge him away.

'Hey, you're squashing me,' she protested mildly. He did not move.

'Rico? Stop fooling, baby, you're about to rupture my spleen.'

Still no movement. Suddenly frantic, she wriggled out from underneath him and tried to turn him over. He was too heavy so she turned his head. His eyes were wide open and she couldn't feel a pulse.

'Tania!' She screamed to his maid. 'Call 911!'

16

The funeral of Enrico Mendoza took place in a quiet cemetery just outside the Bronx. The post-mortem revealed that a massive coronary aneurysm had killed him. Daisy was still in shock, supported by Chico, who had taken his father's unexpected demise far better than she had. For days she had felt guilty, thinking it was her fault, until Chico pointed out that it wasn't exactly a bad way to go. As they stood around the coffin, she saw in the distance a figure, watching by his car. She knew the burly outline of her father anywhere, and she was grateful for his discreet support. He was a changed man. Enrico's untimely departure had made him think about his own mortality. He said he was determined never to alienate himself from Daisy again. For the first time ever, she truly believed him.

She accompanied Chico to the lawyer's office, where the Will was being read. He wanted her there to help him to cope with being disinherited but, as it turned out, Enrico had left the coffee plantation and most of his considerable fortune to his only son after all, with an endnote that had been added on the afternoon of his death. 'Tell him to live his life.'

Within weeks, Chico was seen stepping out with Piers Molyneaux. He dropped his extravagantly camp airs and became quite normal again; as normal as a millionaire playboy could be, anyway.

Enrico had also left a substantial amount of cash to Daisy. She was stunned, because she had never truly appreciated that she meant that much to him. Not five million dollars worth, anyway. After Felix heard that news, he grudgingly admitted that maybe he had misjudged Enrico, ending with, 'I never could understand fucking foreigners.'

Daisy was restless. Her new fortune didn't make any difference to the fact that she needed something to do. Decker had vanished from the face of the earth, but a parcel had arrived via UPS a few days after Enrico's funeral, with ten thousand dollars in it and a note saying, 'now I owe you nothing.' She could sense the bitterness behind the words, and it kick-started the yearning for him that she barely had time to think about until then.

She went to his apartment but it was locked up. The owner said he had left three weeks before, taking only his clothes with him. No, he hadn't said where he was going.

She tried the police next, to see if they knew where he would have gone, or whether he had any relatives, but no one had heard of him. His name wasn't on the computer anywhere. She asked if any green BMWs had been reported stolen. There was nothing on their books. All she had left of him was a dented car and painful memories.

Chico came to see her. Felix had actually rung him to say he was worried about her. He pitched up one evening with a Chinese takeaway and a bottle of Australian Shiraz.

'Love sucks, honey, and I can see it's sucking the life out of you.'

They laid the food out on the table and opened the wine. She wanted to hear about Piers. Was he for real, or a gold digger out for Chico's stack of cash?

'Quite frankly, I don't care,' Chico drawled, immaculate in a dark suit and looking eerily like his father. 'He's a good fuck, and I can afford to keep him happy until I get bored with him.'

She laughed then, for the first time in weeks. 'Honestly, you're the coffee producers' answer to Elton John.'

'With real hair,' he reminded her. 'Anyway, stop circling the subject. You and Max Decker, a pseudonym if ever I heard one. Still no luck?'

'No,' she sighed. 'I just want to see him once more, to explain that who he thinks I am isn't who I really am, and to give me a chance, and . . .'

'To ball his brains out? As much as I'd like to say you're wasting your time, I don't think you are. He sounds like a very damaged human being who needs you, whether he wants to admit that or not. So why don't you go back to Colorado and find him?'

'He's not there, Chico. I've already checked.'

'Well, excuse me, but I haven't noticed you slipping off to the desert recently. How hard did you actually look? Did you ring that cliff dwelling you stayed at? Maybe he's there, looking at the sunset and waiting for you. You can't go on like this, Daisy. You'll end up like I did.'

Daisy shoved a pork ball into her mouth to give her time to answer. The truth was, she was scared to look any further. The trail had gone cold and she had been disheartened by the constant disappointment, coupled with the dread of rejection even if she did find him again. So she had just spent the last month sitting on her ass and moping around. Chico was right. It couldn't go on.

'Fine! I'll damned well go to Colorado and find him,' she declared suddenly.

Chico looked up from his rice bowl with a small smile. 'Better book a flight to Phoenix then.'

Daisy shook her head. 'I'm going to drive it. You've got to help me pack after you've finished your supper.'

Chico looked uncomprehending. 'Drive? Just give me one logical reason why.'

'If I find him, I want to give him his car back, and . . . if it works out, I might not be coming back.'

'Fair enough,' Chico said evenly, 'just don't ask me to explain to Felix.'

The next morning she was on the road, feeling a sense of purpose that had been missing for weeks. Three days she travelled, barely registering as concrete made way for green waving fields of corn and finally, the aspen forests and golden sands of Colorado. She arrived in Durango late one night and booked a room, too exhausted to go to the Chieftain's Rest right away. The day had been hot and humid, sapping the energy out of her despite being in an air-conditioned, automatic car for the last two thousand or so miles. Just before she turned the television off she checked the Weather Channel, as was her habit. Two large areas of low pressure seemed to be on a collision course over New Mexico and threatening severe weather over the next twenty-four hours. It was highly unusual, the newscaster said, and they would be watching developments very closely. Daisy felt slightly uneasy, but she couldn't put a finger on why. Severe storms were hardly uncommon in that part of the world.

The next morning the heat hit her as soon as she walked out of her room. It was a gluey heat, sticking to her skin and making her aware of her own breath. Boiling cumulo-nimbus clouds billowed up in the South and were moving swiftly towards her. And in the East, another storm, even larger and anvil-shaped, was already darkening the sky with thick grey rolls of cloud. Soon she would need to run and duck, but first there was work to do.

She drove to the Chieftain's Rest and stopped outside the small office on the ledge of the cliff, feeling sick with disappointment. Across the large sign with all its dire warnings was another, saying Closed For Renovations in large red letters. The office was locked when she tried the door. There were no other cars, apart from her own. The place was deserted.

She drove to the diner a mile down the road to ask if they knew what had happened. On the way she could hear thunder, distant but constant and foreboding. In her rearview mirror, the storm was moving towards her at frightening speed.

In the diner, two customers stared disconsolately at the television screen, listening to the weather. The bored boy behind the counter served her with a Coke and a doughnut, and she asked about the Chieftain's Rest.

'The old lady sold up about a month ago. She's running a place in Lake Havasu now.'

'Who did she sell it to?'

The boy shrugged. 'Someone from the East.'

'Do you know his name?' Daisy felt the first tremors of sick excitement.

The two old customers looked up. 'Cutter, I think. Dan Cutter. He drives an old Benz. Keeps to himself.'

The other man harrumphed loudly. 'Apart from the hookers, that is.'

Daisy tried to keep her face immobile. 'Hookers?'

'You ain't his wife, are you?'

'Just a friend,' Daisy said, the words choking her.

'Oh, that's OK then. He has hookers there, never less than two at a time. They sometimes come in here afterwards. Whatever he does to 'em, sure makes 'em hungry, heh, heh!'

The younger man must have guessed that she was upset. He gave her a kind, gap-toothed smile. 'None of them look as ladylike as you though, missy.'

'Um, thanks. As I said, I'm just a friend.' She left her Coke and doughnut on the counter and fled back outside. The sky was getting darker by the minute, and every low hanging finger of cloud seemed to be beckoning to some stronger force, as yet unseen but definitely felt, by the absolute stillness of the atmosphere.

Back at the Chieftain's Rest she parked next to two cars that had arrived in her absence. One was a black Mercedes SL500.

She looked around for some way to get down to the dwelling itself, finally finding a wooden gate half-hidden in a brand new fence designed to keep intruders out. But it was unlocked, as if the occupant was around somewhere. She negotiated the slope and scrambled down the ladder, trying to check the shaking in her legs. Looking up, the sky seemed to be almost on top of her, bulging white sacs of cloud that Keith had told her were mammatus. For a moment she hung on the ladder, transfixed by the following grey cloud. Was it rotating in the middle? It was a very subtle, slow movement, but it sent a chill down her spine. Forcing her attention back to the ladder, she reached the bottom and called out. There was no answer.

Something appeared in her peripheral vision, making her spin around. On the adobe wall next to her was a cat. It chirped at her and began washing its paw. She stared at it, its silky fur the same colour as the sandstone clay it sat on. Its face and paws were the colour of bitter chocolate.

'Delilah!' she exclaimed, reaching out to stroke the cat's head. The cat nuzzled against her hand with the beginnings of a deep purr. Then lightning spiked not too far distant and she jumped gracefully away, disappearing deep into the cliff dwelling. Daisy followed her like Alice had followed the rabbit. Wandering through the kiva, she heard rock music coming from one of the rooms above. Nirvana this time. *Come As You Are*, which she thought a tad ironic. The thunder was almost continuous now, accompanied by prolonged flickers of bright lightning. She walked up the steps to the room and looked in.

He was on the bed with two young women, loose-limbed, long-haired, native American girls. She could not see his face because one of the girls was sitting on it, kissing her companion, who was riding his cock. Their breathy sighs were lost under the crashing music echoing around the room. The atmosphere was one seething of raw brutal lust and booze. Two bottles of Jack Daniels, one opened and already half empty, on the table, sat together with an ashtray filled with stale cigarette butts. He began to thrust up into the second girl with brutal force, sharpening her cries. The other girl sucked frantically on her nipple, her hand between her legs. Daisy could see his hands gripping the thighs of the girl on his face, squeezing them cruelly. He slapped her hard.

'Suck my cock,' he snarled, tipping her off on to the mattress. Then he saw Daisy.

His face changed. The mask of lust was wiped away, replaced by dawning horror, mirroring her own. He snapped his fingers at the girls.

'Go!' he commanded, as they scrambled for their clothes. They ran past Daisy, not giving her a second glance. He wiped his mouth to remove the traces of lipstick and whisky and stepped towards her, but Daisy wasn't going to let him come anywhere near her. She turned and fled, hearing him call her name above the thunder. She scrabbled for the ladder, choking back sobs. He had found his trousers with record speed and was pursuing her. She was vaguely aware that it had started to rain, but she paid it no heed. Thunder rolled almost directly above them.

'Daisy, come back! It isn't safe!' He was following her up the ladder. She hit the ground and ran up the narrow path, her feet slithering on mud made slick by the increasingly heavy downpour. The day had suddenly turned black. She didn't know where she was going, only that she had to escape Max Decker.

On the cliff edge he caught her wrist and spun her around. Filled with impotent fury, she punched at his bare chest, screaming that she hated him, over and over again. She went for his eyes and he slapped her hard, knocking her to the ground. All around her the rain had turned into hard little chunks of hail, stinging her skin. It hissed and popped and bounced as it hit the ground. He pulled her to her feet.

'I'm sorry,' he shouted above the wind. 'We've got to find shelter. It isn't safe out here!'

'You're damned right it isn't. How dare you run out on me!'

His eyes widened in disbelief. 'You were the one who went back to Mendoza! What the hell was I supposed to do? Live like a fucking monk?'

'I didn't go back to him, you idiot! I was angry with you for lying to me, but I didn't go back to him. I was asking for his help!'

'What for?'

'It doesn't matter now. You have your floozies and I have enough cash to do whatever I want. Which isn't to be with you!'

'So why did you come?'

She shimmered with inarticulate rage, so much so that the words would hardly come out. The hailstones were getting larger and more noticeable but still they did not hurt as much as the tears, hot on her face. She dashed them away.

'This is my special place, and you've ... stolen it from me! And you're filling it with sluts and banging your way to an early, lonely grave. Well, good luck! I don't need you anyway.'

'Those women don't mean anything to me! I was filling a void ...'

'A void? You were filling a bit more than that!' She

was screaming at him, but her voice sounded tiny against the surrounding storm.

'You didn't want me any more so what was I supposed to do?'

'Not go balling your way through Colorado!'

'Oh, now who's being two-faced? What the hell were you doing two weeks ago?'

'That was different! I didn't know I was in love with you then!'

He advanced on her. 'And what about now?'

The wind was so strong she could hardly stand up, but she brushed away his steadying hand.

'Right now?'

'Yes, goddamnit, right now!'

'I think you're a low down piece of shit!'

'I can't believe you've come all this way just to tell me that.'

'I'd travel a hell of a lot further if I had to!'

'What do you really believe in?' He moved closer so that he did not have to shout above the howling wind. 'Tell me.'

As she opened her mouth they both heard an unmistakable shrieking and the faint smashing of glass. As one they turned to look. Half a mile from where they stood, a wide funnel of debris and dust had obliterated the diner and was heading straight for them.

'Jesus Christ!' Decker yelled, grabbing her hand. He held her tightly, looking for a fast exit from the encroaching turmoil. There was nowhere to run, nowhere to hide except the flimsy low buildings at the edge of the cliff. 'These aren't strong enough. The whole damned thing will be taken away!' The fence was rippling as the wind approached. There was nowhere to go except down, so they headed for the hazardous narrow path. Decker went first, to protect Daisy if she fell. They slithered and slid, their feet scoring into the mud, hanging on to the skinny handrail as the tornado roared ever closer. Daisy was blinded by her hair whipping around her face but somehow she held on and kept going.

It was Decker who fell, slipping on the mud and grasping for the handrail that was no longer secure, the posts loosened by the increasing wind and torrential rain. As he scrabbled wildly at anything he could catch hold of to prevent his fall, she lunged for him, screaming his name. They met and tangled, rolling and rolling and tumbling down the side of the cliff, the screaming wind disorientating her. This was what laundry felt like, she thought numbly, closing her eyes and holding on to Decker's hard, warm body, feeling the jabbing of spiteful stones and spiky pinyon branches attack her as they continued their hectic descent.

Finally, thankfully, they stopped. Daisy raised her head like a wary prairie dog to see where they were.

'Look out!' Decker pushed her head down as something huge and dark soared close over their heads and landed in the trees below with a splintering crash.

'What the hell was that?' Daisy shouted. Decker shook his head. The wind was still roaring, but it was the muted sound of a fast moving train that had already passed them by.

After a breathtaking moment, they looked up again. The sky seemed to be on fast forward, rolling and boiling rapidly in front of them, the lightning causing heat spots in front of her eyes. Decker moved beneath her.

'It's OK, we're on safe land.' He moved her away and sat up. His naked upper body was a mess, beads of blood pricking long scratches on his chest, back and arms. Daisy had faired better, being more protected by her clothing, but she could feel blood trickling down her cheek, and her bare lower legs above the boots looked as if Delilah had attacked her in a moment of feline premenstrual tension.

Decker stood up and looked up at the cliff. They had fallen about twenty feet, though at the time it had seemed much further.

'We're just below the ladder. Come on.' Decker pulled her forwards, back up the side of the cliff. They clawed their way back up to the cliff dwelling, skinning their knees and adding more scratches to the ones they had already received. It was raining again, cold this time and heavy, making them shiver. They breached the wall of the cliff dwelling and fell gratefully over it, then ran for cover.

In the dark shelter of the cliff dwelling all was calm and dry. They huddled under a large, soft alpaca throw and drank belly-warming whisky and watched the rain as it hammered down, turning the dusty ground in the kiva to sludge. The mesas beyond were mere grey shadows beyond the curtain of seemingly solid water pouring from the heavens, but already they could see a break in the cloud, far distant, with a hint of blue sky to come.

They stopped shivering at about the same time, looked at each other, and simultaneously decided that kissing was a better option. They met in the middle, more violently than intended, banging their noses.

'Sorry,' Decker said, pulling away. Daisy pulled him back and planted a gentler, but no less passionate kiss on his lips.

'Apology accepted,' she whispered.

'I didn't mean for that. I meant for the whole damned vacation.'

'And I meant, apology accepted.' She kissed him again. He pulled her on to his lap and held her, drawing comfort from her warmth. She felt something furry rub against her ankles and heard a feline chirp. Delilah had come back. Daisy picked her up and cuddled her delicate body, fussing her chocolaty ears and silky throat. With the three of them huddled together, their damp, cold cave felt strangely cosy, like home.

'So who are you, Max Decker or Dan Cutter?' She asked, pushing her nose into the cat's warm fur.

'Max will do. I've had other names, but I'll tell you about them another time.'

'Fair enough.' She knew he would eventually. 'I wonder what that was that nearly hit us?'

He shrugged and took another gulp of whisky. 'Another piece of my investment, I guess. I don't suppose there's a building worth shit up there right now.'

'So what are you going to do with this place now you've bought it?'

He shrugged again, gulping down more Jack Daniels. 'I don't know. I just didn't want to see it go to some heartless property developer.'

Daisy laughed softly, letting Delilah leap off her lap. 'I'd never put you down as a romantic, Deck. You're worse than me.'

'I'm truly in the shit, then,' he murmured into the whisky bottle. 'Well? What do you think we should do with it? We've got to think of something soon. I've paid for the place, but we need some form of sustainable income.'

She liked his use of the word 'we'. It felt warm and comforting, like one of the wolf fur throws on which they had consummated their affair.

'Hmmm. So what we really need is an enthusiastic millionaire willing to put their trust and cash into whatever project we come up with?'

'Yeah. Like that's going to happen,' Decker said, laughing ironically.

She realised then that he had no idea about her new, independent financial status. She nudged him in the ribs.

'How about me?'

He looked confused. 'You? How come?'

'I'll tell you my secrets when you tell me yours. Let's just say I was honest with someone who loved me. Anyway, I'm not "back", as you so presumptuously put it.'

His face changed, becoming ambivalent. 'So what is this? A social call? An opportunity for you to rub my face in the shit?'

She licked her finger and washed a streak of blood from his chin. 'Sometimes you can be incredibly dense, Max Decker. Either that or too busy being flawed and moody to see past your own nose. When will you stop jumping to conclusions and accept that I never went away?'

He stared at her for such a long time that the dark green of his eyes was indelibly printed on her memory. Then he pulled her on to his lap and held her, his face buried in her hair, his emotions seemingly too close to the surface to risk her seeing them in the raw. Not yet, anyway.

The storm had passed. Hard, refreshing rain was falling, restoring the surviving, dust-strewn trees back to their verdant splendour. She filled her lungs with the sweet, earthy smell of wet stone and ripped vegetation and felt unaccountably content. Outside their shelter, puddles were forming, turning the earth to mud. Debris from the shattered buildings above was scattered everywhere, together with the remains of shredded trees and shrubs. It was, as her father would say, a total fucking mess. One day, she thought, she would let him know where they were so he could see her heaven for himself.

Decker reluctantly let her go. 'Of course, I haven't forgiven you yet for stealing my car. For the second time, I might add.'

'I was going to talk to you about that,' she said as he pulled her to her feet. They went together out on to the balcony, picking their way over strewn pieces of timber and let the rain soak through their clothes onto their skin. They wandered to the edge of the veranda and looked out over the precipice. The storm had moved away to make other poor humans run for cover. The sun breaking through the cloud was already heating the earth again, ready for the next round. A steamy heat haze obscured their view of the horizon, but not the vivid rainbow rising up from the desert floor.

She heard Decker sharply draw in his breath. Following his stare down to the treetops, she understood why. The large object that had nearly knocked them off the path was impaled on a slender fir, the top sticking out through the punched out windshield. All the windows were smashed, and there was terminal damage to the engine. The hood had been ripped right off.

'I bought it back,' Daisy said in a small voice. She bit her lip to stop from laughing. 'Oops.'

'Oops,' Decker repeated with dangerous calm, and turned slowly towards her.

Daisy backed away from him, unable to stop the grin widening on her face. She tried to cover it with her hands, but it was impossible.

'Come here,' he growled.

'No.' She ran skittishly away from him. He pursued her, dodging the debris, lunging for her and missing. They chased each other around the kiva until she had to stop, out of breath with laughing so hard. He watched her bosom heaving through her wet shirt, and the glistening raindrops on her skin.

'Come here,' he said again, rough with desire.

'No!' She made him chase her through the hazardous assault course around the fire pit again. When he finally caught her they tumbled together on to the ground, landing in the middle of a large, muddy puddle. They wrestled, wet sand sticking to their skin and clothes. He finally pinned her down and straddled her, holding her hands firmly above her head. The tiny raindrops felt heavy and incredibly sensual on her naked skin as he ripped her blouse open and dealt with the small hook at the front of her bra, baring her breasts. Leaning down, he licked each drop of rain as it landed on her skin. Coupled with the heat of his mouth, each raindrop lit an intense wildfire of feeling that spread all over her body. The blood and earth-streaked nakedness of his scarred upper body looked primeval, his dark hair as sleek as an otter's pelt. His eyes were fierce as he stared down at her.

'You can mess with my head, my heart and my cock, but you don't ever mess with my vehicle again, understand?' His voice was severe.

'I understand,' she said meekly. He scooped up a handful of wet, red earth in his fingers and smeared it across her breasts in the shape of an "M".

'From now on you're totally mine. No bikers, storm chasers or guys with a Z in their name. Got that?'

'You make me sound like Daisy does Dallas,' she said reproachfully.

'Do you mean it?' He sounded aggressive, his eyes boring into hers.

'You know the answer, otherwise you wouldn't even be here.' As he knelt over her she could see the jutting bulge of his erection. She freed one hand and stroked it, feeling him quiver. She unzipped his trousers and his cock sprang out. No underwear. She remembered he had dressed in a hurry. She also remembered why. She wrapped her hand firmly around it.

'And no pert little floozies apart from me from now on,' she said, talking to his cock as if it were a separate being. Above it, he shook his head.

'No.'

She drew his great, salty cock into her mouth, washing him clean. He steadied himself on the ground above her head, enjoying the feel of being inside her warm, wet mouth. When it became almost too much, he sat back in the mud and pulled her on to his lap again. She wrapped her legs comfortably around his waist.

'Say what you said the other day,' he said. His hands caught hers and crossed them behind her back, trapping her as he had the very first time, rendering her too aroused to answer him. Again he was licking hungrily at her nipples, driving her emotions over the edge of some precipitous cliff from which there was no escape. His cock was insistently questing for her warm, wet entrance, making her squirm and want to let him in.

'Say it!' he commanded again, sucking fiercely at each nipple. His hands on her wrists were tight, and her shoulder blades ached from the pressure put upon them, but she hardly felt it, she was so overwhelmed with desire for this man whom she had known, right from the start, would be her mate.

'I love you,' she whispered, drunk with longing. Their lips met again, their bodies uniting in a slow, undulating dance of painfully exquisite joy. She shuddered with pleasure, saying those three words louder and louder, until they bounced off the rock and floated true and free to join the ever-flowing desert wind.